Second Chances at Samphire Bay

Sasha Morgan lives in a village by the coast in Lancashire with her husband and has one grown up son. She writes mainly contemporary fiction, her previous series having a touch of 'spice', probably due to all the Jilly Cooper novels she read as a teenager! Besides writing, Sasha loves drinking wine, country walks and curling up with a good book.

GW00689560

Also by Sasha Morgan

Lilacwell Village

Escape to Lilacwell
Return to Lilacwell
Together in Lilacwell

Samphire Bay Village

Second Chances at Samphire Bay

Sasha Morgan

Second Chances *at* Samphire Bay

CANELO

First published in the United Kingdom in 2024 by

Canelo
Unit 9, 5th Floor
Cargo Works, 1–2 Hatfields
London SE1 9PG
United Kingdom

Copyright © Sasha Morgan 2024

The moral right of Sasha Morgan to be identified as the creator of this work has been asserted in accordance with the Copyright, Designs and Patents Act, 1988.

All rights reserved. No part of this publication may be reproduced or transmitted in any form or by any means, electronic or mechanical, including photocopy, recording, or any information storage and retrieval system, without permission in writing from the publisher.

A CIP catalogue record for this book is available from the British Library.

Print ISBN 978 1 80436 836 7
Ebook ISBN 978 1 80436 837 4

This book is a work of fiction. Names, characters, businesses, organizations, places and events are either the product of the author's imagination or are used fictitiously. Any resemblance to actual persons, living or dead, events or locales is entirely coincidental.

Cover design by Diane Meacham

Look for more great books at www.canelo.co

Printed and bound in Great Britain by Clays Ltd, Elcograf S.p.A.

1

For Molly and John – finally reunited

Man Killed in Hit-and-Run Accident

Lancashire Constabulary are appealing for any eyewitnesses in connection to the death of Thomas Boyd, who was killed in a hit-and-run accident on Friday night. The collision took place at approximately eleven p.m. outside The Mariners public house on the high street in Carston. A white transit van collided into Mr Boyd, rendering him dead on impact. The vehicle sped off in a northerly direction.

Mr Boyd leaves a widow, Jasmine. Police are urging the public to come forward with any information.

Lancashire Evening Standard, 9 October 2021

Chapter 1

Carrying the copper urn with great care, Jasmine stepped out onto the deck. She gently knelt down on the wooden floor and leant over the side of the narrowboat. Lifting the lid, she slowly tipped the ashes into the canal.

'Goodbye, Tom,' she croaked, face crumpled in grief. She watched the remains hit the dark green water and sink below. A slight puff of grey smoke wafted above. Was it her imagination, or had the shape of a heart formed? Then it, too, faded and disappeared.

Gone. Tom was gone. The love of her life, best friend and husband all rolled into one magical, perfect person, was in fact no more. He'd been snatched cruelly from her in an instant. It was inconceivable; too hideously tragic to be true. Except it *was* true. Her best mate – her *soulmate* – had vanished from her life forever. She was alone, a widow at the age of twenty-nine.

Jasmine turned to look around their beloved boat, aptly named *Moonshine*, on account of the first glimpse she and Tom had had of her...

It had been on a tipsy walk back from the pub one Saturday night. They had taken a shortcut home, past the marina and boatyard, when a full moon had shone a silver beam directly over the narrowboat.

'Oh look!' cried Jasmine, pointing towards the rather dishevelled, lonely looking vessel, begging for attention.

They both moved towards the wire fencing of the yard to peep further in. On closer inspection, they spotted a sign marked:

Marina repossession – to be sold as seen via sealed bids above the guide price

'Are you thinking what I'm thinking?' asked Jasmine, followed by a hiccup.

'What, you mean buy it?' replied Tom, half laughing. 'We don't even know what the guide price is.'

'Bound to be cheaper than the deposit for a house,' she retorted.

True, thought Tom, *but a narrowboat?* They didn't know the first thing about life on the water, only the rather idyllic sense of freedom one assumed when seeing brightly coloured boats chug merrily down a tranquil canal. But then again, he conceded, surely that's just what narrowboats did: peacefully meander their way down the water, with no fuss, taking their time? He was suddenly hit by a mix of realisation and curiosity. Evidently, so was Jasmine.

'Just think, Tom, we could salvage this boat and make it into something really special!' She spoke with excitement. He looked back into the yard and narrowed his eyes in contemplation. 'The money we've saved so far for a house deposit would surely more than cover the guide price?'

'We don't know that, Jas,' Tom cautioned. 'Plus, look at the state of it. It's going to need one hell of a renovation.'

'But even so!' countered Jasmine with gusto. 'It won't cost the same as a house, or the rent we're dishing out. Just think,' her eyes glazed over dreamily, 'our very own floating home…'

Tom stared at his wife and realised at that precise point that her mind was made up. When those big brown eyes held that wistful look, he knew there was nothing and no one who could persuade her otherwise. He ruffled her dark blonde bobbed hair.

'We'll come back here tomorrow, make some enquires,' he tried to appease.

Typically, Jasmine wasn't to be fobbed off so lightly.

'I'll go online when we get home, do some research.'

Tom smiled at her enthusiasm, but was a Saturday night, after a few beers, the best time to be making such an important decision? He was the more practical, sensible of the two. Whilst Tom loved Jasmine's joie de vivre, he was always the one to counsel patience, ever the calming influence to her impetuous, spur-of-the-moment ideas.

Yet, as Jasmine fired up the laptop and went on the marina's website when they arrived home, he too couldn't help but feel a frizzle of excitement. They soon found the advert for the repossession. Reading it in full told them that the guide price was £12,000 and the 'Closing date for all sealed bids to be received by Allied Yacht Brokers at twelve p.m. 1 May 2018. The specification of this boat may be incorrect, as we are not in possession of the full details.'

Tom's hands ran through his auburn curls nervously. Should they? The first of May was tomorrow. Was this fate? As if reading his mind, Jasmine's eyes widened.

'This was meant to be, Tom! We were *meant* to see that poor narrowboat tonight and save it.'

'*Poor* narrowboat?' laughed Tom.

'Yes, it's crying out for love and attention,' she replied, then folded her arms almost in defiance, 'and we're the people to do it.'

So, the very next day saw the pair of them enter the marina yard, clutching their sealed bid. By noon, after much praying, wishful hoping, crossed fingers and anxious gasps, the 'poor' dilapidated narrowboat was declared, by Allied Yacht Brokers, to be the property of Thomas and Jasmine Boyd.

'It's ours!' Jasmine cheered, on the verge of tears, hand clasped tightly in Tom's.

'What shall we call her?' he asked with a smile down at her.

Jasmine cast her mind back to the previous night. '*Moonshine*,' she replied.

The next three months were spent relentlessly renovating *Moonshine*. Aesthetically, the boat was in very poor condition, with a bad paint job all over and a very old, tatty interior. However, the structure was surprisingly sound. The metal hull was thick, with no corrosion, and the interior woodwork was well preserved and solid throughout.

The narrowboat was a cruiser style, which meant it had more outdoor space, a feature Tom and Jasmine were glad of. The interior furnishings were quite basic, making them easy to rip out. Although they worked together on the boat, it was Tom who undertook most of the preliminary manual work, while the interior design was down to Jasmine, who spent lots of time on Pinterest to create a cosy, yet stylish, home – all earthy neutrals, pale browns, greens and creams – with a Scandi-inspired kitchen and luxurious fireplace in the lounge. There was also an outdoor relaxation space on the deck where the couple could enjoy views of the open countryside and waterways.

Moneywise, it had been a no-brainer. Tom and Jasmine had spent a good chunk of their savings on the initial cost of the boat and a few thousand more on the renovation. They also had overheads to consider: the mooring fees, canal and river trust licenses, insurance and the Boat Safety Scheme, but compared to what they were laying out in rent ('dead money,' as Jasmine kept calling it) they were able to manage the finances comfortably.

As a freelance graphic designer, Jasmine loved the freedom of working from home in a job that brought her joy. It didn't seem like work to her, letting her artistic juices flow when designing logos, brochures, adverts, magazine and book covers.

Together, Tom and Jasmine had created a beautiful snug home, which they were both extremely proud of, and rightly so. The friends who had scoffed at their decision to take on the ramshackle of a boat weren't laughing any more, not when they saw the finished article.

Moonshine epitomised just what could be achieved with grit, determination and bloody hard work. She was a joy to behold with her indigo paintwork, complete with a streak of silver running down the side, representing a beam of moonlight, after its namesake. Everybody who stepped aboard loved the little narrowboat, which had been brought back to life with such care and attention; she was an absolute delight.

Until, tragically, all the joy had been sapped from her in one fell swoop. The heart and soul of *Moonshine* had been ripped out. It was no longer a home for the very two people who had saved her. How could it be, when there was only one of them left? Little had Tom known, that dreaded Friday night when he had stepped off *Moonshine* to join his friends at The Mariners, that it would be the very last time he'd be aboard his beloved boat. That it would be the very last time he'd call jauntily to his wife, 'See you later!' When in fact, he would never see her again.

Chapter 2

Robin Spencer drove to the bottom of the limestone track and parked in front of the two cottages for sale to assess for his next building project. When the cottages had been put on the market yesterday, he'd been immediately interested – *very* interested. Truth be told, he'd had his eye on the two derelict cottages for some time now, waiting to jump in and seize the moment they became available.

Situated by the shore, they had a panoramic view of the bay to the Lakeland Fells, a prime location. It had been a travesty to Robin that both cottages had been left unoccupied and unloved for so long. They were screaming to be renovated and cared for. In fact, thought Robin as he got out of his Range Rover, he'd consider knocking the two of them into one, making a really spectacular home.

Standing closer to the flintstone cottages, the idea grew on him even more so. Yes, he would get rid of the two front doors and build one central porch. Obviously, the rooms would have to be reconfigured, which would take time and money, but it would be worth it. The profit he could make on a huge, detached house with stunning views, in such a picturesque, sought-after coastal village would be astronomical.

The Lancashire village of Samphire Bay sat nestled just beneath the border to Cumbria. It offered sheltered walks along limestone paths and amongst woodland, leading to open views of sandy beaches and glittering water. The area was renowned for its flora and fauna, historic buildings and geological features, including a number of springs and wells. Samphire Bay had even caught the attention of the national press a few years ago, when a Viking hoard was found nearby dating back to 900 AD. It was an intriguing and unusual place, with a windswept peninsula between the mouth of the river and bay, which at times was cut off by the tide.

There was only one building that stood on the peninsula itself. A huge, white art deco house built in 1939, sat high on a large piece of land that showed off the architecture perfectly, the modernist curvature of the bow windows, with art deco motifs and parapets on the exterior. The unique history of the place had been lovingly maintained by its owner, Bunty Deville, an eccentric old dear with pots of money, having come from a family of rich wine merchants. Bunty was well known to the residents of Samphire Bay, having lived there since birth, and she'd developed quite the reputation. Perhaps living in such a grand, imposing house high above the crashing waves, periodically unreachable by the tide, gave her that air of mystique. She and the house were like something straight from an Agatha Christie novel.

Bunty relished the mysteriousness surrounding her, often playing up to it. She imagined herself as a bit of a clairvoyant and read tarot cards. In reality, it was all a part of Bunty's imagination rather than any 'gift' she might have, but that didn't bother Bunty. Why ruin a good story by telling the truth? The image of a glamorous, alluring figure was far more preferable to her than a lonely, old lady rattling around a big, cold house.

She was also renowned for her stubbornness. Bunty refused point blank to do the sensible thing and move to a smaller, more manageable, more accessible house. Bunty had far too many happy memories within the curved rooms and polished timbers. She had been born in the master bedroom, as the salty sea air wafted through the great bow window. The house had been a magical place to grow up in, with its many nooks and crannies, listening to the roar of the waves and watching breathtaking sunsets from the balconies. To leave after living there all this time was unthinkable. The place was her world, it was all she ever knew.

To the people of Samphire Bay, Bunty was a quaint, endearing character, albeit a touch quirky. Unfortunately for Robin, it was this quirky, eccentric old dear who also owned these two cottages he was keen to get his hands on. Only once had he attempted to coax Bunty into selling them to him, which had been met with a curt, 'They're not for sale' response. Robin had had the good sense not to try and persuade her otherwise, knowing how obstinate she could be. Instead, he had exercised patience and bided his time, waiting and waiting for the day Bunty would finally relent and put her neglected cottages on the market. It made sense for her to sell them, after all what use were they to her stood empty? She had sold her family's other properties in the village; the pub, which thankfully had been taken over by a local landlord and still served the community, and the Victorian folly which now hosted retreats by the parish. Why keep two rundown cottages which were inhabitable and not serving any purpose? It was a complete waste.

Robin had thought that maybe his request to buy them was the reason why Bunty had stalled. Was she waiting for him to up his offer? He wouldn't put it past the old bird. And why hadn't she just contacted him, instead of advertising them? Bunty knew damn well she already had a buyer – *him*, and a local for God's sake!

Robin had lived in Samphire Bay since he was a teenager, when his parents had had enough of city life and escaped to the country. Robin had taken to Samphire Bay like a duck to water and never felt the urge to leave, despite being tempted now and again by the properties he'd renovated all over the country. Once or twice he had considered actually keeping a house he'd converted and brought back to life, but always the picturesque shoreline village had lured him back and made him stay put. He now lived in one of the flats that he had converted from a grand country house. Luckily for him, his best mate, Jack Knowles, also felt the same way about Samphire Bay. Together they had built up a property developing business. It was Jack that Robin was contacting on his mobile, after having taken a few photos of the cottages.

> Structurally OK, but needs a shed load of money to convert. Pics to follow.

It was soon answered.

> Let's go for it. Do you want me to approach Bunty?

Robin smiled to himself. Did Jack fancy his chances with the old girl? No, he'd do it. Robin knew she had always had a soft spot for him, deep down. Well, with his dark hair, twinkling hazel eyes and charisma, most females did. He'd work his charm on her and win Bunty round this time. He wanted those cottages and wasn't going to let someone else snap them up, even if it meant paying over the asking price.

Chapter 3

'There you go, Jasmine, have a break.' Sue Timpson placed the sandwich and cup of tea in front of her daughter with a worried expression.

'Thanks, Mum,' she replied, still staring intently at her laptop screen. Jasmine was working on the cover of a book entitled *Midnight Murders*. The brief was old, Dickensian England, with a thriller twist. She was thinking dark alleyways with a shadowy silhouette of a cloaked man in a top hat, carrying a dagger, possibly dripping with blood? She'd try without, first, then—

'Jasmine?' Her mum interrupted her train of thought in a dry tone, finally making her look up.

'Yeah?'

'You haven't stopped since eight this morning. You need a break.'

Jasmine blinked. 'What time is it?' she asked, surprised.

'It's two o'clock,' Sue crossed her arms, almost accusingly.

Jasmine glanced at the corner of her screen. So it was. Time had flown. Rubbing her eyes she yawned. 'I'll stop for a bit,' Jasmine agreed and shut down the laptop.

'Do you want to talk, love?' Sue took a seat opposite Jasmine, her forehead creased with concern as she chewed her lip. She scanned her poor daughter's pale face. Jasmine's eyes had bruised circles around them. Her cheekbones were now sharp, jutting out, and her collar-bone protruded where once it lay flat. She'd clearly lost weight. Well, obviously she had. Her beloved, precious child had suffered a traumatic shock. Her husband was dead; Tom had been killed. How on earth was her beautiful girl, who'd been so full of life and laughter, going to cope? For a moment she put herself in Jasmine's position. How would she have managed without Mike? How would she have coped if her husband had suddenly been swept away in the blink of an eye without any warning? Poor Jasmine had been left a widow, and at such an early age! Then a sudden, sharp realisation hit her. It was Jasmine's thirtieth birthday this year. Oh my God, how were they going to celebrate that? Tears stung her eyes and she quickly blinked them dry.

Jasmine didn't seem to register her mum's concern. She stared into space, nibbling at her sandwich, not even noticing what she was eating. Nothing mattered any more. Not what time it was, not what she ate (or didn't eat), not what she was doing (mainly working); all the days and hours blurred together, there wasn't any definition of any kind. Jasmine slept, worked and ate, then repeated the monotonous process again the next day. She was throwing herself into her job – at least the work kept her well occupied and distracted from the torturous thoughts of Tom. Would she ever feel happiness again? Jasmine doubted it. How could she, without Tom? He was her soulmate. Correction, he *had* been her soulmate. Now she didn't have one. She was alone.

'Jasmine, I said, do you want to talk?' The voice of her mum cut through her thoughts again.

'About what?'

'Come on, love, you need to open up. It's been over six months now and you've hardly mentioned Tom's name. The counsellor said—'

'Fuck the counsellor,' Jasmine flatly cut in, making Sue flinch. It wasn't like her daughter to be so vulgar.

'We're all trying to help,' she coaxed, hoping for some form of constructive response.

Jasmine sighed and closed her eyes. Why wouldn't people leave her alone? Her mum, dad, brother, friends, colleagues and the bloody counsellor... she just wished they'd all clear off and *leave her alone*! None of them knew what she was going through. None of them had experienced what she had.

At first, in the days following Tom's death, Jasmine had been glad of the support. Both her mum and dad had been the pillar of strength she'd desperately needed. Sam, her brother, had been a tremendous help in selling the boat. It was he who had liaised the sale with Allied Yacht Brokers, who had originally sold the boat to Jasmine and Tom. *Moonshine* soon sold, being in such good condition. The hefty profit made did little to console Jasmine. She simply couldn't face living on *Moonshine* alone, not when it had been her and Tom's joint dream. Now it belonged to another young couple, and the unfairness of it all cut like a knife. It had been Sam who had ended up handing over the boat keys; Jasmine simply couldn't face it. Her heart was broken enough without having to watch another excited owner step aboard her pride and joy.

Now though, after six months of living in her parents' house, she was beginning to feel a little claustrophobic. Albeit with good intention, her mum and dad were stifling. Jasmine didn't need or want the constant care and attention that was relentlessly being poured on her.

Granted, she had needed assistance early on, but now she had to face the music and start making some decisions. Like where was she going to live. Jasmine had loved living on the canal and still yearned to be near the water. That's about all she knew at the moment.

'Jasmine?' Her mum was persistent, she'd give her that.

'Sorry, Mum, I know you're trying to help.'

'We are, love, that's all we want – to help you.' Sue sat forward eagerly, hoping this was the moment her daughter was about to confide in her.

Jasmine set her shoulders. 'I've come to a decision,' she stated, tone firm.

'Right,' Sue nodded, filled with optimism.

'I'm moving out.'

'What?' The optimism was swiftly replaced with dread.

'I'm going to look for a place to live,' Jasmine said matter-of-factly.

'But… so soon?' her mum spluttered.

'It's been six months, Mum. It's time for a change.' The more Jasmine spoke, the more decisive she sounded.

'Where?' Sue's eyes widened.

Jasmine hummed in thought. 'By the sea I think.'

'The sea?' Sue blinked.

'Yeah,' laughed Jasmine, seeing her mum's jaw drop slightly. Then it struck her – she'd actually laughed.

'Right, let me get this straight,' her mum said. 'You are moving out of here and buying a new home "by the sea"?' Her fingers mimed quotation marks.

'Yes.'

'Where exactly by the sea?' Sue asked in exasperation.

Jasmine shrugged. 'Don't know yet. I'll have a look, see what's out there.'

'Do you need hel—'

'No,' Jasmine interrupted with force, then paused. 'Thanks, Mum, but I'm fine, really.' Her voice softened.

Sue gave a quivering sigh in acceptance. What else could she do? Jasmine was her own woman after all. She had to do things her way, in her time. All she and Mike could do was be there for their daughter; and they would be, every step of the whole damn way.

Chapter 4

Robin drove up the path to the tip of the peninsula, knowing full well he didn't have too long to talk to Bunty. The old girl had granted him an audience, but had insisted it be at three thirty p.m., an hour before the tide was due to cut the peninsula off. She obviously was not going to let Robin stay any longer. He allowed Bunty this condition, let her think she was in control, but he'd soon butter her up.

Still puzzled by her behaviour at not contacting him first, he was keen to get his offer in; even keener to get it accepted. Not for the first time, Robin's imagination was running riot with the possibilities that buying the cottages could bring. He was picturing the finished project and he liked what he saw – so much so, he had begun to think of it as *his* home. As with other renovations he'd completed, Robin grew attached to the place and its potential, but this time it was different. This time the location had a personal connection.

He parked his Range Rover outside the impressive art deco house and made his way up the steep steps to the front door. Ringing the bell, he could soon see the silhouette approach of a figure wearing a caftan dress and bandana through the opaque glass of the double front doors. Bunty opened them with a sly smirk.

'Ah, Robin, do come in.' She stepped aside to let him pass. 'I'm just in the studio.'

The studio was south facing, which meant the sun blasted through the large bow window most of the day. Bunty's father had been a keen artist and paintings surrounded the walls. Scenes of seaside landscapes and family portraits hung all around, including a watercolour of Bunty as a little girl building sandcastles, golden haired and skin kissed by the sun, wearing a polka dot swimming costume, face concentrating on the task at hand. It was hard to believe this cute toddler had once been Bunty.

Turning to face her, Robin took the initiative. They both knew why he was there.

'Bunty, I want to buy your cottages.'

'Yes, I know you do,' she replied tartly.

'Then can we talk money? Decide on a price?' he attempted.

'Yes.'

Robin frowned. Was it really going to be this easy? But then, he hadn't yet given her a figure.

'I'll pay the asking price,' he ventured.

'Which I accept.'

'Really?' he asked, surprised. It really *was* going to be this easy...

'For one of them,' finished Bunty.

'Pardon?' Robin frowned.

Bunty looked at him steadily. 'I'll sell you *one* of the cottages.'

Robin was starting to get a headache. 'But I want both of them.'

'Well you can't have both of them,' Bunty said.

'But... why not?'

'Because I don't want to sell you them both.' She folded her arms defiantly.

'Why not?' he repeated impatiently, then regretted his tone immediately at seeing Bunty's raised eyebrow. 'I mean – I don't understand.'

'Well, it's quite simple, darling,' she explained slowly, her voice saccharine sweet. 'You can buy one of the cottages, but not both.'

Robin glared at her. He knew to try and sway her was futile. Was that a glint in her eye? She was enjoying this, the old minx. He decided to change tack.

'So, who is going to buy the other cottage then?' he asked, tilting his chin up, challenging her. This was greeted with a chortle of laughter.

'You'll have to wait and see, Robin.'

Infuriating, the woman was *infuriating*! Turning on his heel, Robin made his way out, ever mindful of the tide coming in.

'I'll be in touch, Bunty!' he called over his shoulder.

'Goodbye, Robin!' she called back playfully.

Bang went the door.

Oh dear, she thought, smiling to herself, *Robin Spencer isn't used to not getting his own way.*

–

True, Robin Spencer wasn't accustomed to not getting his way – most of the time. There had been one occasion though, when even Bunty had felt a degree of sympathy for him.

Robin had been engaged a while ago – two years, in fact. His business had been growing successfully and he'd poured a lot of money into a property just outside

Samphire Bay. When he'd found it, his then fiancée, Ellie, had fallen in love with the old barn, and then even more so after seeing how well it had been converted, with its glass gable end and mezzanine balcony; and Robin had loved Ellie, so it made sense to make it their home. So once it was completed, and with Jack's permission, Robin paid back Jack his share and changed the deed from the business to his and Ellie's names.

Despite having come from very humble beginnings, Ellie had soon tired of living in the upmarket converted barn. The novelty wore off as she was left alone day after day, waiting for an exhausted Robin to return home late in the evening. When they'd moved, she had handed in her notice working for a firm of accountants, with a view to keeping Robin's books; she liked the idea of knowing how much money he had. Meanwhile, Robin was working manically to maintain his business. It hadn't helped keeping the barn, as the hefty profit it could have fetched would have given the business a much-needed boost. Instead, he had to make up for the loss, creating more pressure.

As Robin grew tired, overstretched and stressed out, Ellie grew impatient, demanding and bored. Her good looks meant she was never short of admirers and the inevitable happened. What hurt Robin the most was that she had managed to claim half of the barn *he* had renovated and paid for.

'It's my home and I'm entitled,' Ellie had thrown at him during their last, vicious argument. To add insult to injury, her new boyfriend was a solicitor, who it seemed was pulling all the strings.

In the end, Robin had been well and truly fleeced. Ellie had basically taken every penny she could squeeze out of him, leaving Robin financially crippled and never trusting women again. It had taken two years of solid, hard graft for his business to regain the loss she'd inflicted. Not to mention the bitterness that had festered away inside him, as he'd also sunk his life's savings into the barn while Ellie hadn't contributed a thing.

Now, just when his business was getting back on its feet, and he thought an opportunity had arisen to start afresh, it was being stamped on. This time by Bunty Deville.

Bunty wasn't a bad person, not really. She was stubborn, yes, and infuriating, but there wasn't a malicious bone in her body. Deep down, Bunty wanted Robin to be happy. She, along with most, had seen the injustice that Robin had endured. He'd been treated despicably by that double-crossing, money-grabbing girl. She knew his parents, he was from a good, honest family and certainly didn't deserve to be treated so dreadfully.

Bunty also knew that Robin had been scarred. Little wonder he didn't trust women, after the way that Ellie had shafted him. Bunty didn't blame Robin, but she, like his parents, wanted him to meet someone. The right one. He so deserved it. She knew he was popular amongst the ladies, with his handsome looks he was bound to be! Bunty might live alone, hidden away in a great big house, but she was sharp and tuned in. She kept abreast of the goings on in Samphire Bay and knew what all its residents were up to.

Secretly Bunty had admired Robin and Jack Knowles and the way they had grown their business converting properties. It was reassuring to know that they would be renovating one of her cottages too. Only one though. Originally, she had intended to sell Robin both properties, but good sense had told her to reach out to an estate agent for an evaluation and to see if there would be interest. And there was – literally within moments of the cottages going on the market, the estate agents had been contacted and a viewing arranged.

Bunty was curious when the agents told her the viewer was not from Samphire Bay, fully expecting a local to have jumped in quickly. No, it was a Mrs Jasmine Boyd, who was currently living in Carston, a market town a few miles away. This piqued Bunty's interest further. Was she viewing the cottage alone? Apparently so, the agents had advised. Then, a distant bell rang in her memories. Bunty was sure she'd remembered reading an article in the local newspaper a couple of months ago, about a Mr Thomas Boyd being killed in a hit-and-run accident. He had been from Carston. There had been mention of a widow, Jasmine. It had to be the same Mrs Boyd who was viewing her cottage, surely?

Bunty being Bunty couldn't resist meddling. All sorts of scenarios ran through her head. Above all, she was keen to meet Jasmine Boyd, there was something 'calling' her to this woman. To most, this would simply have been a chance set of circumstances. Why shouldn't a lady who had appeared in the paper want to view her cottage? It was a totally normal thing to happen. But not to someone like Bunty. No. This had happened for a *reason*. She was convinced of it. As if further conviction was needed, Bunty had read her horoscope earlier that day, as she did every morning and it claimed she would be involved in an 'intervention in matters of the heart'. Yes, fate was definitely rearing its head, as it so often did – in Bunty's mind, that is.

The estate agent had been a touch surprised when Bunty had requested to be present at the viewing.

'Oh… yes, of course Ms Deville, it is your property after all.'

'Yes, I'd like to see what calibre of buyer we're looking at,' said Bunty.

'Well, technically she's not a buyer yet,' the agent corrected carefully.

'No, darling, but she will be,' came Bunty's confident reply.

The agent grinned to herself. Ms Deville had quite entertained the office. Her flamboyant dress sense and dramatic speech, peppered with 'darlings', had caused many a giggle.

'The viewing is scheduled for tomorrow afternoon at one p.m. We'll see you there, Ms Deville.'

'You certainly will.'

So, it was all arranged. Bunty was going to meet Jasmine Boyd. Already she wanted her to buy the cottage. An inner feeling told her Jasmine was the right buyer, the person who was meant to live there. Then her lips pursed mischievously. Would Robin think so too? Doubtful, but with a 'helping hand' from her, who knows?

–

'Are you sure you don't want me and your dad to come with you, love?' Jasmine's mum asked, not for the first time. Jasmine closed her eyes and took a deep breath. How many times did she need telling?

'No, honestly, mum, I'll be fine.' Apart from anything else, it would give her some precious space alone, away from her parents. Her brother Sam had called yesterday and together they'd gone out for a walk. It had been good to breathe in the fresh air and feel the sun on her face. Life on the narrowboat had always afforded Jasmine time outdoors, but these days she was cooped up inside for far too long, to the extent that she now looked pale and withdrawn, devoid of any vitality which had once oozed from her. Workwise, she was producing some of the best pieces of design in her career – hardly surprising when that's all she was concentrating on. Now, after arranging to look at a property, she had something else to focus on.

'Why Samphire Bay?' Sam had asked, as they sat on a park bench.

'It's on a coastal path and I want to be by the sea – need to be by the sea.'

'Right.' Sam nodded, then he hesitated as though he wanted to say more. Jasmine sensed his unease.

'What?'

'Do you ever… regret selling the boat?' He eyed her sideways.

'No.' She shook her head. 'Too many memories.'

'But is that a bad thing?' Sam replied gently. Jasmine turned to face him.

'Yes, it is,' she said almost incredulously. What was it with everyone? Why would she want to remain on *Moonshine*, when all it did was remind her of what she had been cruelly robbed of?

'Sorry,' muttered Sam.

'No.' Jasmine sighed. 'I'm sorry.'

Sam held out his hand and she took it. He squeezed it in comfort.

'Is there anything I can do?' he choked, on the verge of tears. He couldn't help it; his heart broke at seeing his sister in such pain. If the police ever caught the bastard that had driven into Tom, he'd kill him.

'Actually, there could be.'

Sam's head shot up. 'What?'

'This cottage, if it's for me, will need a lot of work doing on it. Basically, it's a wreck, but that's the attraction. I want a doer-upper, just like *Moonshine*.'

Sam looked at her and saw a kernel of enthusiasm glowing in her eyes, which he took to be a good sign. He encouraged her with a wide smile.

'Course I'll give you a hand.'

'I'll have a better idea tomorrow, once I've seen it.'

She took out a printed copy of the house specs from her coat pocket and passed them to Sam. He took in the photographs of the flintstone cottages. Although they had rotten window frames and decaying wooden doors, there was no denying their potential. He totally got the location, with a sun setting in the distance, casting a burnt orange glow over the bay.

'It looks a fabulous spot,' he said in awe.

'I know,' agreed Jasmine.

'Which cottage might you go for?'

'Not sure yet. There's someone else interested in the cottages too, according to the estate agents.'

'They always say that to try and make a sale,' replied Sam.

'Yeah,' laughed Jasmine, 'that's what I thought.'

Chapter 5

Jack Knowles sat by the bar waiting for his friend and business partner to arrive. He had Robin's pint ready for him, knowing what he'd want. It wasn't long before Robin pushed through the pub doors with a foul expression. Immediately, Jack's shoulders slumped – this wasn't going to be good news. Without needing to say a word he passed Robin his drink. Robin nodded in thanks, took a mouthful, wiped his mouth and looked at Jack.

'She'll only sell us one cottage, not both of them,' he stated flatly.

'Why?' Jack asked, surprised. Robin shrugged.

'Because it's Bunty?' he offered dryly. 'Because she can?'

Still, Jack was perplexed. It didn't make any sense. 'But if both cottages are on the market, why not sell both of them to us? We're offering the asking price.'

Robin gave an impatient sigh. 'She says we'll have to "wait and see" who the other buyer is,' he replied, quoting Bunty's words.

'You mean, someone else is interested?' Jack's voice rose.

'So she says.' Robin raised an eyebrow. 'I think it could be a ploy, get us to up the offer.'

'Really?' Jack considered it. 'I'm not sure about that, Rob, not when she's named her price and we're happy to pay it.' Although Bunty could be seen as difficult at times, he didn't think she was greedy or calculating in that way.

'You're probably right, Jack, it's not as if she's short of money, is it?' conceded Robin, his eyes narrowing in contemplation. 'But why not sell us both cottages? It makes better sense to sell to one buyer, rather than two.'

However much Bunty Deville exasperated him, he still thought fondly of her. She had a kind heart and he knew how she had helped various residents in Samphire Bay. She was a long-standing friend of his parents and had given him and Jack work in the early days when setting up their business; it had been Bunty who had stipulated that Robin and Jack convert the Victorian folly into a place of retreat before selling it to the church.

They'd also often done odd jobs for Bunty around her home. Living in such a palatial space, there had been many over the years. She trusted them and in turn they had always maintained a high standard, without charging the earth.

Once, Bunty had been convinced her house was haunted. Robin and Jack listened to her tale of how a ghost made up the fireplace every morning, becoming more and more unnerved as piles of twigs appeared in the hearth each day. Not really taking her seriously, but showing concern, they had offered to stay over one night.

'See for yourselves!' she'd exclaimed.

So the two of them took their sleeping bags and camped out on Bunty's drawing room floor.

'Look at the fireplace, boys, it's empty,' she'd said before bidding them good night.

Robin and Jack exchanged grins before settling down to sleep. Come the morning, though, they weren't grinning. Sure enough, a mound of twigs sat in the grate, ready to be lit. They stared, puzzled, at each other.

'How the hell did that get there?' said Robin, frowning at the mystery.

'Dunno.' Jack scratched his head.

Then, they heard a bird calling down the chimney breast. Robin bent to take a closer look at the wood in the grate, which was covered in soot. A slow smile spread across his face.

'It's a bird's nest,' he laughed, then looked up the chimney. Another bird's call echoed down. 'Jackdaws,' he said, laughing again.

When they'd reported all this to Bunty, she'd burst into hysterics.

'You mean the jackdaws have been building nests and they keep falling down the chimney?'

'Yes, Bunty, that's exactly what's been happening,' Robin said in amusement.

'Oh, thank you so much, darlings. You've set my mind at rest.' She chuckled.

It hadn't taken long for the story to circulate round Samphire Bay, giving everyone a good giggle. Even so, Bunty had been appreciative to both Robin and Jack for their assistance.

All in all, they had a good relationship with Bunty, which made her recent behaviour all the more puzzling. What was the old bird up to?

–

Jasmine sat on the edge of her bed, staring at the photograph album, 'Welcome aboard *Moonshine*!' emblazoned over the cover in Tom's swirly writing in silver marker.

Gulping, Jasmine opened it. There she was, *Moonshine* in a dilapidated state in the yard, waiting patiently for them to collect her. Each photograph depicted the gradual transformation of the boat; a selection of 'before' pictures showing the bare carcass of the vessel, with its inners ripped out, to the 'after' pictures, boasting of a chic and stylish floating house.

Jasmine homed in on the images of Tom – installing the kitchenette, fitting the wood-burner, assembling their bed – and a lump formed in her throat. They'd looked so happy, building their home together. Her absolute favourite shot had to be of the two of them clinking champagne flutes on the deck under a starry sky with a full moon shining behind them. It had been the first night they had slept on the boat, and it was made extra special when the moon was beaming in all its glory. Happy, happy days.

With a determined effort, Jasmine shut the album. Tomorrow, hopefully, would mark the beginning of a new start, a new era.

She so wanted the cottage in Samphire Bay to be the right move for her, needing something to focus on. But was it? Could she just be trying to replicate what she'd done with Tom, only this time going solo? No, Jasmine told herself, she had to live somewhere. Why not in a new place, where people didn't stare at her with sorrowful eyes? She had to get out of Carston, it was suffocating her. There was only so much pity Jasmine could take, however well intended. She'd had enough.

'It's time to move on, Tom,' she whispered, touching the heart pendant necklace he'd given her and which she always wore. She longed to hear his voice, or be given a sign, *anything* to show he was nearby. But no, nothing, just an empty silence.

–

The estate agent stood in front of the cottages and breathed in the fresh, salty air. Well, it was certainly a good day for a viewing. The sun was glistening on the still waters of the bay from a cloudless blue sky. All was quiet and calm, apart from the distant call of the gulls. Blocking the sunlight with her hand, she saw a car making its way up the track. Watching the pale grey Morris Minor, the agent grinned to herself.

As the car drew closer, she could see Ms Deville through the windscreen, living up to her reputation, wearing a lime green bandana accompanied by large sunglasses.

'Hello, Ms Deville!' she called, walking to meet her once the car was parked. 'I'm Cheryl Barrow, we spoke on the phone,' she said, offering her hand to be shaken.

'Good day,' Bunty breezed, barely touching hands. Her attention was on the cottages, giving them a fixed stare.

'They're lovely, aren't they?' the agent gushed, wanting to set a good impression. Bunty lifted her dark glasses from her eyes and looked directly at her.

'No,' she replied bluntly with a cool, dismissive look. 'But they could be. Let's not shilly-shally,' Bunty continued, 'the cottages need a lot of attention and I don't want you to pretend otherwise. You'll put potential buyers off.'

'Yes, I see,' Cheryl replied through gritted teeth.

'Nobody likes a bullshitter, darling,' Bunty finished with a tight smile.

Well, that certainly told her, Cheryl thought, suddenly wishing she hadn't offered to do the viewing after all. A few of the agents in the office had been keen to step in in her place. They obviously thought it would have been entertaining, amusing even, but now she was feeling a sense of dread.

'Ah, that must be Mrs Boyd,' she said with relief, noticing a silver car advancing towards them.

Bunty's head turned sharply. She watched intently, waiting for the figure at the wheel to get out. Taking in the blonde bobbed hair, brown suede jacket, faded jeans and Chelsea boots, Bunty's instincts told her Mrs Boyd had style. Judging by the way she walked, head up, shoulders back, she also had an air of confidence too. Good start.

'Hello, Mrs Boyd. Did you manage to find us all right?' enquired the agent, rushing over to meet her.

That's right, thought Bunty with a roll of her eyes, *imply that the place is hard to get to*. The cottages might be on a secluded coastal path, but that was part of their allure in her eyes. She resented that the estate agent may have hinted otherwise.

'Fine, thanks,' smiled Jasmine.

As the two walked towards Bunty, she got a better look at her. Bunty gave a sharp intake of breath. My, what a beauty she was! Immediately she saw Mrs Boyd through a young man's eyes. Robin's, in particular. An innate sense told her they would make a perfect match. Then, Bunty steadied herself. She didn't definitely know if this was the same Mrs Boyd she was assuming it was.

'I'm Ms Deville, the owner,' she announced holding her hand out. 'Call me Bunty.'

'Hi, I'm Jasmine,' came the reply as she shook hands.

Bunty gave one of her most enchanting smiles and held Jasmine's hand a fraction too long.

Hmm, not quite the reception I got, thought Cheryl, before giving a slight cough.

'Right, shall we make a start?' she asked politely.

The agent turned the key in the lock and the door gave a loud creek as it opened, making her wince. They entered the hallway, brightly lit by the rays beaming in through the windows, but also illuminating all the dust in the air. Jasmine seemed undeterred, fully expecting to see dirt and dust in a building that had been left derelict for years.

They were in the right-side cottage, nearest to the sea, but Jasmine had asked to view them both. Her eyes darted about, taking in the bare wooden stairs, a spindled banister (with some spindles missing), the damp blotched wall-paper peeling from the walls, two rotten window frames either side of a decaying wooden door. The floorboards appeared solid underfoot though, Jasmine noticed, as her boots walked along them.

'As you can see, the cottages are in need of a lot of attention,' remarked the agent, quoting Bunty's words.

'Yeah,' nodded Jasmine. 'That's why I'm here,' she replied in a quiet voice, not particularly directed at anyone, more to herself.

Bunty narrowed her eyes in interest. This Jasmine Boyed intrigued her and she was desperate to find out more about her. In typical Bunty fashion, she plunged in regardless.

'Are you looking to live here alone, or—'

'Just me,' interrupted Jasmine, disliking the question. It felt intrusive. It *was* intrusive – and what was she here for anyway? She'd organised the viewing with the estate agents, not the owner.

'I see.' Bunty tried to hide just how pleased she was with the answer, as it further confirmed her suspicions.

Then, almost in retaliation, Jasmine asked, her chin raised slightly, 'How come the cottages have been left empty for so long?' She felt a degree of satisfaction at seeing the woman's expression, clearly taken aback at the direct question.

'Err… well the last tenants left one or two years ago and I hadn't quite decided what to do with them. Rent out again, or simply sell them,' answered Bunty.

'Hmm.' Jasmine thought it rather a lame answer and didn't believe it to be the whole truth. The cottages looked like they had been derelict far longer than 'one or two years' and why take so long to decide their fate?

Cheryl smirked to herself, sensing a slight tension in the air. A part of her was pleased that Ms Deville had been put on the spot and was tasting her own medicine.

'Let's see the kitchen,' she said to break the awkward moment.

They were greeted by an Eighties style kitchen, with a tiled floor, tiled patterned walls, even a tiled cooker hood. The units were made from a honey coloured mock wood with metal strips running on the doors to open and shut. Jasmine had to suppress a giggle. A short silence followed, each waiting for the other to break it. In the end, it was Bunty.

'It's dreadful, I know,' she sighed, making Jasmine turn to her and openly laugh. Bunty gave a despairing sort of look. 'But the state of the place is reflected in the asking price—'

'Well,' the estate agent jumped in, a touch anxiously. Bunty put her hand up to silence her.

'But I am open to conversation. I will be flexible,' she continued.

Jasmine's head tilted to one side. What a strange creature this Ms Deville was, not quite deciding if she liked her or not. However, she admired her honesty. Not all sellers would openly admit to their property as being dreadful. Something told her to put in a cheeky offer. Was it Tom's voice? Was this the sign she'd been waiting for? To be honest, Jasmine had practically made her mind up on the journey there. Driving through such idyllic scenery had won her over and then seeing how amazing the location actually was once parked up had clinched it. The cottages weren't exactly crumbling down. Structurally, they seemed in good shape. It was the internal space that needed all the work, as she'd fully anticipated.

'Are both cottages still on the market?' asked Jasmine, mindful of what she'd been told about another buyer.

'Yes,' Bunty replied. 'Take your pick, darling.'

Jasmine couldn't help but laugh again. She could hear Tom's voice in her head once more. *Make a cheeky offer, Jas!* it whispered, even though the viewing hadn't even finished.

'I'd like to see both cottages before having a conversation,' reasoned Jasmine, refusing to be rushed. She was forcing herself to stay calm and rational, despite the rising exhilaration inside her. Could that really have been Tom's guidance? Or just her own wishful thinking?

Bunty loved it when a plan came together. A sale was in the bag, she *knew* it! The trouble with Bunty was that she lacked a person in her life to keep her in check. Had she a partner, they would have told her to back off and let people live their own lives. They would have instructed her to mind her own business and exercise discretion. But Bunty didn't have that sensible, wise counsel. And Bunty didn't do discrete.

The rest of the viewing carried on in the same vein. The bathroom was in a similar sad, Eighties condition as the kitchen and each of the three bedrooms smelt of damp, had flaking paintwork and peeling wallpaper. The whole place needed gutting and starting again. The absolute winning factor, though, was the view from the master bedroom. The full vista of the bay, stretching out onto the horizon was magnificent. It took Jasmine's breath away. Looking out of the bedroom window down onto the back lawn, she was also delighted with the size and position of it. South facing meant plenty of sunshine and she would soon have the grass cut and maybe install a paved terrace or decking for outdoor furniture. She pictured herself spending hours out there. Perhaps installing a studio to work in? That rising exhilaration was bubbling over. She turned to look at Bunty, who seemed to be studying her. A strange sensation came over Jasmine. Had they met before? It was as though the woman knew her in some way. Bunty gave her a warm smile, wrinkling the corners of her eyes. Jasmine suddenly felt in a safe place.

'I don't need to see the other cottage, Ms Deville,' she told her. 'Let's talk money, shall we?'

Chapter 6

Robin was busy driving when a call from Jack came through the car's Bluetooth.

'Bunty's sold one of the cottages,' he stated flatly, making Robin sit up sharply.

'What?' he spat out.

'There's a Sold sign put up outside it,' Jack replied dully.

'Which one?'

'The right-hand one.'

Typical, thought Robin, the cottage with the best view of the bay. Given a choice, he'd have chosen the very same. Actually, given the choice, he'd have bought them both.

'Right,' he sighed, 'well, there's nothing we can do about it.'

There was a slight pause before Jack spoke. 'Do you think we should both go and talk to her?'

'Not much point now, mate. She's sold it and that's that.' But who to, he couldn't help but wonder. Jack was obviously thinking along the same lines.

'It'd be interesting to know who's bought it, though,' he said.

'Hmm, it would,' Robin agreed, eyes narrowing. Maybe he'd pay Bunty another visit after all. Would it be cheeky to ask how much she'd sold it for? Of course it would, he reasoned – and no doubt rankle Bunty into the bargain. The last thing he wanted was a disgruntled Bunty to deal with. Not if he fancied his chances of still buying the remaining cottage.

After the call to Jack, he changed direction and drove up the coastal path, as if needing confirmation from his very own eyes. Within a few minutes, he had it. Robin sighed again at seeing the Sold sign standing purposely in the front garden. He ran his hand through his dark curls in irritation. For the hundredth time, he asked why. Why had Bunty done this?

With an air of impatience, he turned the car round and headed for the peninsula road to Bunty's house. A glance at his watch told him it was ten thirty a.m. – at least it was low tide and he wouldn't be rushed off this time.

–

Bunty saw Robin's Range Rover park up outside on the drive and smirked, having fully expected him to put in an appearance sooner rather than later. She knew the Sold sign would spark a reaction.

Even Bunty had been a touch surprised at how swiftly Jasmine Boyd had negotiated and dealt with the purchase of the cottage. Mrs Boyd was clearly a lady who knew her own mind; a woman after her own heart, thought Bunty with contentment.

Opening the front door, she gave Robin one of her most winning smiles.

'Robin, do come in.' She swept the door wide open.

He stepped inside and turned to her, taking in the large, hooped earrings and bright red lipstick. Unusually, her grey hair was loose, running wild.

'Bunty, you know perfectly well why I'm here,' Robin started, getting straight to the point.

'I do.'

Robin waited for her to elaborate, but nothing was forthcoming.

'Why, Bunty?' His expression showed genuine confusion. It simply didn't make sense to him, why Bunty wouldn't let him buy both her cottages in the first place.

'Robin, it's just bricks and mortar we're talking about!' she exclaimed in exasperation. Truth be told, she hated seeing him look this way, however convinced she was that her actions were for his own good.

'I don't get it,' he frowned, further adding to her discomfort.

'Oh Robin, let's talk, darling.' Bunty's voice was soft and assuring. She tipped her head towards the drawing room door. 'Come on, let's have a drink.'

She led them into the spacious room, blazing with sunshine through the large, south-facing bow window. She made her way to the mirrored drinks cabinet and rustled up huge glasses of gin and tonic; her favourite tipple, so refreshing, no matter what time of day it was. Bunty prided herself on always having fresh cucumber, neatly sliced to accompany them, stored in the mini fridge with lots of ice in the small freezer compartment.

'There you go, darling.' She passed Robin his drink and sat down in the armchair opposite him. 'Now don't be cross with me for selling one of the cottages,' she began, leaning forward in her earnestness. 'In time, I'm sure, you'll thank me.'

'Will I?' Robin replied in a deadpan voice.

'Yes, there's method to my madness, you see,' Bunty tried to explain. 'The lady who's bought the cottage is a Mrs Jasmine Boyd.' She looked expectantly at him.

'And...?'

'Doesn't that name ring a bell?' Bunty pushed.

'Should it?' he replied, frowning.

'Her poor husband was killed in a hit-and-run car accident, it was all over the papers,' she told him. For now she knew for certain it was indeed the Mrs Boyd she'd suspected, the estate agents had confirmed it.

'Right...' said Robin, a touch confused where this was going.

'Well, I wanted to help the girl, she was very taken with the cottage and...' Bunty paused.

'What?' Robin asked, taking a large gulp of his gin and tonic.

'I think you'd make a good couple,' she finished assertively, making Robin splutter on his drink.

'What?!' His eyes widened in disbelief.

'It makes perfect sense to me,' Bunty told him calmly. 'You buy the other cottage, become neighbours and see what happens.' Her hands spread out, like it was all so simple.

Robin blinked. Bunty's matter-of-fact tone made it all the more incredulous. She could have been telling him the weather forecast, not matchmaking him with a woman he'd never set eyes on. Unbelievable.

'So,' he sat forward, 'let me get this straight. You deliberately sold one of the cottages to a vulnerable, young widow, with the intention of lining her up for me?'

'In a nutshell, yes. Obviously, you won't want to rush things—'

'Hell no, that would just be madness, wouldn't it?' Robin cut in sarcastically.

'Yes, it would,' agreed Bunty, ignoring the jibe. 'This will need sensitive handling.'

Robin let out an incensed yelp. 'And supposing I don't want to buy the other cottage now?' He looked defiantly at her, one eyebrow raised.

'But you do, darling,' she chuckled, eyes twinkling.

The old bird was enjoying this, thought Robin furiously. How dare she play with people's lives like this? The way she was acting beggared belief.

'You've gone too far this time Bunty,' he stated, then took another gulp from his glass.

'What's wrong with wanting to help two people who I believe will be good for each other?' she asked innocently.

She still didn't get it. Robin took a deep breath.

'Bunty, what makes you think me and this...'

'Jasmine,' chipped in Bunty.

'Me and this Jasmine will be good for each other?' he asked, trying to reason with her. She was right, he did still dearly want to buy the remaining cottage.

'I feel it.' Bunty knocked her fist against her chest with conviction, causing Robin to roll his eyes. He had an urge to tell Bunty to cut the dramatics but knew full well it was futile. Bunty was an eccentric, deluded old dear, whose intentions might be honourable, but no less outrageous. 'Don't worry, I'll sell for the same price Jasmine paid for her cottage.'

Robin's stare narrowed in interest.

'Which was?'

'Ten thousand less than the asking price,' she casually replied.

'What? *Ten grand* less?' Robin cried out.

'Hmm, so what do you say, darling? Are you in, or are you out?'

Living on a narrowboat meant Jasmine didn't possess too much in the way of belongings, something she became grateful for as she packed up for her move to Samphire Bay. Most of her stuff had still been in boxes from the move off *Moonshine*, never having had the inclination to unpack. The storage boxes were neatly stacked in her parents' garage. Now all Jasmine had to collect were the everyday items she used, mainly toiletries, clothes and her work equipment.

The first thing she needed to do, besides bottoming out the cottage with a good clean, was to install an internet connection, as she couldn't work without it.

Despite both her parents' reservations, Jasmine had wanted to move as soon as the money had transferred and she'd signed for the deed on the cottage. As neither the owner nor the buyer was involved in a chain, the transaction had been straightforward and only taken a matter of weeks. Jasmine had been a cash buyer, so hadn't needed to sort out a mortgage, and a quick survey that showed no structural damage allowed the process to move quickly. Tom's life insurance had seen to that. Plus, with the sale of the narrowboat, which had made a hefty profit, Jasmine had ended up with quite a tidy sum. Not having any money worries didn't compensate for not having her husband, though. Yes, being financially solvent meant she could press on with renovating the cottage, but with no Tom to do it with, Jasmine would gleefully return every penny to have him back.

As promised, Sam was going to help with the initial renovation; the kitchen and bathroom were the top priority. Although every room needed attention, Jasmine wasn't in any particular rush. As long as the place was safe, she'd deep clean the cottage and take her time. The banister in the hall had to be repaired and the window frames replaced, as did the front door. Jasmine had already ordered replacements, having taken measurements, so she and Sam would start ripping out the kitchen while they waited for the deliveries.

To her mother's horror, Jasmine intended to pitch a tent in her back garden and live there for the first couple of weeks, managing with just a camp stove.

'Jasmine, there's no need to do that!' she'd exclaimed.

'But I *want* to, Mum,' she'd countered.

So, with everything packed and ready to go, including a tent and camping gear, Jasmine and Sam set off, followed by their parents.

–

'It is a gorgeous spot,' Sue conceded, gazing out of the car window as they entered Samphire Bay and drove along the scenic coastal track. The bay lay before them, glistening in the sunlight, looking cool and inviting.

'It certainly is,' agreed Mike. For once, in what seemed a long, long time, his shoulders relaxed. His girl was going to be all right here, he could feel it in his bones. He gently patted his wife's lap. 'She'll be OK,' he soothed.

Both cars parked in convoy outside the cottages. Sam tipped his head towards the other cottage.

'Looks like you've neighbours.' He pointed to a second Sold sign in the adjoining garden.

'Oh, yeah,' Jasmine replied, her thoughts instantly turning to who they might be. A smidgen of disappointment entered her. She'd rather welcomed the idea of being

44

alone for a while out here. Just her and the beautiful coastline. Now it looked like she'd have to share it. Oh well, never mind. She felt a tinge of curiosity, perhaps it was a young family, wanting to create a perfect place to raise children?

'At least you won't be on your own,' her mum remarked as they started to unload the cars. It had bothered her knowing her daughter was out here, alone, in a *tent* for goodness' sake.

After a few hours, all the storage boxes had been shifted inside the cottage and the tent had been put up. The four of them were sat on deck chairs, drinking a well-earned cup of freshly brewed tea from the little camp stove.

'What a view!' trilled Sue, looking out towards the burnt-orange sun, now slowly setting over the water.

'I know.' Jasmine smiled, certain she'd made the right decision. She longed to hear Tom's voice again, telling her so. Ever since convincing herself that he had guided her into buying the cottage she'd listened in earnest, ready to follow his advice; but no, there hadn't been anything, just a steady, empty silence.

All four of them drank in the scenery, listening to the sea gently lapping the shore. Jasmine caught a whiff of lavender and scanned the garden to see where it was growing but couldn't spot any trace of the plant. Leaving the others who had now started to chat, Jasmine got up to peek over the hedge into next door's garden. Maybe the fragrance was coming from there.

Sure enough, it was. A line of lavender was growing along the edge of the garden path leading from the back door. It had obviously been planted some time ago, to look so full and lavish with its green leaves and bright purple blooms. Jasmine closed her eyes for a few moments and breathed in its sweet aroma. She opened them abruptly at the sound of a cough. A tall, dark haired man stood before her.

'Oh, hi.' She blushed, a little embarrassed to be caught looking over the garden hedge.

'Hi,' he smiled back, putting down a toolbox. He wore a white fitted T-shirt, emphasising his tanned, muscular arms, and faded jeans which were worn at the knees. He must be some kind of workman.

'I was just… admiring the lavender,' Jasmine said, cringing at how lame she sounded.

'Yeah, the garden's in far better shape than the inside of the house,' he laughed, finding her blush rather endearing. Then, moving closer towards the hedge, he offered a hand to shake. 'I'm Robin.'

'Jasmine,' she replied with a polite nod. On impulse, she asked, 'Are you working on this property, or do you own it?' Suddenly realising how nosey she must appear, she quickly added, 'Sorry, I didn't mean to sound so—'

'Both,' he interrupted with a grin, his hazel eyes twinkling. 'I'm the owner and I'll be renovating the cottage. It's what I do, property development.'

'I see,' Jasmine replied, chewing her lip.

'And you?' he asked gently.

'Sorry?'

'I see you've set up headquarters,' he teased, tipping his head towards the pitched tent in her garden.

'Oh, right.' She laughed. 'Yes, I'm the owner, and me and my brother are doing up the cottage. Well, giving it our best shot anyway,' she explained, a touch self-consciously, feeling slightly inadequate compared to this property developer.

'Jasmine!' her mother shouted.

'Better get back,' she said quickly, not wanting her mum to come and join them. If he thought she was nosey, what on earth would he make of her mum's inevitable interrogation?

'OK, well nice meeting you Jasmine,' Robin replied, picking up his toolbox. Jasmine's eyes homed in on his broad shoulders.

'You too, bye!' she called, then shooed her mum away as she was fast approaching.

'Who were you talking too?' she hissed.

'Just the next-door neighbour,' answered Jasmine, as nonchalantly as she could.

'And? Who is it?' her mum asked eagerly.

'Shush, I'll tell you later,' Jasmine said in a hushed tone and led her back down the garden to the others.

–

Robin closed the back door behind him, then leant on it. So, that was Jasmine Boyd. And what a beauty she was. Jasmine obviously hadn't noticed him walk up the side of the cottage to the back garden. He'd certainly noticed her though, head slightly titled, eyes closed, dark blonde hair blowing gently in the breeze. He'd admired her slender neck and shoulders covered only by the thin straps of her sun top. She looked so serene... so captivating. He could have stood there staring at her for hours. Then he let out an impatient sigh. Damn Bunty, this was exactly the reaction she wanted from him.

Chapter 7

Robin was knackered. He'd spent all yesterday in the attic of his cottage. Wanting to make good use of the space, he and Jack had decided to strengthen the floorboards and put a skylight in the roof, maximising the splendid view it would give. They also needed to install a set of stairs leading up, which meant reconfiguring the landing slightly, as at the moment, stepladders were propped up to allow Robin to climb back and forth as he carted up the wooden planks.

It had been such a warm day and he'd opened wide all the windows to let the breeze in, now and then catching snippets of conversation from Jasmine's garden, unable to help but listen. Fair to say, he was more than curious about the girl next door.

Listening shamefully, Robin had gleaned quite a lot. He levelled it in his mind as being neighbourly, wanting to learn more about Jasmine – and after all, she herself had been caught taking a good peak at his property.

It was evident she had very caring parents, the way they both fussed over her, and pretty obvious that the brother was protective of her too. No wonder, thought Robin, given what the poor girl had gone through. It was blatantly clear how resilient she must be, summoning up the strength to renovate a new home and start again, all on her own.

He cast his mind back to how hurt and forlorn he'd been when his ex-girlfriend had royally dumped him and ripped him off. His wounds would be nothing compared to Jasmine's.

Although only having met his next-door neighbour briefly, she had made quite an impact on him, probably due to the fact he knew of her heartbreaking background. Human nature did that, thankfully; made people kinder to those in need, no matter how well you did or didn't know them. And Robin *did* want to help her; he knew he could, very easily. He had the resources, as a property developer, to make Jasmine's life a whole lot easier. They were both in the same position, renovating adjourning cottages. Although Jasmine had a brother to help, Robin doubted he'd have the same skills he and Jack had, as implied by her comment that they would be 'giving it their best shot'.

A skip was being delivered that morning and, knowing that Jasmine and her brother were about to rip out the kitchen and bathroom (from his eavesdropping), he intended to offer its use to her. He had originally ordered a smaller skip, but he'd called and changed it to a larger one to make extra room.

It had tickled Robin that Jasmine and her brother were camping out in the garden. But why not? It made sense to take advantage of the good weather, rather than being cooped up inside the cottage which would be full of muck and dust whilst working on it.

Yawning, he made his way into his kitchen and filled the kettle. He always took a full flask of coffee and sandwiches with him when working on a job, fuel for the day. His mobile rang, and looking at the screen told him it was Jack.

'Hi, mate,' he answered.

'Hi. The window's arrived for the skylight,' Jack informed him.

'Good. I'll knock through the roof today and get it fitted.'

'Need a hand?'

'Nah, don't think so. You OK to go to the reclamation yard?' They had decided to try and source original fittings for the bathroom and wanted a cast iron, rolled top bath along with sinks and shower mixer taps. They'd also wanted an old fireplace to install in the living room.

'Yeah, sure, leave it with me.' Then Jack added, 'Any sign of next door?'

Robin paused, having expected this question from Jack. Part of him was tempted to deny he'd met Jasmine, knowing how inquisitive Jack would be about her. The last thing he wanted was for Jack to go snooping about, hoping to catch a glimpse of her. For some reason, he felt quite defensive of Jasmine. He'd never mentioned to Jack that he'd gone to Bunty to get answers, so he was left in the dark about her matchmaking schemes.

Although he had eavesdropped on her family yesterday, rather hypocritically, he didn't like the idea of Jack's interest being satisfied.

Instead of outright denying what happened, Robin played down his answer.

'Just exchanged names over the hedge,' he said in an offhand manner.

'And?' Jack's voice rose in anticipation.

'She seems nice enough,' came the neutral reply. 'Like I said, we only introduced ourselves, didn't talk for long.'

'Oh.' Jack was obviously disappointed not to have had a more detailed account. 'What does she look like?' he persisted.

Robin rolled his eyes, typical Jack. He was damned well not going to tell him that Jasmine was without doubt one of the most attractive women he'd ever set eyes on. This would only raise Jack's interest further.

'Well… shortish hair, friendly face. Her brother's there too, helping out apparently. Built like a brick shithouse,' added Robin unnecessarily, but it seemed to do the trick.

'Oh, right.'

Robin grinned wryly, changing tack. 'So, if you go to the reclamation yard, I'll get the skylight done.'

'OK, will do, bye.'

'See ya, mate.' Robin hung up then laughed, shaking his head at Jack. He knew how to handle him, having been his best friend for years.

When Robin's parents had chosen to leave London and all its pressures behind, they couldn't have picked a more ideal spot than Samphire Bay. Although only a teenager at the time, Robin instantly became accustomed to the tranquil, coastal village, which held so much charm. He'd loved the quirkiness of the peninsula and the way it could be cut off by the tide. The place intrigued him with its folk tales of stolen contraband hidden in secret coves by smugglers, or shipwrecks out at sea waiting to be discovered. It had all been such a huge contrast to the busy suburb in north London where he'd grown up.

Together with Jack, who he'd immediately gelled with, they had got the most out of the place; barbeques with friends on the beach, dancing until sunset to go skinny dipping under a moonlit sea. They'd had a ball. Having a small community meant people really knew each other well and solid friendships formed.

Looking back, Jack always did have an eye for the ladies. His good looks and natural charisma meant he'd been popular, but perhaps never taken too seriously, while Robin had been the quieter of the two in comparison, but still well-liked; and where Robin was dark, swarthy and with a tendency to brood, Jack was fair haired and the more boisterous.

It had been Jack who had warned Robin of Ellie, his ex-fiancée. Although appearing to have a devil-may-care attitude, it was he who'd had the intuition to see straight through her, especially when she had tried to flirt with him. That, in Jack's book, was bang out of order. It was one thing chatting up women, but best mate's girlfriends were most definitely out of bounds. He'd tried several times to caution Robin, without actually telling him just what his girlfriend was capable of. Robin's friendship was important to him and the last thing he wanted was any kind of rift between them, especially as nothing had come of her flirting.

'Don't put her name on the deeds, mate, just yours,' he'd said, knowing it was Robin's money which was being poured into the renovation of the barn they had planned to live in.

'But it's going to be her home too,' Robin had reasoned, thinking his friend was acting a touch mercenary. But for all Jack's advice, which Robin had ignored, he'd been proved well and truly right. If only he had listened to his best mate, he'd have saved himself a whole load of misery and money.

Still, that was in the past and time had moved on. So had Robin. At least Ellie had done the right thing and beggared off, out of Samphire Bay, leaving him free to get on with his life. He laughed to himself when thinking about Bunty and her idea that playing cupid was going to help him. Despite it being totally outrageous the way she was trying to engineer the situation, he could see she meant well. Then again, after seeing Jasmine yesterday, maybe Bunty wasn't too far off the mark after all.

Jack had left the new window propped up against the side of the cottage and was gone by the time Robin arrived. He couldn't help but be a tad relieved, feeling reluctant to introduce Jack to Jasmine just yet. He knew how playful his mate could be at times, especially around attractive ladies, and didn't want Jasmine to feel uncomfortable in any way.

He picked up the glass and walked to the back of the cottage. On doing so, he saw another face peering over the garden hedge.

'Hi, there!' called the man he assumed was Jasmine's brother.

'Hi,' replied Robin. He leant the window against the back door and went over to him. 'Robin,' he supplied and held out his hand.

'Sam, Jasmine's brother.' The men shook hands.

'Heard you're doing this all yourselves. I've got a skip being delivered this morning, feel free to use it,' Robin offered.

'Thanks, appreciate it, that'll be a big help. We've just started ripping out the kitchen units.' He pointed to a pile of damaged wooden doors and an old Formica worktop in the garden.

Robin smiled. 'I'll be doing the same before so long.'

'You from Samphire Bay?' asked Sam.

'Yeah, moved here when I was seventeen.'

'It's a lovely spot,' Sam remarked, gazing out towards the bay.

'The best,' agreed Robin.

'Will you be living here, or selling once you've finished renovating the cottage?'

Robin paused for a moment, surprised at Sam's directness. Was he sizing him up? Sussing out who could be living next door to his sister? Originally, he had wanted to buy both cottages and renovate them into one spectacular house. Then, he *would* have been tempted to keep such a stunning property as his own home. As that hadn't panned out, he was still considering his options.

'I may live here, haven't decided yet,' he answered, looking Sam in the eye. He refused to feel intimidated in any way, albeit understanding Sam's brotherly concern. He also didn't feel the need to explain himself, either.

'I see.' Sam nodded. 'Well, thanks for letting us use your skip. Best get back to work.'

'No worries,' replied Robin, and he turned back to the cottage, ready for a full day's work.

–

Bunty poured herself another generous glug of gin, added tonic, a slice of cucumber and lots of ice, then turned to gaze out of the huge bow window in the drawing room. This was her favourite spot, overlooking the panoramic view of the bay.

Many a time she'd stare out to sea, watching what it had to offer that day – whether it be a raging storm with metal grey clouds hovering over its dark waters, flashes of lightening illuminating the whipped-up waves, or a serene sunset peacefully settling down, reflecting deep orange and soft pink hues over its gentle ripples. No two days were ever the same.

Today, the sea was calm. What was the saying? *Still waters run deep*, echoed a distant voice in her head, causing her to take a big gulp of gin. Her eyelids closed, allowing hazy memories to morph into sharper focus, refusing to be forgotten...

Bunty had watched the little red fishing boat chug out on a limpid sea. All was quiet apart from the distant echo of seagulls calling in the distance. She squinted, shielding her eyes from the sun and saw the figure on the deck wave – no, he was saluting her. She froze for a moment, suspecting the gesture was a final one, the last goodbye, a dismissal. With her chest pounding, Bunty raised her hand to wave frantically at him. *Come back!* she wanted to scream, but knew it was pointless. He'd never hear her and, besides, would it make a difference if he had? She paused, then tried again, this time with both hands, crossing each other urgently in the air. But no, he'd turned his back, refusing to look at her any longer. Hot tears poured down Bunty's face as she watched the stern of the boat bob gently through the waves, slowly distancing the space between them. She stared numbly, rooted to the spot, her heart breaking. He'd be back she told herself, he *had* to come back.

Chapter 8

Jasmine took off her face mask once all the dust had finally settled. Turning to her brother, who was covered in as much debris as she was, a contented sigh escaped her.

'Well, that's the kitchen and the bathroom gutted now,' she said with satisfaction.

'Yeah, pretty much a blank canvas to make your own mark now, sis,' Sam grinned. It was good to see his sister so full of optimism. Jasmine had been right; buying this house had definitely given her motivation, a reason to get up in the morning besides just pouring her energies into work. Over the last few days, he'd noticed the dark shadows surrounding her eyes gradually disappear and the gaunt harshness of her cheekbones become less stark as her face began to fill out again. Jasmine was slowly but surely returning to her usual self. Deep down, Sam was pleased to be helping her, but also glad his sister was keen to do the renovation at such speed. He did have a job to hold down, after all, and there was only so much annual leave he could take. Now that they had cleared the kitchen and bathroom, leaving them ready for fresh fittings, he'd soon be heading home, that had been the deal.

Jasmine was more than happy for her brother's assistance, but she was so looking forward to moving into the cottage alone. Camping out in a tent was fun, at first, but now she craved the comfort of a warm bath after a long day's hard slog. And hard slog it was, pulling out the old bath, toilet and sink, manoeuvring them down the stairs, through the gardens to next door's skip. The kitchen units had been easier to dismantle, and thankfully on ground level, but still tiring work.

Whilst Jasmine had enjoyed choosing the simple but stylish shaker kitchen, she knew it would need a professional to put it all together. Thoughts of Tom installing their kitchenette in *Moonshine* briefly haunted her, but she refused to dwell on them. Jasmine would need to employ a plumber for the bathroom too. Plus, she didn't like the idea of her and Sam bundling the new white porcelain sink and toilet up the stairs. It was one thing ripping out old fittings, but she wanted the professionals to handle the expensive equipment she'd recently purchased.

Once the kitchen and bathroom had been fitted, she did fancy having a go at the tiling. She was thinking of laying tiles halfway up the walls, then plastering the rest. Already deciding to make the most of the space, she hadn't gone for any upper wall units, just floor ones, and wanted to hang thick oak shelves with cast iron brackets. For Jasmine, it was all about character, giving the place definition, a story. She was keen to retain the history of the cottage.

Jasmine had since discovered from chatting to the locals that the cottages had been built as homes for fishermen. Hardly surprising given their location. She tried to picture how her house would have looked, all those years ago, as a humble dwelling for them. She laughed to herself, not imagining such fishermen bothering with the shades of kitchen worktops, styles of door handles, or deciding between brass or brushed copper taps. Then, she paused. Laugh, she'd actually *laughed*, once more. It still sounded strange to hear it. Incredulous even, never thinking she would hear that sound again.

It had been almost a week since Jasmine and Sam had started work on the cottage. Luckily, the weather had held out, but the forecast told them a storm was brewing. Neither of them fancied camping outside in the heavy rain, so time was of the essence. The kitchen and the bathroom had to be fitted, or at least the plumbing did, and fast.

Originally, Jasmine had been recommended workmen from the kitchen and bathroom suppliers, but they'd unfortunately let her down; their current job had gone 'belly up' and they were way behind schedule. Jasmine, not particularly warming to the description of their workmanship, had tactfully withdrawn, stating she'd find someone else. Now that both rooms were empty shells, ready to be fitted, she badly needed someone reliable and trustworthy to do it.

Again, from chatting to the locals yesterday, Jasmine had learnt that her very own next-door neighbour was in fact the man, or indeed the contact. It was amazing what a shopkeeper could inform you of, she had thought whilst walking back from the mini supermarket. Of course, she knew Robin was a property developer, but would he be interested or have the time to help her? He was busy working on his own cottage. When she'd voiced this to Sam, he seemed positive.

'I think he would help you, Jas, look how he offered the use of his skip. It's worth asking him,' he said. Jasmine chewed her lip in contemplation and, sensing her unease, Sam had quickly offered, 'Do you want me to have a word for you?'

'No. I'll do it thanks,' she answered decisively.

Quickly brushing her hair and climbing out of dusty overalls, Jasmine made her way next door. The back door was slightly ajar, so she knocked and tentatively poked her head round it. Nobody was there, but the sound of loud hammering in the hallway told her the cottage was occupied. Deciding to venture further in, she walked through the entryway and stood at the bottom of the stairs to see Robin knelt over the top step. Once again she took in his broad shoulders plus his bulging biceps as he swung the hammer against nails into the wood. Jasmine coughed and he suddenly turned.

'Hi, sorry, I did knock,' she explained.

He stopped what he was doing, looking pleasantly surprised. 'Hi, Jasmine.'

'Sorry to interrupt, but I was wondering if you might be able to help?' she started, a little awkwardly. He really did look busy and she was beginning to regret having to ask for a favour. 'It's just that I've been let down by the guys who were going to put the kitchen and bathroom in and—'

'You want me to do it?' finished Robin with a grin.

'If you're too busy that's—'

'I'll do it,' he interrupted again, still smiling.

'Are you sure?' she asked, wide-eyed with hope and filled with relief.

'Of course.' He chuckled. 'It's what I do, remember?'

'Thanks so much.' She grinned, then added, 'But what about your cottage?'

Robin shrugged. 'It can wait, there's no hurry.'

'I'll obviously pay you the going rate,' Jasmine was at pains to point out.

Robin gave a nod. 'We'll sort something out, don't worry.'

'Are you definitely sure?' she repeated hesitantly.

Robin crossed his arms and arched an eyebrow.

'You doubting my workmanship?' he teased.

'No!' Jasmine shouted, then, when realising he was joking, commented, 'Actually, you've come highly recommended.'

'Oh yes, by whom?' His hazel eyes twinkled mischievously.

Jasmine couldn't help but laugh. Again, the second time that day, she'd noted.

'Trish,' she said, knowing perfectly well he'd know her. Everybody knew everybody in Samphire Bay, she was fast learning.

'Ah yes, good old Trish.' Robin nodded, then looked into her eyes, holding her gaze. A few moments passed before either of them spoke. 'So, I'll start tomorrow, first thing,' he confirmed, breaking the pregnant pause.

'Thanks so much,' said Jasmine. 'See you tomorrow then.' She left, feeling somewhat… unsettled? But in a good way, she concluded.

Robin certainly wasn't feeling unsettled in any way. Quite frankly, he couldn't wait to start work on Jasmine's cottage, or see her again.

–

Robin was very careful about what he told Jack. As his business partner, he obviously needed to be informed of the delay in work on their cottage, so Robin had been honest, but not completely open. He'd explained that the 'next-door neighbour,' as he referred to her – not Jasmine – was in desperate need of her kitchen and bathroom fitting and how badly she'd been let down.

Jack had been fine about it, but the inquisitiveness in his voice had been evident.

'So, what's she like then, this Jasmine?' he'd asked, with a wry grin on his face. Despite Robin's blasé tone, he knew damn well when his best mate was being evasive. He could tell Robin was acting deliberately casual in an attempt to keep him at arms distance. Sending him to the reclamation yard, telling him to drop off the skylight window – Robin wanted him well out of the way, he could tell, and the man was putting their own project on hold to help her out. All this could only mean one thing, suspected Jack: Robin had the hots for this Jasmine Boyd. Good for him, he thought. It was about time Robin met someone. He more than most deserved to be happy.

Despite his Jack-the-lad reputation, deep down he cared a great deal, especially for his best friend. He had seen first-hand just what Robin had been subjected to, and even though it had been a few years ago, the scar that his ex-girlfriend inflicted had only just healed. Robin had turned down many an attempt on Jack's behalf to get him back on the dating scene.

'Come on, Rob, it'll be fun,' he'd tried to coax him, whether it be blind dates, double dates, or even a dating app. But his attempts had always been met with the same response.

'I just don't feel like it, mate, but thanks.'

Jack had started to worry about him. It pained him to see his friend so impassive, so *defeatist*. Gone were the carefree days they had enjoyed in their teens and twenties together. Robin had morphed into a solemn, quiet figure, eager to work, but not to play. He knew Robin's parents had been worried too, seeing their son so devoid of his usual free spirit.

Jack's resentment towards Robin's ex-girlfriend had grown to hate. He had *despised* what Ellie had done to his friend, not only cheating on him, but ripping him off as well. Jack knew just how much time, energy and money he'd poured into renovating that barn. He also knew how much Ellie had brazenly taken from Robin. She'd robbed him of his pride, money, but more importantly, his trust – big time. Little wonder Robin had been so reluctant to meet someone else. How could he put his faith in another relationship?

Yet now, maybe Robin had met someone. It certainly appeared that way to Jack, and whilst he was pleased for his mate, he was also damn curious as to just who had finally caught Robin's eye.

Jack decided he'd call round at the cottage and take Robin unawares. Well, it was his cottage too, wasn't it? He did have a right to be there, it had been bought as a joint business venture. Besides, he needed to take the fireplace surround he'd got from the reclamation yard.

All was quiet when he reached the cottage. Whilst there was no sign of Robin, it was clear how busy he'd been. The skylight window was neatly inserted in the roof and when Jack entered the cottage, he could see how Robin had reconfigured the stairs in the hall, with extra wooden steps installed to lead up to the attic.

'Good job, Rob,' Jack muttered to himself, admiring the workmanship. He shared Robin's vision for the place. Once they had completed the renovation, it would be worth a small fortune. The profit they'd make would be handsome indeed, especially as Robin had actually got the property for ten grand less than the asking price. Just how had he managed that? Bunty really must have a soft spot for him, he thought with a grin.

Hearing voices coming from elsewhere, he made his way back outside to the garden, but stopped in the kitchen. Looking through the window, he saw Robin and another bloke – who he assumed was the next-door neighbour's brother – slowly carry an old bath down the garden, before manoeuvring it into the skip. They were followed by the lady herself, who was laden with what looked like an old shower, towel rail and toilet seat. She too threw the lot into the skip. *Their* skip, thought Jack. So, they were paying to get rid of her rubbish too? Jack watched the three of them. They seemed to be easy with each other, chatting and laughing. Then he homed in on Jasmine. It was easy to see what he supposed Robin was drawn to. He took in her petite figure and blonde hair; her arms, poking out of rolled up overall sleeves, looked smooth and tanned, her nails polished a bright pink. Her face looked to have freckles… then she turned just as Jack was assessing her. She froze with a startled expression. Quickly Jack went outside to join them all.

'Hi,' he breezed, approaching them.

Robin introduced him. 'Meet Jack, my mate and business partner.'

Sam nodded. 'Hi, Jack.'

Jasmine, still looking a tad uncomfortable at being stared at, managed a tight smile but didn't say a word.

'I've fetched the fireplace surround,' said Jack turning to Robin.

'OK, thanks,' he replied, but didn't offer to do anything with it. Right now, he was up to his eyes clearing away Jasmine's old bathroom, then he was going to start on the plumbing and get her new toilet and sink put in. There was an awkward silence.

'I still need to get hold of a cast iron bath. There wasn't one at the reclamation yard. I'll try going further afield, see what I can find,' Jack continued.

'Great, thanks,' Robin answered. Still he wasn't elaborating, anxious to get on with his work for Jasmine.

'Right, I'll get going.' Jack knew where he wasn't wanted. It was pretty obvious the three of them just wanted to press on. He turned to go, then stopped. 'Oh, good work on the stairs Rob.'

'Cheers, mate.' Robin smiled. 'I'll call you later, yeah?'

'Yeah, no worries, bye.' He waved towards Sam and Jasmine.

'Bye Jack,' Sam said. Jasmine gave another rigid smile.

Robin frowned, noticing Jasmine's reluctance to speak. Although it puzzled him slightly, he couldn't help but feel somewhat pleased. If Jack had come here today expecting to smoothly introduce himself, it hadn't gone to plan. It was clear Jasmine hadn't been too at ease in his presence.

–

By the end of a very long and laborious day, Robin had successfully fitted Jasmine's bathroom, not only putting in the new sink and toilet, but bath too. The shower would have to wait. Sam had been a big help, fetching, carrying and holding things in place. The two had worked well together, whilst Jasmine had kept them fully refreshed with endless cups of tea and sandwiches the size of paving slabs.

'Blimey, they'll keep us going,' joked Robin, as the three of them sat in the sunshine on camp chairs. They'd been enjoying a well-earned lunch break.

'A token of my appreciation,' replied Jasmine, ever mindful of Robin's generosity. Although she would obviously be paying for his assistance, the fact he'd treated her cottage as a priority was something she'd be ever grateful for.

'Yes, thanks, Robin,' Sam chipped in. He was warming to Robin, too; he really did seem a decent chap. So much so, Sam was beginning to wonder how much he was needed now. Fitting the kitchen was going to be more straightforward than the bathroom, there'd be no lugging up and down the stairs for a start. When Sam had tentatively voiced his thoughts, he'd been a touch surprised at Jasmine's reaction. He had wondered if she'd be hesitant about him going. But no, she had simply shrugged.

'We could probably manage,' she said.

Hmm, that told me then, chuckled Sam inwardly. He looked again at his sister and a wash of relief came over him. Yes, she was definitely growing back into her old self again. Maybe Samphire Bay was just the tonic Jasmine needed.

Chapter 9

'Come in, Trish!' Bunty trilled, ushering her friend through the front door. Eager to hear the latest village gossip, she soon had the shopkeeper ensconced in the drawing room, equipped with a large glass of Pimms. Bunty had made sure she was well stocked up with the drink, knowing how much it loosened Trish's tongue. Keeping her well-oiled was the plan.

'So, what do we know?' enquired Bunty with a wide smile. By 'we' she obviously meant 'you' but wanted Trish to feel a sense of camaraderie, involving her too. It didn't take too much effort to get Trish to chirp like a canary, a couple of stiff drinks and a little flattery usually did the trick. 'Love that dress by the way, is it new?'

'Oh yes, thank you,' Trish replied. 'I got it in the sale at—'

'Yes, yes,' interrupted Bunty, 'drink up darling, then tell me all the gossip.' Her eyes twinkled eagerly in anticipation.

After taking two large gulps of Pimms, Trish was off.

'Well, I've met your Jasmine Boyd.' She leant forward.

'She's not *my* Jasmine, dear,' Bunty corrected in a flat tone, not caring for the reference.

'No… well, your… you know,' faltered Trish.

'And how did that go?' Bunty pressed, keen to learn everything she could.

'Very well,' Trish's response made Bunty sit up. Sensing she'd got Bunty's full attention, she cranked up to full flow. 'Jasmine came into the shop the other day. She bought bread, milk—'

'What did she have to say?' interrupted Bunty impatiently again.

'She wanted to know if I could recommend anyone to work on her house.'

'Ooooh.' Bunty clapped with delight. This earned her a big grin from Trish.

'Yes, well, of course I mentioned Robin, just like you told me to,' Trish tapped the side of her nose conspiringly at Bunty, who winked back in approval. 'And she seemed to take everything I said on board, what a brilliant renovator he was, what a good reputation he had, how well you thought of him—'

'You mentioned me?' Bunty butted in sharply.

'Well… you know… you and everybody else in Samphire Bay who thinks well of him,' Trish corrected in haste.

'Hmm.' Bunty narrowed her eyes in contemplation.

'Anyway, he put her bathroom in yesterday apparently,' she finished triumphantly.

Bunty's eyes flew wide open. 'Really?'

'Yes, Jack came in the shop this morning and I quizzed him. Just like you told me to,' she added.

'And what exactly did he say?'

'He confirmed that Robin had been so busy helping his next-door neighbour, he was putting his own renovation on hold.'

Promising, thought Bunty with satisfaction. She knocked back her drink. She didn't offer Trish a top-up, the shopkeeper had told her enough, everything she needed to know.

'So, about that charity event...' Trish gave a nervous cough. She'd promised the vicar to enrol Bunty in the annual Tea by the Sea fundraising party.

'What? Oh, that,' replied Bunty dismissively. She vaguely remembered someone mentioning something about it weeks ago.

'You did promise,' whined Trish.

'Yes, yes of course I'll help, but I'm not serving cups of tea all day long, darling,' Bunty said stoutly, remembering how her feet had ached like billy-o last year.

'Oh, but—'

'Leave it with me. I'll think of something.' She glanced out of the drawing room window. 'I think you'd better be making tracks, Trish. Looks like an early tide could be coming in,' she lied.

–

Once left alone, Bunty's mind began to race, as it often did. Living alone in such a large, secluded house meant that sometimes she looked to alternative methods for comfort and company. Tarot cards was one channel that Bunty used. It had started off as a novelty at first, just a bit of fun, and now it had become more of a habit. One or two of her friends questioned her behaviour, but she'd waived away their concerns.

'The cards are as safe or dangerous as you make them,' she'd say. 'They deliver a message, they don't create them.'

Bunty had learnt that the symbolism in the cards was what she needed to pay attention to in order to gain clues and insight into her own subconscious. The cards themselves never caused any harm. Or so she thought. The truth was, Bunty was lonely. She had too much time on her hands, hence her meddling into other people's lives.

What Trish had told Bunty earlier on only encouraged her further. Convinced her plan of pairing up Robin and Jasmine was forming nicely, she couldn't resist drawing the tarot cards for more information.

Moving to the hall, she opened the drawer in the console table and took the pack out. Shuffling them, she then pulled one out. Turning it over, she saw The High Priestess, a woman wearing plain blue robes, sitting with her hands in her lap. A lunar crescent appeared at her feet and she wore a horned crown with a globe in the middle. This card represented mystery, stillness and passivity – time to retreat and reflect upon the situation and trust inner instincts.

Hmm, did she trust her inner instincts, though? Yes, thought Bunty, when it came to others, but did she when it came to herself?

More and more, Bunty's mind had started to rewind, back into the past. Was it because of all this matchmaking she was trying to accomplish? The cold, hard truth hit home with force. *Yes!* a voice from within yelled. She was concentrating on other people's love lives to compensate for so badly neglecting her own. Mistakes, misunderstandings and misgivings tumbled inside her head, building momentum. Those memories came floating back up to the surface of her psyche once more. That red boat, that final salute…

'Oh Perry, where are you?' she whimpered.

–

Jasmine sighed happily and sank further beneath the bubbles. She was at last luxuriating in her bath. She had been waiting for this moment, when she could finally relax and let the warm water soothe her aching muscles – and ache they did. Never had she done such physical labour. Yes, she'd pitched in with Tom when renovating *Moonshine*, but everything had been on a much smaller scale. She pictured the tiny bathroom they'd had on the boat, compared to the one she was bathing in now.

Looking around the room, Jasmine couldn't help but be proud. Gone was the grimy old toilet, sink and bath, dirty lino, damp wallpaper and peeling paintwork. Now, thanks to Robin, a new white suite had been installed. Together with Sam, they had sanded the wooden floorboards down and stained them mahogany, presenting a striking contrast in colour. The original tiles which ran halfway up the wall, Jasmine had rather liked, being a classy dark green, so she'd scrubbed them clean and regrouted in between. She had stripped all the tatty wallpaper off and simply painted over the rest of the walls with a chalky-white paint.

Once the accessories of a wooden towel rack with matching dark green towels, a large mirror hanging above the sink and a wooden bath shelf holding green candles and white blocks of soap had been added, the room looked complete. Job well done, thought Jasmine with satisfaction.

Of course, none of this would have happened so swiftly if it hadn't been for Robin. Thinking about him comforted her; it was good to know there was someone so kind nearby. Sam, as her protective older brother, had even given him his seal of approval. Jasmine knew that he wouldn't have left earlier than planned had he not liked her neighbour.

As it was, Sam had jelled well with Robin when working together on the bathroom. After packing up the tent and waving his little sister goodbye, he'd been comforted she wasn't completely alone. It had also been a huge comfort to their parents when he had relayed to them the news of how much Robin had helped, too.

In the soapy water, Jasmine closed her eyes, basking in the peace and quiet. For once, there wasn't the sound of knocking and banging to be heard from next door either. Whilst Robin had been busy fitting her bathroom, Jack, his business partner, had apparently been dismantling and replacing a fireplace. It sounded like the chimney breast was being bashed through. Jasmine hadn't altogether warmed towards Jack. His first impression left her feeling uncomfortable, having caught him staring at her through the kitchen window. She also noticed that Robin had been keen to press on, rather than keep him talking. Once again, she was reminded of the consideration Robin showed, willing to put her cottage first, before working on his. She wondered if this had caused any difficulties with Jack, especially as Robin was about to start fitting her kitchen.

After a good, long soak, Jasmine stepped out onto the new bath mat and wrapped a thick, fluffy towel round her. Barefoot, she tiptoed into her bedroom and almost laughed at the comparison. This was definitely going to be the next room to get the treatment. For a start, she was sick of sleeping on a camp bed. That novelty had long worn off and now she was desperate to assemble the double bed she'd had delivered. Apart from stripping the walls and painting them, plus replacing the carpet, there wasn't too much involved in this room. Just taking out the heavy, dark curtains would make a huge difference, letting the natural light flood in. Jasmine couldn't understand why anyone would want to restrict such a fabulous view. She intended to put up a Roman blind in the window, maximising as much of the clear window as possible. But all that would have to wait until the kitchen was finished. One room at a time, she told herself. So, for now, a camp bed it was.

Her thoughts were interrupted by the sound of high-pitched drilling. After quickly dressing, she pulled back the curtains to see Robin's Range Rover parked outside. He must be doing something next door. It sounded like it was coming from upstairs. Blimey, didn't he ever stop? It was early evening, surely he must be tired by now? Yesterday he had finished putting in her shower and had gone straight back to his cottage to assist Jack with something. The guy was constantly on the go. Then the drilling stopped. Jasmine listened for any further noise. All was quiet.

Her thoughts turned to the chilli which was ready to be heated up in the microwave. It was seven o'clock and she was starving. Would Robin have eaten yet? Deciding to show some appreciation for all he was doing for her, she made her way next door.

Jasmine was about to knock on the back door, when Robin came out of it.

'Oh,' she hastily stepped back. 'I just came round to see if you've eaten yet, only I'm about to have a chilli and there's plenty for two?'

Robin stopped and looked at his watch. 'Hell, is that the time?'

Jasmine chuckled. 'You've not had dinner then?'

He gave a slow smile. 'No, but chilli sounds wonderful.'

'Go mad and have a glass of wine with it,' Jasmine said with a twitch of her lips.

'I just might,' he replied.

Robin genuinely had lost track of the day, having worked flat-out – the stairs leading up to the attic were finished, and the floorboards strengthened. The skylight window gave extra light, making the room feel airier. All they had to do next was clear away the storage trunks which had been left in there and it would be a clear, open space.

Jasmine's kitchen was crowded with various boxes containing kitchen unit parts waiting to be unpacked and made up. She managed to squeeze in a couple of camp chairs by one which acted as a makeshift table for them. After heating up and serving the chilli, along with microwave rice, Jasmine opened a bottle of red wine and poured them each a generous glass.

'There you go, you deserve it,' she said passing Robin his glass.

'Cheers!' Robin took a large gulp, savouring the rich and fruity flavours hitting the back of his throat. Glancing down at his steaming plate, he suddenly realised how hungry he was. 'Thanks for this Jasmine. It's good of you.' What would he have eaten at home? Probably just cheese on toast, something quick. He looked up to see her studying him. He cocked his head to one side and frowned slightly. What was she thinking?

'Robin, why are you helping me?' she asked.

The question floored him, it was so unexpected. Stalling for time, he chewed on his food before answering.

'Because I want to.' He shrugged. 'Why do you ask?'

'I do appreciate it, don't get me wrong, but you don't know me and… well… it's a big favour, isn't it, when you've got so much on?' She was still scrutinising his face.

Robin looked down, avoiding eye contact. He was beginning to feel a little put on the spot. What could he say? Tell her that Bunty had basically set them up to meet? That from the moment he had clapped eyes on her, he'd felt an innate compulsion to help her? No, she'd run a mile, and rightly so.

For Jasmine, the penny had just dropped. 'You may not know me, but you know *about* me, don't you?' It wasn't an accusation, more a recognition. Her voice was quiet and soft, making Robin shift in his chair awkwardly. There was a silence. Then Robin came clean.

'Yes, Jasmine, I know about you,' he answered honestly.

'I see.' She gazed out of the kitchen window, chewing her lip. Her hand reached up to clasp the heart pendant on her necklace. Robin sat still, not knowing what to say. 'I suppose it's common knowledge. Tom's death was in the paper after all,' she said, turning back to him with tears in her eyes.

Robin resisted telling her that he'd in fact learnt from Bunty about her poor husband.

'I'm so sorry, Jasmine, it must be… awful for you.' Robin winced at how lame he sounded, but words really did fail him. Still, he pressed on, 'I would have helped you anyway. We're neighbours and that's what neighbours do, isn't it, help each other?' he gently replied, then pointing to his plate, '*You've* made me dinner, and very nice it is too.'

'Thanks.' She gave a shaky smile.

Their eyes met for a moment. Jasmine swallowed, a strange sensation washing over her.

'Let's have a top-up.' Robin took the wine bottle and refilled their glasses. Then he sat back and surveyed the chaos in the kitchen. Jasmine's lips twitched, guessing what he was thinking. 'Well, I've got my work cut out here, haven't I?' he teased, trying to make light of the situation.

'I'll be your glamorous assistant,' she replied dryly.

Robin smiled compassionately whilst admiring this young, beautiful widow, who was valiantly restarting her life. Yes, he was attracted to her, of course he was, but equally he couldn't help but value her strength in spirit.

Chapter 10

Robin was up early the next morning. Considering he had drunk so much wine the evening before, he was feeling surprisingly cheery. He'd thoroughly enjoyed being at Jasmine's last night. After her initial question, which had caused a thorny moment, the atmosphere had lifted, conversation had flowed, and it hadn't been long until another bottle of wine was opened.

As the drink flowed, both Jasmine and Robin had relaxed more in each other's company. Robin had had her giggling at the scrapes he and Jack had got themselves into as teenagers living in Samphire Bay. Jasmine envied them, having such a beautiful location to grow up in, as well as the strong bond between the two friends. The alcohol had given her enough Dutch courage to be open and frank about Jack.

'To be honest, I didn't like the way he was staring out of the kitchen window the other day. Why not come out straight away and introduce himself?' she'd confessed. This had caused Robin to throw his head back and laugh. 'What?' asked Jasmine, perplexed.

'Because that's typical Jack,' he'd replied. 'He was sussing you out on the quiet.'

This explanation didn't do anything to mend her opinion of him.

'What do you mean?' she asked almost indignantly. Still Robin couldn't help but laugh.

'Don't be offended, Jasmine. He's just curious about you, that's all.'

'Curious, or just plain nosey?' Jasmine arched an eyebrow.

'Curious. To be honest, everyone in Samphire Bay will be wanting to know all about you.' He grinned.

'Yeah, well, that sounds about right, if the shopkeeper's anything to go by,' Jasmine muttered with a heavy dose of sarcasm, 'not to mention that Bunty Dev… Dev…' Her head was a touch fuzzy from the wine by this time and she struggled to remember Bunty's full name.

'Deville,' Robin supplied, suddenly looking serious.

'Hmm, Bunty Deville, she's a character.'

'She certainly is,' agreed Robin quietly. If only Jasmine knew just how much a character Bunty was. How would she react if she knew of Bunty's attempt to play cupid? Deciding to quickly change the subject, Robin moved the conversation back to Jack. He couldn't help but think Jasmine had got the wrong impression. Whilst a small part of him was glad Jasmine hadn't exactly fluttered her eyelashes at Jack, he still didn't want her to think badly of his best mate. 'Don't be too hard on Jack though, he's a decent bloke.'

'If you say so,' Jasmine replied, still unconvinced.

'No, he is. He wouldn't be my best mate or business partner otherwise.'

'I'll give him the benefit of the doubt then.' She smiled, not wanting to cause any offence.

'And it's only natural for people to be interested in a newcomer to Samphire Bay. You're new blood,' he said with a grin.

Jasmine tilted her head to one side in contemplation. 'I suppose so,' she replied, remembering how nosey her mum had been about Robin, plus how quick her brother had been to introduce himself. It worked both ways, Jasmine conceded.

And so the evening had continued, with easy chat and banter. Robin couldn't remember when he had last enjoyed himself so much. Usually he'd be sat in front of the TV, or working late. He was still reluctant to venture out on dates, despite Jack's encouragement. Even he had stopped trying to coax his best mate into some sort of social life. It wasn't that Robin didn't want to enjoy himself, he really did, but the mere threat of encountering the stress he'd endured with his ex-fiancée left him cold. It had sapped him dry in every sense – emotionally, physically and financially – and his bad experience dampened any enthusiasm for future relationships. Until now.

Jasmine had a certain quality about her which Robin couldn't define, finding it hard to put his finger on what made her different. He hardly knew her and yet his gut instinct told him he could trust her. Why? Was it because she, too, had been dealt a blow in life? Well, more than a blow, acknowledged Robin, considering what had happened to her late husband. Yet despite the horrific circumstances surrounding Jasmine, she was obviously a fighter, willing to carry on and start again.

Respect. That's what he had for Jasmine; he admired and respected what she was doing, and you trusted those kinds of people, didn't you?

–

In the meantime, Jasmine hadn't slept well at all. The heavy head she'd gone to bed with had kept her awake most of the night. That, and the way her mind refused to stop spinning. A peculiar sensation was slowly breaking through, leaving her confused.

For the past eight months, all Jasmine had felt was bleak desolation – a sad, empty crater, refusing to be filled. She had dismissed the words people tried to comfort her with. 'Time is a healer,' seemed such a ridiculous platitude. But here she was, in a new house, in a stunning location, actually *looking forward* to seeing her home fully renovated. A chink of light was starting to break through the bleakness.

But with it came other, difficult thoughts – should she be feeling this way? Should she have enjoyed the evening with Robin? It had been all too easy to unwind with a glass of wine and listen to his tales. He was interesting, entertaining and not threatening in any way.

A wave of guilt hit her. Instinctively her hand went up to the heart pendant on her neck, her default any time she thought of Tom, where she felt closest to him. She longed to hear his voice, ever convinced she had heard it that day, in this very room, telling her to put in an offer for the cottage. Jasmine had tossed and turned till the early hours, until she finally fell into an exhausted sleep.

She woke the next morning tired and bleary-eyed. Deciding to have breakfast straight away, she took a couple of headache tablets with her tea. She had a busy day in front of her.

–

Jack entered the shop and Trish immediately turned in his direction from behind the counter. With a wry grin he braced himself, knowing what he was in for. Trish was a renowned gossip and it was common knowledge that the local shopkeeper was a friend and spy for Bunty Deville. It didn't take too long for him to pick up the bread, butter, milk and cans of lager and head for the checkout. As predicted, Trish was on him straight away as she scanned the contents of his basket.

'So, I hear Robin's getting along nicely with his new neighbour,' she said, glancing up at him.

He sent what he hoped was a neutral smile her way. 'Yes.'

'Has he finished working on the cottage next door?' Trish eagerly asked.

'Give him a chance,' replied Jack with a laugh. 'He's good, but not that good.'

'So where is he up to then?'

'He's about to start the kitchen I believe.' Jack placed his items in a carrier bag.

Trish, desperate for more information before he left, halted and held the loaf of bread hostage.

'Does he… you know…' she faltered, keen to have at least some juicy morsel of tittle-tattle to give Bunty.

'What?' Jack asked, eyes wide and lips twitching.

'You know… fancy her?' she blurted out, startling herself.

'Pardon?' Jack laughed, causing Trish to blush.

'Just asking. We all want to see Robin happy, that's all. It'd be ideal if he got together with Jasmine. They'd make such a good couple,' Trish was at pains to explain.

Jack shook his head in awe.

'Trish, we all want Robin to find happiness,' he said patiently, 'but I'm not sure he'd thank you for inter—' he quickly changed the word interfering, 'taking an interest. Maybe just let nature take its course?'

'Yes, I suppose so,' mumbled Trish, disappointed not to have any feedback for Bunty. She finished scanning the bread and Jack paid. Just before stepping out of the shop, he turned.

'And Trish?'

'Yes?' she answered sharply with anticipation.

'You don't always have to listen to Bunty.' He smiled and closed the shop door.

Huh, thought Trish, *easier said than done.*

–

Meanwhile, Robin was indeed busy fitting Jasmine's kitchen. Surrounded by empty cardboard boxes, he was putting together the base units.

'Don't you need to read the instructions?' asked Jasmine, watching as he screwed the joints of wood together without any hesitation.

'Nah, I've assembled enough kitchens in my time.'

Jasmine had been impressed with the speed and efficiency Robin showed. So much so, she was beginning to feel a tad surplus to requirements.

'Can you pass me those?' He pointed towards a plastic bag containing metal hinges. She supposed it must be handy for him to have a fetcher and carrier so he could focus on the important stuff. Jasmine noticed he'd brought his own packed lunch.

'I can make lunch, you didn't need to bring your own,' she told him, nodding towards his butty box. He looked up to face her.

'It's fine, you made me dinner last night.'

'As a thank you, Robin,' she explained in exasperation, as well as humour. 'Seriously, I can't just stand here doing practically nothing, give me a job,' she insisted. Robin looked around.

'OK, I'd love a cuppa.' He grinned.

With a laugh, she headed for the counter. 'Coming up.'

Whilst waiting for the tea to brew, Jasmine thought back to the days when Tom had fitted *Moonshine*'s kitchenette. It seemed a long time ago somehow. A lump formed in her throat which she tried to swallow. She blinked her eyes rapidly. The last thing she wanted was for Robin to see her getting emotional.

Taking both cups of tea, she handed Robin his.

'Ah, thanks.' He stood up and lent on one of the boxes. He could see her eyes were slightly red-rimmed. Was she tired, or had something upset her? Not knowing how to react or what to say, he looked away and concentrated on drinking his tea.

Jasmine chewed her lip. Then, not really knowing why, began talking about her narrowboat. Robin was instantly interested, eager to hear all about it.

'We named her *Moonshine*,' she said with a wistful smile, remembering that very first glimpse of the neglected boat, illuminated by the shaft of silver light. 'I persuaded Tom to buy her. She was a wreck, in need of salvaging.' She chuckled softly.

Robin stood and listened, hands clasped round his mug, head slightly tilted, absorbing her words. Truth be told, he'd been more than interested in Jasmine. After hearing about her from Bunty and seeing her for the first time, he'd searched the internet for her background. It hadn't taken too long for the tragic story to appear. Newspaper articles had been in abundance concerning her husband, Tom Boyd. He'd read about the hit-and-run accident rendering him dead. It was sickening. How could anyone leave someone to die in the road after ploughing into them? It beggared belief. All the while he had thought of poor Jasmine, left a widow so young. How on earth had she dealt with it? Now, listening to her, he felt almost privileged to be privy to her memories – they must be so precious.

'I'll never forget our first night on the boat,' continued Jasmine, now in full flow, as if an emotional dam had burst within her and all the pent-up tension was spilling out. 'It had been a full moon that night and we drank champagne under the stars, bathed in its light.'

'Obviously meant to be,' murmured Robin. She looked at him, a touch surprised, like she'd forgotten he was there in the kitchen with her. It was almost as if she'd been talking to herself.

'Yes, yes it was,' Jasmine agreed. 'Everything was meant to be. Meeting Tom, getting married, buying our narrowboat, all of it…' Her chin quivered.

Robin froze. Hell, please don't say she was going to cry; he'd never felt so bloody useless. Except he wasn't useless, was he? He was here, offering his services, putting her kitchen in. Still looking at her, he finally offered some sort of comfort.

'Jasmine, I think you're incredibly brave,' his voice was hoarse and he gulped.

Her gaze rested on him. 'Thanks.' She gave a sad smile.

'If there's anything I can do…'

'Apart from renovate my cottage you mean?'

He gave a half laugh.

'Only your bathroom and kitchen.'

'Only?' Her eyebrow rose.

'That aside, I mean…' he puffed out his cheeks. 'I don't know what I mean really.' His brows furrowed in confusion. 'I guess… if you need to talk, I'm only next door.' He blinked at his own words, not quite believing the conversation had taken such a dramatic turn. He certainly hadn't been expecting it and suspected that neither had Jasmine.

She let out a sigh of gratitude.

'Thanks, Robin.'

–

The rest of the day was spent constructing the rest of the units, putting on the doors, then lastly, fitting the oak worktop. Robin had used his jigsaw to cut it into shape for the sink area, which took time and precision. Jasmine watched his face, etched in concentration. He really was a master craftsman. For the second time that day, she'd been hugely impressed with his work. As she looked round the kitchen she was delighted with the result. Solid oak cupboards ran round two sides of the room. A white ceramic butler sink with brass taps stood under the window. The wooden worktop finished the look off beautifully. It was clean, practical, stylish and gave the country feel she wanted. Choosing not to have wall mounted cupboards, just floor ones, meant the room felt more spacious too. Jasmine planned to hang her copper pans and fancy crockery from sturdy oak shelves, adding to that country look.

After a full, industrious day they both stood back and admired their work. Jasmine had proved herself useful, not only fetching, carrying, holding things in place and making tea but, on her insistence, had made a tasty lunch. Once Robin had caught a whiff of the quiche cooking in her new oven and saw the colourful salad and crusty French bread, he'd soon ditched his butty box.

Now it was early evening and they were both in need of a drink. Jasmine opened another bottle, this time prosecco.

'You seem to have an abundance of booze,' smiled Robin, remembering the two bottles of wine she'd had at the ready the previous night.

'I was given a crateful from Sam, a house-warming present,' she replied, popping the cork. Pouring the fizz into two flutes, she gave one to Robin. 'Cheers, Robin. The kitchen's amazing.' She clinked his glass.

'My pleasure,' he answered, and truly meant it.

Chapter 11

'Agenda item number three, Tea by the Sea,' announced the vicar with enthusiasm, looking round the table expectantly. He was hoping for a good response. Last year's Tea by the Sea fundraising event had made a hefty sum, and the church roof wasn't going to mend itself.

There was a brief moment before Trish coughed and began the conversation.

'Well, I have put the word out and enrolled a few volunteers.'

This gained her a big beam from the vicar.

'Splendid,' he said, then looked directly at Bunty, who up until now had been unusually quiet. 'And Bunty, have you anything to add?'

Bunty had anticipated being roped into the event. Since Trish had asked her, she had given the matter some thought and was rather pleased with the result.

'Actually I have vicar,' she replied.

'Oh, and what's that, pray tell?' he asked with a charming smile.

'I intend to read tarot cards.'

The vicar's eyes widened and a stony silence followed. 'Sorry...?'

'All in good taste. I'll dress up as a fortune teller, I thought, and read people's fortunes. As long as they know it's all tongue-in-cheek, the punters will love it,' she stated.

'But... couldn't this be seen as playing with the dark arts?' asked Trish, mouth gaping open. Bunty gave a bark of laughter.

'No, darling. It'll be seen as me playing the fool. I intend to attract customers for fun, that's all. And besides, I won't come cheap.'

'How much would you charge then?' Ned, landlord of the village pub, laughed heartily while a few smirks were exchanged around the table.

'Ten pounds a reading,' Bunty said, almost defiantly.

Hetty, who drove the mobile library, gasped. 'Ten pounds!' she exclaimed.

'I'll be worth every penny. They'll get the full monty: me dressed up as a gypsy, called Rosy-Lee, I'm thinking, in a cosy caravan and reading the tarot cards. I'll even throw in a crystal ball,' she said with gusto.

'A crystal ball?' the vicar questioned with a frown.

'Well, an old goldfish bowl. I'll turn it upside down and fill it with fairy lights, it'll do.'

'And whose cosy caravan?' asked Jim, a local farmer.

'Yours. I'll use one of your shepherd's huts.' Bunty locked eyes with Jim, as if challenging him to object. He didn't.

'But Bunty dear, do you really think people will pay ten pounds for a reading?' Trish tentatively asked.

'Yes I do. They'll be curious,' came the forthright reply.

The vicar mumbled in thought, hands steepled together. This could well be a money spinner... and they did need the funds.

'I say let's go for it,' cheered Ned. If anything, he was dying to see Bunty Deville dressed up as a gypsy, in Jim's shepherd hut, with a goldfish bowl full of fairy lights and a deck of tarot cards. Hell, he'd pay twenty pounds for a reading! He'd also make sure there were photographs of her, when they put snapshots of the charity event on the church website.

'Let's take it to a vote,' advised the vicar. 'All those in favour, raise your hand.' He looked round the table. Ned's arm shot up, in unison with Bunty's. Trish, after getting a firm nudge from Bunty's other arm, reluctantly raised hers too. As did Jim, when receiving Bunty's threatening glare. Hetty, refusing to be intimidated, remained still. The vicar took stock.

'That's four votes in favour, one against and I wish to abstain from the vote,' he said.

'Motion carried,' cut in Ned, not even trying to conceal his laughter. 'Bunty's going to be gypsy Rosy-Lee,' he chuckled.

'All for a good cause,' countered the vicar, not quite sure how this was all going to pan out. He wiped his perspiring forehead and gulped. 'Now, item number four, Tea Duties…'

–

Robin was struggling to move the remaining trunk which had been left in the attic. The first one had contained old pictures, a few books and some bed linen and had been light enough to haul down the stairs. But this one weighed a ton and no matter how hard he tried the trunk refused to budge. He stood back to inspect it. Made of dark wood with elaborate patterned carvings, it had a brass lock, keeping whatever was inside sealed shut.

As far as he knew, the previous occupants of the cottages had been fishermen, all tenants of Bunty. Why would anyone leave a locked trunk behind? Surely they would want to take their possessions with them? Did Bunty even know the trunks were here? Probably not, tucked away in the rafters. He doubted she would have ventured up here. Still, it puzzled him as to what could be inside the trunk and more importantly, how he was going to get the thing out of the room.

It was clearly going to be a two-man job, so he reached for his mobile and rang Jack to see if he was free to give him a hand. It hadn't taken long before he heard his mate enter the house.

'Up here Jack!' called Robin.

Jack climbed the newly installed steps up into the attic.

'Hi, what's the problem?' He frowned.

'It's this, I can't budge it.' Robin kicked the side of the trunk.

'Why? What's in it?'

'No idea, it's locked.'

'That's odd,' said Jack moving nearer to inspect the trunk. 'Why leave something if it needs to be under lock and key?'

'My thoughts exactly.' Robin nodded. 'Do you think we should tell Bunty about it? It must have belonged to one of her tenants.'

Jack knelt down to scrutinise the lock.

'We own the house now, so technically it belongs to us,' he replied, eyes narrowing to get a closer look.

'Should we open it?' asked Robin. 'There's no sign of a key.'

'We could use a crowbar.' Jack stood up. 'I've got one in the van.'

They looked at each other, both curious as to the contents of the trunk.

'Yeah, OK, let's force it open,' Robin said decisively.

After a few attempts at pushing down heavily on the crowbar, the lid eventually creaked open. Both eagerly peered inside.

'An anchor?' Robin's voice held slight surprise.

'Look, it's got initials engraved on it.' Jack pointed to the curved bottom where the letters B and P appeared in the steel. More interestingly, the shape of a heart was positioned in between. There was a slight pause as they took stock at their find.

'This must have belonged to a fisherman who lived here once,' Robin remarked. Then he noticed a brown envelope lying flat underneath it. He carefully pulled it free and opened it. Inside were photographs, slightly damaged by age and damp. Jack came to stand behind him to take a look.

They were pictures of a couple, taken some years ago judging by the Sixties clothes. A preppy looking young man wearing a double-breasted blazer with straight-legged slacks and loafers, stood next to a girl in a geometric shift dress and kitten heels. Both wore dark shaded glasses and big grins for the camera. Another shot showed the couple on what looked to be a day trip out, with Blackpool Tower in the background, splashing in the seawater. The man had his trouser legs and turtle-neck shirtsleeves rolled up, whilst the lady laughed, also barefoot in Capri pants and a button-down blouse. Robin smiled at their sense of style and fun. Each picture depicted how much the couple were openly in love; the way their eyes held, arms wrapped tightly round each other's body, always touching, connecting. The photos had been taken over a period of time, some in winter with snow-capped hills in the backdrop, or in summer picnicking in meadow fields. One was taken in a fairground, eating candy floss with a brightly lit Waltzer whirling behind them.

Robin and Jack studied each picture with interest.

'I wonder where they are now?' Robin's eyes darted from one image to the next.

'And why they left such treasured memories,' Jack said. 'Maybe one died and the other couldn't bear such painful reminders?'

Immediately Robin thought of Jasmine and he gulped. He put the photographs back in the envelope.

'What should we do with it?' He tapped the trunk with his foot.

Jack scratched his head. 'It doesn't seem right to get rid of it…'

'We could polish it up, it'd make a nice piece. The anchor would be a good feature in the garden, part of the cottage's history,' Robin suggested.

'Yeah, but what about the photos?' asked Jack.

Robin shrugged. 'Just keep them I guess. I'll take them home for now.'

Between them they carried the anchor down and propped it up against the back of the house for the time being. Robin decided he'd lightly sand the trunk down and varnish it, in which case it was as good there in the attic than anywhere else. He even considered keeping it, thinking the piece would look good at the bottom of his bed, plus it would make for handy storage space.

On his way home late afternoon, he called at the shop for something to eat that evening. Trish was busy serving other customers, so hadn't seen him come in. Robin stared into the freezer cabinets with little relish. He knew he really ought to make himself something fresh, packed with vitamins and goodness, but just didn't have the energy. It was times like this that he missed having someone to come home to. It would be lovely to return to his flat for once and have that special person to greet him with a welcoming smile and a delicious cooked dinner to share, or vice versa. Instead he was faced with a line of frozen meals to choose from, which he'd microwave, alone. Great. Just what he needed after a hard day's work.

An image of Jasmine suddenly flashed into his head. He wondered what she was eating tonight, alone too. Maybe he ought to return the favour and cook her a meal? Why not? Deciding he'd call on her the next day and do just that gave him a touch more zest.

Opting for the chicken curry and rice, he made his way to the till, where Trish – who by now had spotted him – was keenly waiting.

She smiled as he approached. 'Robin dear, how are you?'

'Good thanks, Trish, and you?'

'Oh you know, can't complain,' she replied whilst scanning his ready meal. 'How's the work coming along next door?' she enquired as casually as she could. Robin looked up from digging in his back pocket for money.

'Jasmine's? Fine, the kitchen and bathroom are in.' He paid, waiting for his change, which Trish was in no hurry to give.

'How are you two getting along?' she brazenly asked.

Oh, I get it, thought Robin, knowing where this was going and, more to the point, where it was coming from.

'Who wants to know?' he replied with an arched eyebrow.

'Just asking, that's all,' said Trish innocently. Robin wasn't convinced. He knew full well Bunty was behind Trish's questioning. Honestly, that woman! Then, deciding to play along for devilment, he leant forward.

'Can you keep a secret?' he asked in a hushed voice.

'Of course!' trilled Trish.

'She cooked me dinner the other night,' he whispered, trying to keep a straight face.

Trish's eyes went wide. 'Really?'

'Yes, I won't tell you what was for afters, if you get my meaning.' He winked, causing Trish to gasp. Robin couldn't help but openly laugh.

'Robin Spencer, you're teasing me, aren't you?' she huffed, folding her arms.

'Yes, I am.' He chuckled, took his ready meal and left the shop.

'Well, really,' said an indignant Trish.

Chapter 12

'Oh darling, it's fabulous!' cried Jasmine's mum as she entered the kitchen.

'I did the tiling,' Jasmine said proudly.

'Really?' Her mum looked amazed.

'Absolutely, it's surprising what you can pick up on YouTube.'

It had taken her hours to do, even though it was a relatively small space between the worktop and shelves, but still, she'd done it all by herself and was pleased with the result.

Jasmine's parents had arranged to visit and were most impressed with what they'd seen so far. Just having the tent gone made a difference, her dad had joked. Now, stood in the newly renovated kitchen they couldn't believe their eyes. The transformation was astonishing.

'Wait till you see the bathroom,' she boasted.

As predicted, her parents were stunned.

'And the next-door neighbour installed this too?' asked her dad. He'd learnt from Sam how helpful the man in the next cottage had been.

'He did,' replied Jasmine. 'I can't thank Robin enough.'

'Hmm.' Her mum was pensive, thoroughly liking the sound of this Robin. By all accounts this young man had been a Godsend. Then, on cue, there was a knock at the back door. Jasmine went to answer it.

'Oh hi, Robin, come in.' She stood back to let him enter. Immediately her mum was hot footing it down the stairs at hearing his name. Slightly out of breath, she halted before joining them in the kitchen to listen.

'Sorry, have you company? I noticed a car in the drive,' Robin asked.

'Yes, it's fine, my mum and dad are here.'

'Right, I was just wondering if you'd like to come to mine for dinner? Not tonight, obviously if you're busy—'

'Tomorrow then?' cut in Jasmine.

'Great, about seven? I'll come for you.'

'Are you sure?'

'Yeah, I'm not working tomorrow, so I'll have plenty of time to pick you up,' Robin told her.

'Shall I bring anything?' Jasmine asked.

'No, it's OK.'

'I'll bring a bottle at least,' grinned Jasmine.

Robin smiled, remembering that crate of wine she'd told him about.

'Sounds good, see you tomorrow,' he laughed and made his leave.

Interesting, thought Jasmine's mum, who by now had decided to enter the kitchen.

'Who was that, darling?' she asked innocently. Jasmine smirked wryly to herself. As if her mum hadn't listened to every word of the conversation.

'Robin. I'm having dinner at his tomorrow evening,' she explained unnecessarily.

'He can cook as well, then?' her dad said, joining them. Jasmine looked from one to the other. Clearly she was expected to divulge more on the Robin front.

'He's just being neighbourly, that's all,' she stated.

'Of course,' agreed her mum with a big smile, delighted that her daughter had met such a nice chap. Even her dad had a look of smugness about him.

'We're just friends,' Jasmine persisted.

'Good, good.' Her dad nodded. 'Now then, how about putting the kettle on in that new kitchen of yours?'

–

Robin was more than pleased with Jasmine's reaction to his invitation. She'd appeared pretty keen to come to his. Now he just had to decide what to cook. Hell, he wasn't much of a chef, but even he could stick a casserole in the oven and not burn it. He'd thought twice about buying anything from the local shop though, wishing to avoid Trish's questions and speculation. No, he'd have to go further afield to buy everything.

First things first, he'd better get his flat clean and tidy. It had been a while since he'd entertained. Correction, he'd never entertained since moving into the place. Not that he didn't value his home, he did. Being in the property business, Robin appreciated the high ceilings and cornices, loving the Gothic influences and intricately designed woodwork the large Victorian house had, before being made into separate flats. Fortunately, the developers who had renovated it had been sympathetic to its origins. The outside appearance was equally aesthetically pleasing, with patterned brick and decorative barge boards on the gable ends. The name of the building was rather grand too, Augusta House, in keeping with the era it was built.

Robin had been one of the first to view the flats once they'd been converted. He had managed to secure one of the larger ones, containing two bedrooms and a balcony at the rear which overlooked the bay. This, like it was for Jasmine, had been the deal breaker.

Although Robin had loved his new home, he'd never had the time to truly put his stamp on it. The walls were plain, clean white and the kitchen still looked brand new, not having been used that much. At least his bedroom had a more lived-in look, with the plush king-sized bed covered with paisley patterned linen, a few tasteful pictures and an old rocking chair he'd inherited from his grandmother, which stood by the balcony doors. There was a small bistro set outside on the balcony. Robin had contemplated eating there with Jasmine but felt uncomfortable with them having to access it through his bedroom. Instead, they'd use the dining table under the window in the lounge and make the most of the view that gave.

Robin was a mixture of nerves and excitement to be having a visitor – and not just any visitor, but Jasmine. It really mattered to him what she thought of his place, wanting to set the best impression. He was pleased to have tomorrow off to give himself plenty of time to prepare.

There was something else bothering him; he had to give Jasmine the invoice for his work. Left to him, he probably would have done it for free, under the circumstances. But he had a business and knew he had to run it as such, especially having Jack as his partner. Even so, he couldn't help but feel a touch uneasy.

By the next evening, Robin had accomplished everything he'd set out to. The flat was immaculate, the casserole was cooking nicely and smelling delicious, and the lemon cheesecake was chilling in the fridge, along with a bottle of champagne (he'd decided to push the boat out) and the prawn cocktail for starters he'd bought ready-made but put them in large wine glasses and added sliced lemon on the rims to look homemade. Not bad for a single bloke who didn't cook, he thought. Now all he had to do was go and pick up his guest.

–

Jasmine was looking forward to the evening ahead. Not just to have a nice meal made for her, but she rather fancied having a look around Robin's home. She assumed he'd have good taste, being in the property development line of business.

Putting on the finishing touches to her make-up in front of the bathroom mirror, a sudden wave of guilt gushed through her. She stopped midway applying her lipstick. *What was she doing?* She stared at the reflection in the glass. Her blonde hair was highlighted by the sun and a rosy complexion glowed from her face. Big brown eyes stared back at her, no longer surrounded by dark shadows. She had a radiance about her. The sunshine, fresh sea air and exercise had had an effect on her. That, and having her mind occupied with the jobs on her new house.

'It's not a date,' she told herself. Of course it wasn't. It was just two neighbours enjoying a meal together, that's all. Placing all manner of doubt behind her, Jasmine finished applying her make-up. There, it was time she made an effort on her appearance anyway. She was making an effort for *herself*, that's all.

Robin arrived on time and took it to be a good sign that Jasmine answered the door without delay. She was obviously ready and waiting. Standing on the doorstep, Robin gulped at the image before him. Jasmine looked striking in a chocolate brown, fitted halter-neck dress. It totally complemented her slim figure, sun–kissed skin and brown eyes.

'H–hi,' he almost squeaked.

'Hi, thanks for picking me up.' She offered him a soft smile.

'No problem.'

He'd actually spent an hour cleaning his Range Rover inside and out. It'd been littered with all kinds of snack wrappers, tools and muck. He hardly recognised it once finished, and neither had Jack when he'd called round that afternoon. When Robin had explained why he'd made an effort to clean his car, Jack had looked up rapidly from his scrutiny of the clean paintwork.

'You're finally going on a date?' he'd asked in amazement.

'Yeah, well not a date as such, just—'

'Good on you, mate,' Jack interrupted, so pleased his best friend had at last ventured back onto the dating scene. Seeing Robin appear a touch self-conscious, Jack quickly changed the subject and hadn't stayed long, leaving Robin to 'spruce up'.

Robin was surprised at how nervous tonight's not–date was making him. It's not as if he wasn't used to female company, far from it. Before his previous relationship, Robin had had plenty of girlfriends. He and Jack had never been short of admirers and, like most young men, they had made the most of it.

Despite feeling tense, another part of Robin felt buoyant. He genuinely enjoyed Jasmine's company. She was easy to be around, calm and placid, all the things Ellie was not, or certainly not with him at least. Horrendous memories flared into his mind; the venomous rows they'd had, her pretty face contorted with fury and spite;

the cruel, hurtful things she had screamed, leaving him wounded and crushed.

Now, standing on Jasmine's doorstep, he had to remind himself those days were gone. It was time to move on. And whilst he had told Jack this wasn't exactly a date, he dearly wished it was, in every sense.

'It smells nice in here,' Jasmine commented as she strapped her seatbelt on.

'That'll be the new air freshener. It's not always this clean and tidy,' Robin replied dryly, making her laugh out loud. This is exactly what he liked about Jasmine, there was no need to stand on ceremony. When they arrived, Jasmine took in the Augusta House sign on the cast iron gate by the entrance. The grand Victorian building looked imposing, standing proudly flanked by tall fir trees. Jasmine glanced sideways to see Robin wind his window down and scan a fob to gain entry. It all looked very sleek and classy, she thought.

Entering his flat, her impression didn't change. That too was elegant and stylish, however more minimal than she was expecting, lacking a homely touch, in her opinion.

'So, I've made a casserole,' said Robin, reaching in the fridge for the chilled champagne, 'but first let's open this.' He popped the cork and poured into two flutes.

'Lovely, what's the celebration?' Jasmine asked, surprised to see the champagne.

Robin shrugged. 'No occasion, just thought it'd be nice.'

Taking her glass, she clinked it with his.

'Cheers, Robin, and thanks, again.' She gave a half laugh, conscious of all that he'd done, which then reminded her. 'By the way, how much do I owe you?'

Robin paused, not wanting to ruin the moment, he waved her question away.

'Oh, don't worry about that now—'

'No, really,' Jasmine cut in firmly, 'I need to pay you for all your hard work.'

She looked sternly into his eyes.

'Yeah, OK, I'll drop off the invoice,' he finally said, feeling a little awkward.

'No, just give it to me now,' she insisted.

'But—'

'Please Robin, it's no big deal, really.'

'OK.'

He went to the kitchen drawer to take the envelope with the duly made out invoice in. There was also the brown envelope in the drawer from the old chest containing photographs. As a talking point, he decided to show them to Jasmine after handing her the invoice. Her face lit up with interest when he explained how he'd come across them.

'Oh look!' she cried, casting her eyes over them. She paused at the black and white shot of the couple in dark shades grinning into the camera.

'What?' Robin frowned, watching her closely examine this particular picture.

'Doesn't she remind you of anyone?'

Robin's forehead creased in bafflement.

'Look at the cheek dimples and the cleft chin.'

Still Robin frowned.

'Imagine this woman forty-odd years older,' said Jasmine almost exasperated, to her it was blatantly obvious.

Then, the penny dropped. Realisation hit Robin.

'Oh my God, it's Bunty!'

'Exactly! That's what I was thinking. But who do you think she's with?'

Then, Robin remembered what else he'd discovered.

'I found an anchor in the chest too, it had been engraved with the initials B and P,' he told her.

'So, mystery man's name begins with a P?' Jasmine was intrigued.

'And he was a fisherman, hence the anchor, and Bunty did rent out the cottages to fishermen,' concluded Robin, gaining momentum as he spoke.

'Well, well.' Jasmine narrowed her eyes. 'It looks like Bunty had a thing going with one of her tenants.' She looked at the photos again. Turning to Robin, she asked, 'How long had the cottages been empty?'

'Ages, they've been unoccupied since I moved to Samphire Bay, at least seventeen years.'

Jasmine distinctly recalled Bunty saying the cottages hadn't been lived in for 'one or two years' when asked. She hadn't believed her at the time, considering the state they'd been in.

'Do you think we should give her the photos?' asked Robin, now beginning to feel uncomfortable that they were in his possession.

Jasmine looked into his troubled eyes, admiring his integrity. She also admired the colour of them, a rich hazel, framed with dark lashes making them stand out…

'Jasmine?'

'Hmm? Oh… sorry, yes of course. Give them to Bunty, it seems the right thing to do.'

'What about the anchor? Should I give her that too do you think?' He tried to hide his disappointment, as he really thought that would have been an excellent feature for the garden.

'Not necessarily. That obviously belonged to mystery Mr P, but the photos are personal, aren't they?'

'Yeah, you're right,' Robin replied, feeling justified in keeping it. 'Right, let's eat.'

As the two of them dined, the late evening sun shone its final rays over the bay, to finally give way to a panoramic sunset.

'Such stunning views, I can see why you bought this place,' Jasmine remarked, in awe as she gazed out of the window.

'I know, but the cottage is nearer to the sea. I prefer that location.'

'Are you tempted to keep it then?' she asked, a touch taken aback at hearing this. She observed his expression, he seemed to be brooding over the answer. It suddenly occurred to her that she didn't want another neighbour. She wanted Robin to stay.

'I—I'm not sure. It was bought as a business venture, but the more I'm there, the more I'm lured.' Was he ever, especially having her as his next-door neighbour.

They looked at each other, no words exchanged, just a contented stillness. Jasmine experienced a serenity she hadn't felt in a long, long time.

The rest of the evening continued with the same easy pleasant ambience and time flew by. So much so, Jasmine looked startled at her watch when the taxi she'd booked had buzzed through to the flat to take her home.

'Thanks so much for a lovely evening,' she said, as they both made their way to Robin's door.

'My pleasure,' he replied. They stared at each other, not quite knowing what to do next.

'Well… good night.' She smiled hesitantly.

'Good night, Jasmine.' He smiled back. 'Text me when you get back home.'

'I will, bye.'

Closing the door behind him, he lent on it and exhaled. He was falling under Jasmine's spell. But what did she think of him? Was he about to have his heart broken all over again?

Chapter 13

The vicar's prayers had been answered and a glorious sun shone in a cloudless blue sky for the Tea by the Sea charity event. An area of grass ran along part of the bay before sloping down into sand dunes. Opposite it stood a row of pretty white cottages, with colourful front lawns divided by picket fences, a medieval church and a village hall. There was a cobbled square containing a large stone cross. The grass area was large and flat, making it the perfect place to set up the tables, chairs and the tea tent. Various stalls containing cakes, books and bric-a-brac had also been put up. Jim, the local farmer, had supplied his shepherd's hut for Bunty, as arranged at the church committee. She had dressed it up with bunting and made the interior as cosy as possible, whilst adding an air of mystique. Well, she'd covered the table with a silver cloth and lit a few tea lights. The 'crystal ball' looked surprisingly good, considering she'd kept to her word and tipped a goldfish bowl upside down and filled it with fairy lights. Her fortune teller costume really finished the whole effect off nicely. She had an array of bandanas to choose from but opted to put her hair up in a bun, not wanting to seem her usual self. She wore large, gold hoop earrings, a long, black dress and a red shawl. She added more rings and bracelets and her make-up was a touch bolder: brighter lipstick, heavy eyeliner, lots of blusher and black nail varnish. All in all, Bunty was quite pleased with the result.

Ned had made sure he'd taken enough photographs of her and the gypsy caravan for the church website. He was going to have enormous fun choosing from all the pictures he'd snapped of everyone involved in the event.

'Well, Bunty, you certainly look the part,' grinned the vicar.

'Yes I do, don't I?' She gave a toss of her head, enjoying how her earrings swung dramatically with the motion. 'Just you wait, vicar, we'll soon have that church roof repaired,' she quipped with a nudge.

'Hmm, let's hope so.' With a faint smile, he turned and moved on.

Down of the beach, Jim had also brought Melvin, his cute little donkey, for the children to ride on. Poor old Melvin was carted out twice a year for Samphire Bay, once for the outdoor Christmas nativity and this Tea by the Sea occasion. He took it in his stride and plodded on. Today Melvin wore a jaunty straw hat, out of which poked his ears.

Trish was in the tea tent getting more flustered by the minute. She rather envied Bunty sat down nicely in her gypsy caravan without all this commotion. Already dreading the busy day ahead, she promised herself a sit down and decided she'd get a 'reading' from Rosy-Lee, despite her original reservations.

Meanwhile Jack and Robin had showed their support by buying plenty of cake and sat scoffing them at one of the tables.

'So, how did the big date go then?' asked Jack between mouthfuls of Bakewell slice.

'I told you, it wasn't a date,' Robin said, before swilling the rest of his tea down.

'Yeah, yeah, course it wasn't. So, how did the friendly-meal-with-your-neighbour go then?'

Robin couldn't help but grin. In spite of Jack being a pain in the backside a lot of the time, he did enjoy the banter they'd always shared.

'It was good.' he said with a nod.

'How good?' Jack arched an eyebrow.

Robin laughed. 'Just… good. Time flew. Jasmine's really good company.'

'Did you kiss?' Jack asked directly, as only he would.

'No. Not that it's any of your business.' Robin stared him out.

'I get it, not a friend with bene—'

'Hello, Jack, Robin,' a voice interrupted from behind, causing them to startle and turn around abruptly.

'Hi, Jasmine,' Robin said, getting up. 'Here, sit down, I'll get another chair.' He left them momentarily to fetch one.

Sat facing Jack, Jasmine saw he at least had the grace to blush, having caught the tail end of the conversation. She felt sure Jack was referring to a 'friend with benefits' and didn't care for the expression. Even more so when she suspected he may have been talking about her, albeit teasing Robin. None of this did much to change her opinion of him. Looking at Jack now, it was pretty clear he knew this too, judging by the way he shifted uncomfortably in his chair.

'So, how are you settling in on Samphire Bay?' he attempted polite conversation.

'Fine, thanks,' Jasmine replied, looking him straight in the eye.

Thankfully for Jack, Robin soon reappeared.

'Have you seen Bunty?' he laughed, thumbing behind him to where her gypsy caravan was.

'Yeah, I think I might just pay her a visit,' said Jack, taking the opportunity to leave.

Jasmine couldn't help but snort at the idea. 'What, get your cards read?'

'Why not? It's just a bit of fun,' he replied, a touch defensively.

'And for a good cause too,' joined in Robin, then turned to Jasmine. 'Fancy getting a reading?'

'I will if you will,' she countered with a grin.

'You're on.' He held out his hand to shake on the deal.

Jack left them to it, feeling somewhat of a gooseberry. Regardless of what his mate said, the chemistry between those two was palpable. Reaching the shepherd's hut, he read the sign outside it:

£10 for a tarot card reading. Let gypsy
Rosy-Lee reveal your fortune!

Ten quid? Bloody hell, Bunty better give him good news, thought Jack as he reached for his wallet and climbed up the wooden steps into the hut.

Stifling a laugh, he sat down to face Bunty.

'Hello, Bunty,' he said, straining to keep a straight face when seeing the goldfish bowl.

'It's Rosy-Lee,' she corrected, reaching for the pack of tarot cards.

'Of course, sorry Rosy-Lee,' he replied, pursing his lips.

She placed a row of cards face down on the table before him.

'Pick a card, Jack.' He did as she told him and pointed to the middle one. 'Ah, the Lovers,' announced Bunty as she turned it over. The card showed a man and woman stood in the Garden of Eden, with the tree of life behind the man and the tree of knowledge behind the woman. She described what the figures represented. 'Relationships and choices, Jack,' she declared in a mystical voice.

'What relationships?' Jack said flatly.

'Not an existing one,' continued Bunty, 'but there'll be a temptation of heart, or choice of a potential partner.'

'I see,' said Jack, not wholly convinced. It was a good job this was for charity, or he'd be demanding his tenner back. Outside the hut he could hear giggles. Recognising them as Jasmine's he got up to go. 'Thanks Bunt— Rosy-Lee.' He smiled and made his leave.

Outside, Robin and Jasmine stood grinning like Cheshire cats. Jack gave them a cynical look with a raised brow. 'All yours,' he told them.

Jasmine went in first, not quite knowing what to expect. At seeing her, Bunty's face lit up.

'Ah, Jasmine, come and take a seat,' she welcomed.

Jasmine too was trying hard to conceal laughter at seeing the whole set-up. She stared into Bunty's face and was instantly reminded of those photographs Robin had found. From the first time she'd met Bunty Deville, Jasmine had believed there was more to her than met the eye.

Bunty placed a row of cards on the table and requested Jasmine to pick one. On doing so, Bunty then turned it over.

'The Moon,' she said with interest.

'What does that mean?' asked Jasmine.

'It represents emotion, reflective and mysterious.' Bunty held her gaze and Jasmine blinked, a little taken aback. 'It's a feminine sign, the yin… to a future yang,' finished Bunty in a gentle voice. She reached out a hand to touch Jasmine's arm. 'Don't be alarmed, I'm not really a fortune-telling gypsy,' she whispered, eyes twinkling with mischief. Jasmine smiled.

'I know,' she said, then added, 'but you are quite a character, aren't you, Bunty?'

'Am I?' The corners of Bunty's mouth twitched.

'Yes,' Jasmine said resolutely, but she couldn't resist asking: 'Have you ever found a yang to *your* yin?'

The question floored Bunty. Jasmine took in the initial shock, then the sadness of her expression. There was a long pause before Bunty spoke in a hoarse voice.

'It's your cards I'm reading, not mine. Could you send the next person in please?'

Clearly dismissed, Jasmine left the hut feeling rather odd. Robin was waiting outside.

'You OK?' he asked with concern.

'Yes, fine. Your turn.' She gave a tight smile.

When Robin entered he was a little puzzled to find Bunty looking subdued, still and staring into space.

'Bunty?' he queried. She turned at hearing him.

'Robin, come in.' She forced a bright smile. Shuffling the cards, she did the same as before and placed a row in front of him. 'Now then, let's see what's in store for you.' She indicated for him to choose one. When she flipped it over, a slow beam spread across her face, followed by a soft chuckle. 'The Sun,' she revealed. 'The best card, Robin.'

'Really, why?' he asked, peering at the card as if it would tell him its secrets.

'Yes, it represents good fortune, happiness, joy and harmony.'

'I like the sound of that,' laughed Robin.

'Hmm, it also represents the universe coming together and agreeing with your path and aiding forward movement into something greater.'

'Blimey, the whole universe, eh?'

Bunty sat back in reflection. To her, it was no coincidence that the card that came before Robin's Sun was Jasmine's Moon. The yin and yang cards, together they symbolised a time of growth and transformation, as well as a need for balance and harmony; so fitting in her eyes. Together, Jasmine and Robin had only reconfirmed what she already truly believed: they made the perfect couple.

'Worth every penny,' Robin chirped.

'Glad I cheered you up,' Bunty said but then noticed him stall, as if wanting to say something. 'What is it, Robin?'

'Err… Bunty, I found an old chest in the cottage attic and it contained an envelope with old photographs in it.' He could tell this had made an impact, as her expression shifted.

'Photographs? What kind of photographs?' she asked sharply.

'Of a young couple, probably taken in the Sixties,' he replied. 'I think they may be of you,' he quietly added.

Bunty blinked, dumbfounded. This was the second time that afternoon she'd been caught off guard.

'I'll give them to you,' Robin spoke softly.

Bunty coughed, still not knowing what to say. There was a pregnant pause.

'Yes, thank you, Robin,' she murmured.

'Right then, I'll let you get on.' Robin tried to sound as assertive as possible. Bunty didn't respond, just silently nodded.

Chapter 14

The glorious, warm weather rolled on well after the Tea by the Sea event and into mid-August. Jasmine had made the most of it and had taken to early morning swims in the sea. She loved watching the sunrise, giving a rose gold glow over the waves, finding it rejuvenating and lending her a sense of optimism.

Gradually, day by day, Jasmine was beginning to feel a little more like her usual self. Buying and renovating the cottage had clearly been the right decision, not only giving her purpose, but she loved being part of Samphire Bay; it was helping her to heal. The coastal village was a beautiful setting and she now considered it home, a place to lay down new roots.

The cottage was slowly taking shape. At last she was sleeping in a double bed, which was a blessed luxury after weeks of roughing it on a camp bed. Sam had helped her assemble it and also given her a hand stripping the wallpaper in her bedroom and redecorating it. After a new carpet and Roman blind had been fitted, the room was completely transformed. No longer a dark, damp place, but a light and airy one, the duck egg blue walls providing a fresh, calming feel.

Now, as she woke to see daylight, Jasmine stretched her limbs ready for a morning dip. She climbed out of bed and moved to the window to pull up the blind. It was promising to be another balmy day. She looked out onto the back lawn. All the grass looked yellow and singed from the heat, and Jasmine didn't fancy working in that all day again. She'd previously sat outside with the laptop in the garden but was now tiring of it, thinking it would be ideal to have a separate workspace. The idea of a studio came back into her mind and, instead of heading to the beach for her morning swim, she decided to make a start on her new studio project. The rest of the house could wait. What she really needed next was a proper, designated space to work.

As the garden sloped down, it would need to be levelled for the studio to sit on. She'd have to hire a professional with a digger. Searching the internet, she rang the number of a local business and, after explaining what she needed doing to her garden, the man on the phone seemed keen to help.

'No problem, I've a Bobcat that can soon sort that out,' he'd said.

'Great! When can you come?'

'Early next week?'

'That's fine,' she replied.

'If you just give me your details, I'll write them down.'

'I'm Jasmine Boyd and I live—' she stopped at hearing a sharp intake of breath. There was a short silence. 'Hello?' she continued.

'Sorry, I can't do it,' said the man tersely.

'But you just said—'

'Sorry.' Down went the phone.

What was all that about? frowned Jasmine. She made a note of the business, A.R. Hall Services Ltd, clearly one to avoid. Shaking her head she looked down the list. After several attempts she gave up. They were either too busy or too far away. Feeling despondent, she decided to go for that morning dip after all.

–

Robin had made an early start that morning. He and Jack had decided to knock through their kitchen wall into the adjacent room, making it a large kitchen diner, and today his task was to install a wood burning stove into it. From the kitchen window, he watched Jasmine as she left through the back garden gate, onto the footpath that led down to the beach. She was carrying a small rucksack. He knew she would be going for a swim, as she had told him it had become a morning ritual. He was so tempted to join her. He could just do to sink his aching limbs into the crystal clear shore. The sea water would be good for his bones, or so his mother always told him. Looking at the cast iron stove before him, he made an impromptu decision. He was leaving it. He'd fit it in the afternoon when Jack was there. The bright, warm sunshine and the glittering waves beckoned him. That and Jasmine. He'd swim in his boxer shorts, then go back home and change afterwards. Grabbing a towel from the downstairs loo, he headed off for the beach.

He could see Jasmine climbing down the dunes and soon caught her up.

'Hey, Jasmine!' He waved when she quickly turned.

'Robin, hi!' she called back.

He ran the small distance between them and climbed down.

'Thought I'd join you, if you don't mind?' he asked, shielding the sun from his eyes.

'Course not.' Then she looked him up and down before giving a cheeky grin, 'Not about to go skinny dipping though, are you?'

'Nah, I'm wearing a very respectable pair of boxers,' he laughed. He couldn't help but admire her body in the black tankini she wore. The morning swims had obviously toned her muscles and her skin had gained an overall honey glow; she looked amazing.

As they reached the shore, Robin quickly whipped off his trainers, T-shirt and jeans. Now it was Jasmine's turn to appreciate the sight before her. Trying to stay focused on the swim, she was unable to ignore Robin's firm thighs and broad shoulders, the dark shadow of hair on his chest, his taut stomach. A tingle shivered through her – and it wasn't due to the cold water.

Robin pelted into the sea at full blast, splashing as he charged past her. She laughed, loving his style, no pussyfooting around for him. He pushed himself under the waves, then up again, wiping his hair back, before moving into a crawl swim. She treaded water, mesmerised by his energy and movements as his biceps thrust in and out of the sea. She swam towards him, keeping her head above the water.

'When did you last come here?' she panted once she caught up to him.

'Too long ago,' he said, turning to face her.

His eyelashes were dark and wet, outlining the sparkle in his hazel eyes. Jasmine swallowed, then looked away towards a flock of noisy seagulls.

'Come on, I'll race you,' Robin said with gusto.

'No way, you'll easily win,' she replied with a half-laugh.

'I'll give you a head start, go on.' He tipped his head out to sea. Jasmine ventured a few metres ahead of him then looked back, smiling. 'Ready, steady, go!' he shouted. The two of them swam frantically towards the horizon. Robin easily overtook her, grabbing her waist on the way, putting her off stride.

'You cheat!' she spluttered.

'I am not,' Robin tried to sound indignant, but couldn't keep a straight face.

They eventually swam back and waded out of the sea. Shivering, they wrapped towels round themselves and sat in the sun on the dunes, quickly drying in the summer heat.

'That was so revitalising,' said Robin. 'I can see why you do it every morning.'

'It's brilliant,' replied Jasmine, taking out a flask from her rucksack. 'Want some coffee?' He nodded and she passed him a small plastic cup.

He blew on it. 'Thanks.'

'Actually, I hadn't planned to swim today,' Jasmine remarked, then went on to explain the studio project she had planned and the conversation she'd had with A.R. Hall Services Ltd. Robin frowned, he knew who that was; Adrian Hall, they'd gone to the same college.

'That's odd,' he said when Jasmine had relayed how the man had abruptly changed his mind.

Jasmine blew out a breath. 'And now I'm stuck with no one to level out the garden.'

'No you're not. I'll do it.'

'But you don't have the machinery,' Jasmine said.

'We can hire one. Jack'll probably know someone with a Bobcat.'

'But you're too busy, Robin, and besides, you've helped me more than enough already,' she tried to reason with him.

'No, honestly, it won't take too long,' he insisted, still rather puzzled by Adrian's behaviour.

–

A storm was brewing, the spell of sunshine and heat reaching a heady climax. Bunty watched the dark clouds seep through the sky, like ink blotching out the daylight. Rumbles of thunder echoed in the air. She counted between each growl to estimate the distance, a method her father had taught her years ago, each second representing a mile. Seven – the storm was getting nearer and nearer. The seagulls dashed across the unsettled waves, their squawks piercing over the bay.

The tempest reflected Bunty's mood: foreboding. Turning her gaze from the window, she looked down towards the table, where the photographs lay all in a row like her tarot cards. These pictures told a story too, not of the future, but of the past. She sighed and sat down, staring at the set of black and white camera shots, all depicting happier times. Reaching out, Bunty picked up the one of her paddling in the sea. How chic she was in her Capri pants and such shapely legs! Then her eyes swept towards the handsome young man beside her, also very stylish, but then Perry always had been rather dapper. She examined his face, the creases by his eyes as he squinted in the sun, the dimples in his cheeks as he laughed, the *love* shining from his very existence.

Bunty's throat clogged with emotion. No matter how long ago it was, the pain of losing him still cut like a knife.

Once more, the image of him sailing out to sea in his little red boat drifted into her mind, that final salute, and all over circumstances that should never have been…

'Marry me, Bunty.' It was more an order than a proposal. His voice was firm, to the point of indignant. He'd asked several times before, but only to be met with the same response.

'I can't leave Daddy, he's all I've got.' She searched his face, hoping he'd understand her predicament.

Perry had understood all right. He'd learnt early on just how selfish Hamish Deville was. Selfish and quite disturbing. Perry could see plain as day how he manipulated his daughter. Bunty was his only child and she belonged *to him*.

From the moment he had stepped foot into the huge art deco house, standing proudly on the peninsula, Perry had been in awe of the grandeur of the place. Having come from a humble fisherman's cottage, he'd never experienced the likes. His qualms hadn't been calmed by the presence of the owner either. Hamish Deville had taken one look at the hesitant young man his daughter had brought into his home and his distaste had practically oozed from him.

Standing at the top of the sweeping staircase, Hamish had frozen, his eyes narrowed.

'And who's this?' he demanded, glaring down at the young couple.

Perry stared up at the man towering above them.

'This is Perry, Daddy!' trilled Bunty excitedly. 'He's come to meet you.'

'Has he indeed,' Hamish said flatly, then proceeded to walk past onto the landing into an upper room, clearly dismissing them and leaving Bunty a touch embarrassed.

'He'll come down later,' she tried to smooth over the situation. Perry didn't want him to. In fact, he'd rather not have to see him at all. He'd caught the man's measure; he was clearly trespassing on *his* territory and with *his* daughter.

Now matter how much Bunty had tried to coax her father into liking or even accepting Perry, Hamish refused point blank to cooperate. He rebuffed the boy's presence and eventually banned him from the house. Hamish's control over his only child was unhealthy – obsessive even. He had attempted to forbid Bunty from seeing Perry, on the grounds he was 'simply not good enough' for her, but not even he had the power to stop his formidable daughter. Bunty still met him, albeit in secret, something Perry had resented.

And that resentment began to build momentum. Bunty was forever clock watching, anxious to return home when she was with him. Her father had way too much influence over her; it wasn't natural for a woman of twenty-one to be treated in such a way. When he'd voiced his thoughts, Bunty became defensive, eager to protect her father. Daddy was on his own; Daddy didn't have Mummy any more; she was all he had.

What about him? Didn't they have a future together? Would they constantly have to meet in hiding, only enjoying snatched time? Why shouldn't she be able to live a normal life, have a boyfriend, one day get married? The whole scenario verged on the ridiculous and was totally unfair on Bunty.

Then it had all come to a head one summer's evening. They were having a picnic on his little fishing boat. Enjoying the champagne he had bought, they sat together on the deck, gently bobbing up and down, listening to the water as it lapped against the sides. Perry had suddenly presented a ring, a stunning aquamarine diamond which glittered in the last of the sun's rays. Bunty gasped at its beauty.

'Marry me, Bunty,' Perry had said, praying this time it would be different, that by producing a ring, it would sway her. For a brief moment, the light in her eyes told him it had – that *he* came first – but then the shadow of defeat cast over her face. And it was at this point he knew he'd lost. Hamish Deville would always come first place.

He had to leave, get out of Samphire Bay. There was no way Perry could carry on with the status quo, pretending he was happy, or even tolerated the impossible situation her father had callously created. It wasn't natural. It was toxic. Two young people in love ought to be allowed to be together. Of course they should. But Perry knew that was never going to be, not with Bunty and her controlling, vindictive father.

In the end he sailed away. He collected all his belongings from his rented fisherman's cottage, put them in his boat and set off for a new beginning. The only possession he left was his trunk containing some of their most treasured memories.

He'd seen her though, waving frantically, calling out for him. Too little, too late. Bunty had made her choice. He raised his hand and flicked the side of his head, an acknowledgment and a final goodbye.

Hamish Deville was delighted at the boy's move. He even bought the fishermen's cottages, thereby making sure

Perry could never come back and live there again. He took Bunty away on holiday, the French Riviera, in an attempt to cheer her up. It didn't. As the years went on, even Hamish had to admit that his daughter would in fact never get over losing the wretched boy. *Such* a waste to see Bunty so miserable, but still, at least she was here with him.

Chapter 15

Jack saw the transit van drive up to the cottage, pulling a trailer with the digger he'd hired. He went out to help direct the machinery into Jasmine's back garden. She was out, so all was quiet. Robin was due to arrive later that morning, so he'd be the one levelling the garden. Jack was going to be busy installing the cast iron bath he had finally found in a house clearance.

After the trailer had safely been parked at the bottom of Jasmine's garden, Jack gave the driver the thumbs up.

'OK here?' called the driver, getting out of the van to unload.

'Yes, thanks mate,' nodded Jack.

Soon the Bobcat was being slowly driven down the slope of the trailer onto the lawn. Once finished, Jack went to join the driver.

'Cheers, we'll be done with it by tomorrow afternoon I'd say.'

'No worries, just give us a call,' he replied, climbing back into his van.

Jack looked at the brand new vehicle.

'Business doing well, Adrian?' he asked, tipping his head toward the shiny, new van.

Adrian turned his head sharply.

'Er… yes. The old one was knackered, sold it for scrap,' he answered a tad abruptly, then quickly started up the engine. Without any hesitation he drove off, and Jack frowned. Clearly a busy man, he thought.

Later, when Jasmine came back from her swim, she was pleased to see the Bobcat had been delivered. She was keen to get on with the studio and was looking forward to creating her very own workspace.

Meanwhile, Robin had just arrived next door. He too was pleased to see the digger in situ, ready to start work.

'Hi, Rob, the digger's arrived,' Jack told him as he entered the kitchen.

'So I see,' Robin said, peering out of the window.

'Fancy giving me a hand with this bath before you start next door?' asked Jack.

'Yeah, course.'

The two men heaved the heavy cast iron bath up the stairs to the bathroom, leaving them out of breath.

'Blimey, it weighs a ton,' huffed Jack as they straightened it up against the wall.

'This job certainly keeps us fit,' Robin said, laughing. 'Just think of the money it's going to make us.'

'Speaking of, Adrian must be making some money. Just seen his brand spanking new van. That must have set him back a bit.'

'Adrian Hall?' repeated Robin.

'Yeah, that's who's hiring out the Bobcat.'

'But… he couldn't do it when Jasmine contacted him.' Robin's brow puckered in confusion.

'Well, maybe he's busy, but could still hire out the digger?' suggested Jack. 'He's the most obvious choice, being local.'

Robin paused, thinking it was still a little strange. Why didn't Adrian offer the hire of his Bobcat to Jasmine in the first place?

Once the cast iron bath was situated in the right position, Robin left for Jasmine's. He tapped on the back door.

'Come in!' she called. She was cooking a hearty breakfast after her morning swim, making enough for two.

'Something smells good.' Robin's mouth watered at the bacon, sausage and eggs in the frying pan.

She grinned. 'Fancy a full English?'

'Absolutely.' He rubbed his hands together.

They sat at the kitchen table enjoying the fry up.

'I could get used to this,' Robin said, tucking into his breakfast, then stopped, realising how that could be misconstrued.

'Us breakfasting together?' ribbed Jasmine. She could tell by the slight blush that he knew how clumsy he'd sounded. Robin looked into her warm, brown eyes, which held a twinkle of mischief, then slowly broke into a grin.

'I meant you cooking for me.' He laughed at hearing his own words. That sounded even worse!

'Not just breakfast then?' Jasmine arched a playful eyebrow.

'Never mind out there,' he pointed towards the garden, 'I'm already digging a big enough hole in here,' he joked.

Jasmine threw her head back and chuckled. 'Listen, if I can cook then it's the least I can do for all your help, seriously,' she said with sincerity.

Their eyes locked. Time stood still. Jasmine reached up to touch the heart pendant around her neck and Robin noticed the action. He also noted that she had done that before. It seemed to be a gut reaction of hers and it didn't take Sherlock Holmes to deduce the necklace was acting as some kind of talisman, presumably a gift from her late husband. He looked down, all the light-hearted banter suddenly lost. They were interrupted by the sound of Jasmine's mobile phone.

'Sorry, it's my mum,' she said, reaching to answer it.

'I'll make a start,' mouthed Robin, clearing the plates away before he headed out to the garden.

Within a couple of hours, a huge pile of earth had mounted up. Robin looked around the garden, thinking some of it could be used to make a rockery, if not for Jasmine's garden then maybe his next door. He suggested as much when he completed the job late in the afternoon. They were sat on deck chairs having a well-earned cup of tea. Whilst Robin had been scraping and digging the earth, Jasmine had been sanding down the hallway banister, ready for a fresh lick of varnish. She had decided to get the floorboards sanded down too, wanting them to be varnished also, rather than carpeted.

'A rockery?' she said in response to Robin's proposal.

'Yes, I think it'd be a good focal point for the garden,' he replied taking a sip of tea.

'Hmm, I think I'd prefer raised vegetable beds.' That was something she and Tom had missed, living on a canal boat, not being able to grow their own vegetables. It was something she'd always fancied doing.

'Good idea,' nodded Robin, liking her thinking.

'But there's plenty to do both, if you want to build a rockery next door,' she said.

'Yeah, I think I will.' He pictured the anchor he and Jack had found in the trunk. It would look good in a rockery. For a moment his thoughts turned to Bunty and those photographs he'd given her. Never had he seen her so melancholy as when he'd handed them over.

'What are you thinking about, Robin?' asked Jasmine, seeing emotions flicker across his face.

'Hmm? Oh… just about Bunty and the photographs we found of her. She looked so sad when I gave them to her.'

'Poor Bunty.' Jasmine felt a surge of pity for the old dear. Then an idea came to her. 'Why don't I cook for her? Invite her round for a meal?'

'That'd be nice. I'm sure she'd love the company,' Robin said.

Jasmine shook her head. 'I mean the three of us, a mini dinner party?'

'Lovely, I'm sure she'd appreciate that. She'd be interested to see what you've done to the place too.'

'Yes, she would,' laughed Jasmine, already imagining Bunty striding through her home, offering up her opinion unasked. 'I'll let you invite her.'

Robin narrowed his eyes in thought.

'No, why don't you pay her a visit? She'd like that.'

'Oh, right.' Jasmine blinked, not expecting that response, but why not go and see Bunty? She often wondered what that impressive big house on the peninsula was like inside. Well, now was her chance to step inside and see.

–

The next afternoon Jack had called Adrian to collect his digger as promised. Robin had finished all the levelling of Jasmine's garden and it was now flat for the studio to be installed. Jasmine had bought a contemporary, wooden cladded studio with large patio doors. It was to be erected by the company she had bought it from within a matter of days, which meant that she was looking at having a much-needed workspace very shortly.

Jasmine had spent hours looking at various websites to give her clues on how to furnish it inside. As the studio's exterior was going to look quite modern, she decided to keep the inside minimalist and sleek. She wanted a large, simple desk in there with a swivel chair and a noticeboard to pin up sketches and prints of ideas for her work. The studio's glass doors would be positioned at the back, so facing the view of the bay would be a good enough distraction for her. As always with Samphire Bay, it was all about the view.

Robin, who had wheelbarrowed half of the mounted-up earth to his garden, was busy constructing his rockery. He stopped shovelling when he spotted Adrian pick up his Bobcat next door. Robin watched with interest at the way he flinched when Jasmine came out to see him.

'Hello, I'm Jasmine, we spoke on the phone,' she told him.

'Oh…' Adrian stumbled to a halt.

Robin narrowed his eyes at the way Adrian was acting. Was he shaking slightly? His shoulders hunched and he clearly couldn't even look Jasmine in the face, let alone shake her offered hand.

'I'm glad we managed to borrow your digger. I thought you said—'

'Yeah, a job got cancelled,' Adrian interrupted brusquely, then ran a hand through his hair nervously.

'Ri-ght,' said Jasmine, a touch puzzled by this man's demeanour. 'Well, here's what I owe you.' She handed over the money for hiring the machinery.

'No,' he said, pushing it back to her. 'I don't want paying.'

Jasmine blinked.

'Sorry?'

'You don't owe me anything, really, it's fine,' he insisted, then got into his van and started up the engine.

'But…' Jasmine's mouth gaped open as Adrian drove off as quickly as possible.

Alarm bells began to ring inside Robin, who had witnessed the whole scene, followed by a horrid sensation that seeped into his very being. Something was most definitely not right here. *Why* was Adrian acting so strangely? And more to the point, why did he refuse Jasmine's money? It was the fee she owed him, not charity. The man was supposed to be running a business and a lucrative one at that, according to Jack. Then another dark thought hit him like a bell toll. The van, that new one Adrian was driving. He remembered the one which had been replaced, and his heart began to thud. It had been a white van. He took out his mobile from his jean's pocket and walked to the side of the cottage, out of any possible earshot. The last thing he wanted was for Jasmine to hear him.

'Jack?'

'Yeah mate, I'll be with you in half an hour, just—'

'Listen, Jack, what did Adrian Hall say about that old van of his?'

'What?'

'You said he'd bought a new van, what was up with his old one?' asked Robin with urgency.

'Rob, are you OK?'

'Just answer me Jack,' hissed Robin impatiently.

'He–he said his old van was sold for scrap… Why? Robin what's the matter?'

'Gotta go.' Robin ended the call. With a pounding chest, he climbed inside his Range Rover and drove towards Adrian's work yard with grim determination.

It didn't take him long to catch up to the van and trailer. Luckily there was a car in front of Robin's Range Rover, so Adrian wouldn't notice he was being followed. Eventually, Adrian's van turned left at a junction, leaving the car in front to set off in the opposite direction. Robin stayed behind the van at a reasonable distance, all the while adrenalin was pumping through his veins. A film of perspiration covered his skin at what he suspected he was about to uncover.

Robin waited discreetly at the side of the road whilst watching Adrian drive into his work unit. There was quite a lot of land at the back of the property. He noticed an outbuilding and an old garage at the rear end. He slowly drove closer to get a better look but stopped immediately when Adrian jumped out of his van and into a car parked next to it. Robin ducked his head down as Adrian began to drive past his Range Rover.

Taking a deep breath, he got out warily, looking around and making sure the coast was clear before quickly jogging into the yard. He glanced through the window at the front of the building, checking nobody was inside. It was empty. Then he made his way round the back. He tried the door of the outbuilding but it was locked. Walking to the side, he saw transparent panelling at the end of the roof. An old oil drum stood nearby and he pushed it to the edge of the building wall, climbing onto it to hitch himself up onto the roof. Looking through the translucent plastic, all he saw was machinery, obviously the outbuilding was just used for storage.

After getting down carefully, Robin then went to the garage behind the building. Wooden and clearly in need of repair, he easily pushed the doors open and stood in shock at what he'd found.

A white transit van.

What's more, it had a large dent on the bonnet. Robin froze, gulping at the sight before him. He had to clear his head and act quickly. Taking his mobile, he pressed the camera on and took several pictures of the van, particularly the registration number. Then he speedily closed the doors behind him and ran back to his Range Rover at breakneck speed. He couldn't be caught by Adrian if he came back, or anyone else that might be on these premises.

Panting, he leapt into the driver's seat and drove back, his mind rattling with what he'd discovered. A white transit van, with a dent in it. It had obviously been involved in some kind of collision – not sold for scrap as Adrian had told Jack. He cast his mind back to Adrian's strange behaviour and refusal of money. Was it all out of guilt?

Once back at the cottage, he sat on the doorstep, forcing himself to calm down. He then took his phone out again, this time to search the internet. He soon found the article he wanted.

Man Killed in Hit-and-Run Accident

Lancashire Constabulary are appealing for any eyewitnesses in connection to the death of Thomas Boyd, who was killed in a hit-and-run accident on Friday night. The collision took place at approximately eleven p.m. outside The Mariners public house on the high street in Carston. A white transit van collided into Mr Boyd, rendering him dead on impact. The vehicle sped off in a northerly direction.

Mr Boyd leaves a widow, Jasmine Boyd. Police are urging the public to come forward with any information.

Lancashire Evening Standard, 9 October 2021

Oh my God. It had to be the very same van. It all added up: Adrian's skittish behaviour, not taking Jasmine's money, lying about his van… What the hell was he to do?

Just then Jack arrived, and he stopped short at seeing Robin sat on the doorstep looking pale and shaken.

'Rob, what's going on?' He crouched down to look at him.

'Jack, I've… found something out…'

'What, mate?' asked Jack with concern.

'It's Adrian Hall, he killed Jasmine's husband,' he whispered.

Jack's eyes bulged in shock.

'What?'

'He lied about his old van. I've just seen it. Look, here.' He showed Jack the photographs he'd taken. Jack let out a gasp, lost for words. 'See, look at that, Jack—' Robin pointed out the dented bonnet, 'that'll be where he hit him.'

'But… we can't just assume—'

'Adrian said he'd sold his old van for scrap!' cut in Robin, making Jack halt.

'Yes, he did,' he conceded. He inhaled deeply before looking Robin in the eye. 'So, what do we do now, tell Jasmine?'

'Hell no! Not yet,' cried Robin. 'We need to report it to the police first, let them investigate, make sure it's definitely him. My money says it is though.'

Jack nodded in agreement, then asked, 'Do you think we should confront Adrian beforehand?'

'What? And give him chance to torch the van? It's evidence, Jack, and it's in his bloody garage!' rasped Robin.

'OK, OK,' Jack tried to pacify Robin, although he too was beginning to feel on edge. 'We'll go to the police together. I'll drive, you look shaken, Rob.'

All the while, Robin was trying to anticipate Jasmine's reaction to the news that would inevitably follow. Deep down, Robin knew he had stumbled upon something sinister the likes of which Samphire Bay had never seen.

Chapter 16

Living on a peninsula with a cross tidal road meant that Bunty's guests always had to plan their visits carefully. Jasmine was doing the very same thing. She looked at the tide times which were propped up on the kitchen windowsill. After studying them, she decided the best time to visit would be ten thirty in the morning, at low tide, giving her a few hours to get back home safely.

Jasmine had been genuinely saddened to hear how upset Bunty was when Robin had given her the photographs. It both touched and surprised her how a larger than life, gregarious, tell-it-as-it-is character could react in such a way, given the length of time it had been since those photographs had been taken. It must have been over fifty-odd years ago, judging by the looks of her and the man in the pictures. Jasmine wondered, not for the first time, who the man was; who had made Bunty smile and laugh so carefree and wantonly? And what had happened to him? He certainly wasn't on the scene any more, mores the pity, she suspected.

Travelling down the tidal road, it amazed her how flat and clear it could be one minute yet was so easily covered by the racing tide as it reached its highest point. It was incredible, really, how quickly the conditions changed. So much so, photographs of stranded cars in the sea were displayed on a notice board at the beginning of the road, to act as a warning for anyone daring or foolish enough to try and beat the rushing water.

Jasmine had allowed herself plenty of time as she breezed down the road with the wind blowing through the car windows. She breathed in deeply, smelling the salt in the sea air. She saw the magnificent art deco house standing high above the estuary, showing off its 1930s architecture. Jasmine admired the curvature of the bow windows and the parapets of its exterior. It was all so tasteful and intriguing; she was curious to see inside it.

After parking her car, she climbed up the stone steps and rang the doorbell. It wasn't long before Bunty's outline appeared in the glass door. She opened it with a big beam at seeing who it was.

'Jasmine! Lovely to see you.' She held the door open and ushered her inside.

Jasmine instantly took in the high, cherry yellow ceiling with a glamorous chandelier in gold leaf and chrome finishing, the full-length fan wall mirror and the sweeping staircase. The rooms leading off the hall had the typical art deco sunburst mantels above the door frames and the light switches had the original brass cases. It was all so captivating and very fitting of the era it had been built. Jasmine almost expected a pretty young maid to come scurrying in, dressed in a black uniform with a white frilly apron and headdress.

Her fascination continued when Bunty led them into the drawing room with high dusty pink walls, covered with two elaborate mirrors and various watercolour paint-ings in ornate gold frames. She wafted over to a retro glass drinks cabinet and began making drinks.

'Gin and tonic, darling?' she enquired, already pouring into two tumblers.

'Just the one please,' answered Jasmine.

She glanced at the sea landscapes and noticed their tiny signature in the corners: *Hamish Deville*. She assumed this was Bunty's father, or maybe an uncle.

'Daddy was a brilliant artist,' announced Bunty passing her drink. She'd seen Jasmine squinting to read the painting's signature.

'Ah, I see. Yes, they're wonderful. Thanks,' said Jasmine taking her glass. Then, as they sat down by the table, she noticed the photographs that Robin had found. They were all positioned neatly in a row. Jasmine looked at them, then slowly lifted her head to face Bunty who was staring at her.

'Have you already seen these?' asked Bunty, pointing towards the black and white pictures.

There was no point in denying it, so Jasmine came clean.

'Yes, Bunty, I have. Robin showed them to me,' she admitted, then took a sip of her drink. *Hell, it was strong!* She coughed at its sharpness.

Bunty nodded her head.

'Yes, I thought he might have,' she said, appreciating the girl's honesty. They both looked back at the snapshots on the table, stories from long ago. 'Why are you here, Jasmine?' Bunty asked a tad abruptly, interrupting any sentimental impression that might have been on the brink of emerging.

Taken aback by Bunty's briskness, Jasmine blinked and took another sip of her drink before replying, refusing to be intimidated.

'I was wondering if you would like to come to mine for dinner one evening?'

At this Bunty gave a delighted — if not somewhat surprised — smile.

'Dinner? At yours?' she repeated, her face lit up with glee.

Jasmine smiled. 'Yes, I'd love to have you round and show you what I've done with the place.'

'I'd love to, darling, how kind,' Bunty cheered, thoroughly pleased with the invite.

'Great, well I was thinking one night next week perhaps?'

'Absolutely,' nodded Bunty.

'Saturday OK with you?' Jasmine suggested, preferring the weekend so at least Robin wouldn't be working the next day, which then reminded her to mention he'd be there too.

'Saturday it is,' replied Bunty, then added with a sly grin. 'I take it I won't be the only guest?' Her eyes twinkled with mischief.

'Er… actually no, I've invited Robin along, too,' said Jasmine, frowning slightly. Why was Bunty looking so playful? And more to the point, how had she guessed about Robin being invited?

'I thought he might be there.' Bunty gave a knowing smile and arched an eyebrow.

'Sorry?' replied Jasmine rather confused.

'Getting along nicely, are you?'

'Well… yes, I thought it would be neighbourly to include him,' answered Jasmine.

'Of course, darling, of course,' chuckled Bunty. Then, changing the subject completely, she reached out to one of the photographs on the table. 'Perry,' she blurted out. 'His name was Perry.' Her eyes filled with emotion. Jasmine sat in silence, not quite knowing what to say. 'But he sailed away,' she murmured to herself. Jasmine coughed and shifted uncomfortably in her chair. 'Anyway,' said Bunty, quickly snapping out of her reverie. 'Saturday sounds lovely. I'll look forward to it.'

'Good,' said Jasmine, relieved that Bunty was back in the room. For a moment she'd thought she had lost the old woman, she seemed so distant and vulnerable, not at all her usual self.

Driving home, Jasmine was pondering the man's name Bunty had revealed: Perry. Quite an unusual name. Then she reflected on her other words, *but he sailed away*.

She also remembered the anchor Robin had found in his trunk – he'd obviously been connected to the sea in some way. Jasmine's eyes narrowed in contemplation. A man named Perry, with sailing connections. Why did that sound so familiar...

–

Robin and Jack stood at the bar ashen-faced.

'Right, lads, what can I get you?' asked Ned the land-lord.

'Two pints of Dizzy Blonde please, Ned,' replied Jack.

Once served, they went to find a quiet corner, away from the hustle and bustle of the pub. Both sat in silence, drinking their beer, until Robin heaved a sigh.

'What do you think is going to happen now?' He looked at Jack for the answer. They'd just been to the police station to report all that Robin had uncovered. The officer in charge had listened intently, interested in everything they had to say. He had paid particular atten-tion to the photos on Robin's phone and asked for him to send them onto the constabulary email account. He had clearly taken the pair of them extremely seriously, recording Adrian's workplace address as well as Jasmine's home address. Finally, once the police officer was happy with their version of events, he took their contact details and they left the station feeling somewhat dazed.

'I think they're going to get Adrian in for questioning, can't see what else could happen,' Jack said, finishing his pint. He tipped his head towards Robin's glass. 'Fancy another?'

'I'll get these,' said Robin, getting up from his chair.

Although knowing he'd absolutely done the right thing, he couldn't help but worry about how all this was going to affect Jasmine. He, more than most, had seen how she was beginning to blossom, how she had seemed to be settling into Samphire Bay. He pictured her laughing that morning they'd gone swimming in the sea, how joyful and bright she'd been. Then he pictured her sat opposite him talking animatedly when he'd cooked her dinner that evening. How she'd just got on with renovating her cottage, with a cheery, positive disposition. Would this revelation change all that? Would it reopen a deep wound and suffocate all her positivity?

'What's up, Robin? You're looking damned serious mate,' Ned said from behind the bar.

'Same again thanks, Ned.' Robin offered a half smile, but no explanation. He could hardly tell the pub landlord his troubles. *But you need to tell Jasmine*, said the voice of reason inside his head.

-

Meanwhile Jasmine was sat at the kitchen table with her laptop open. She had spent the past hour searching the website of Carston Marina, where *Moonshine* had been moored. She had also searched various canal and narrowboat Facebook pages. She and Tom had been members of the various groups when living on *Moonshine* and the pages had proved extremely useful, being novices, to have a forum where they could query or discuss aspects of narrowboat living. Some of the members were very experienced and had a lot of good advice to offer. It had also been handy when buying and selling boat equipment.

She and Tom had needed a manual water pump and had looked online to find a good second-hand one. Luckily, one was for sale via the Carston Marina website. Jasmine remembered the owners name, Perry. Could there be a connection?

Not having much to go off, Jasmine had scoured Facebook, page after page, with all things related to canals and narrowboat living, eyes running across each member's name, but there wasn't anyone by the name of Perry. Surely he had to be somewhere? If he had used the Carston Marina's website, then he must have moored there at some point, or at least have some connection to it. She tried going back to the marina's Facebook group page, this time scrolling way back to when they had bought the water pump, over three years ago. It took a while, backtracking to the period she wanted. Various photographs of fellow narrowboaters flashed before her; stunning sunsets in fire-lit skies, colourful boats chugging serenely along the canal, festive deck parties, barbeques… and there was one, a group of older men huddled together round a wood burner, clasping tankards of ale. They were celebrating someone's birthday, a *Happy 70th!* banner was displayed in the background. Under the picture read the caption, 'Great birthday party last night. Big thanks to Geoff, Brian, Perry and Trevor.' Perry! At last, she had stumbled across the name.

Jasmine's mind went into overdrive. This Perry was the right age to be Bunty's man. She clicked on the photograph and enlarged it as much as possible, studying the four men. She homed in on the third man in the group, assuming this would be Perry, in name order. Did this look like the man in the photographs Robin found? It was hard to tell, obviously fifty-odd years on, but he still had a sense of style about him, with his jaunty neckerchief and granddad shirt. Or was she just clutching at straws? His grey hair was thick and quite long with a slight wave to it. He definitely had an air of charisma about him. Almost a nomadic magnetism, she thought to herself with a giggle.

Then a bright idea struck her. If Perry had a narrow-boat, she might be able to trace him. She quickly went onto the website for the register of canal boats, Canal Plan. All she knew was his first name. The search needed a full name, or at least the name of the boat. Refusing to give in, Jasmine used her initiative. Perry was a fairly uncommon name, could he have used it when naming his boat? It was possible, people did incorporate their name. In any case it was worth a try. Jasmine typed in the name 'Perry' on the search tab. A list of names came up: *Periwinkle, Peregrine's Place, Peri-Peri* and *The Merry Perry*.

Her eyes scanned each name and she clicked on every one to be thorough. *Periwinkle* was a brand new boat, so that was ruled out. *Peregrine's Place* was owned by a Todd Walker, maybe he'd either inherited the boat, or had bought it without renaming it? *Peri-Peri* was a Portuguese floating restaurant. Then came *The Merry Perry*, owned by a Perry Scholar. Yes! What's more, his address wasn't a million miles away either, it was Lancaster. Could this be Bunty's Perry?

Chapter 17

Robin stood back and admired his and Jack's handiwork. It had been a great idea to knock the dividing wall down and create the large kitchen diner. The wood burner at the far end really finished the room off nicely.

Whilst pleased with the progress he and Jack were making on the property, Robin was still in a state of anxiety. He needed to talk to Jasmine – and fast. Now that the police had all the information regarding Adrian Hall's van, he knew time was of the essence. Being absolutely convinced that he'd found Tom Boyd's killer, he felt the need to forewarn Jasmine so that, when the police suddenly turned up, she wasn't shocked or triggered by memories of them calling in the past.

Knowing he had to broach the subject with hypersensitive care, Robin thought carefully about where, when and how to have the conversation. This was potentially going to have a catastrophic effect on Jasmine and, once again, he became very aware of his feelings for her and just how protective he felt. Yes, he could tell Jack he was merely being neighbourly and try to disguise his true emotions, but he couldn't kid himself, could he?

Robin was slowly coming to terms that Jasmine had most definitely got under his skin. His thoughts permanently gravitated back to her and flashbacks of their time together forever played in his mind. But this wasn't just any woman he could make a move on. Jasmine was a vulnerable, young widow. He was reminded of how her hand frequently reached up to touch that heart pendant she wore. Was he wrong to want a dead man's wife?

As if on cue, his thoughts were interrupted by Jasmine herself tapping on the window.

'Hi!' she called through the glass.

'Come in, door's open,' he mouthed, thumbing towards the back door.

She soon joined him in the kitchen diner.

'Wow! This looks amazing!' she exclaimed as soon as she saw the new space.

'Yeah, I'm quite pleased with the result.' Robin nodded modestly.

'Quite pleased? You should be ecstatic, it's fantastic.' She laughed and Robin looked into her warm, brown eyes and melted. Was he about to change all this? Would those gorgeous eyes soon be filled with tears? He gulped.

'You OK?' Jasmine asked, puzzled by his expression.

Robin inwardly shook himself. 'Yeah, fine.'

'Right, well, I've seen Bunty,' she said positively.

'Ah, good,' he replied.

'And is Saturday night good for you?'

'Yes, that's great.'

'That's settled then. Bunty's looking forward to it.' She hesitated, as though wanting to say something further. Now Robin frowned, sensing an awkward pause.

'Robin...?'

'Yeah?'

'If–if you thought you had information... important knowledge concerning someone... would you...' She stalled again.

'Would I what?' asked Robin, suddenly beginning to feel alarmed. Had she got wind of his dilemma? Did she know exactly what was on his mind?

'Would you tell them?' she finished, staring at him intently.

Robin let out a nervous sigh and ran a hand through his dark curls.

'I think so,' he answered cautiously.

'Yes, I thought you'd say that,' Jasmine said, sounding somewhat reassured.

'Can I ask what the information is?' Robin asked tentatively.

Jasmine blew out a breath. 'It's about Bunty.'

'Bunty?' Robin was surprised but, in equal measure, relieved.

'Hmm, those photographs were spread out on a table when I went to visit her. They're obviously precious to her. She looked so sentimental about them, even told me the man's name.'

'Really?' Robin said, wide-eyed. He thought Bunty, more than anyone, would have kept quiet about such a personal detail.

'Yes, he's called Perry. Does the name ring any bells with you?'

'No, but it wouldn't. I only moved to Samphire Bay in my teens. This Perry had most probably been long gone by then.'

'Yeah, probably,' she agreed. 'But it resonated with me. So much so, I did a bit of—'

'Snooping?' Robin laughed at the irony; he knew all about snooping.

'Researching,' corrected Jasmine and told him all she'd uncovered.

'I'm impressed, Sherlock,' Robin laughed again.

'But don't you see? It's left me in a bit of a quandary,' Jasmine pointed out. *You and me both*, he thought wryly. 'Do you think I should contact this Perry from Lancaster?'

Robin breathed in, considering his reply.

'I think…' he hesitated.

'Yes?' she prompted eagerly, leaning forward.

'I think, if you believe it's in Bunty's best interests, then yes, maybe you should contact him.'

Jasmine nodded as though Robin had confirmed her decision.

'Although, it very well might not be him—'

'In which case, no harm done,' she interrupted.

'Yes, but if it is him and he's a wife and family, would he want contact?' warned Robin.

'As an old friend he might,' Jasmine countered.

'And more importantly, what about Bunty? Would *she* want contact?' he pressed.

'Hmm, a lot to think about,' Jasmine said contemplatively.

A pensive moment passed, then Robin decided this was the right time, and inhaled deeply.

'Jasmine… there's something I need to tell you actually.' He looked at her gravely, hating that he was about to bring this storm onto her.

'What?' She sensed something ominous from Robin's manner. He looked troubled, uncomfortable.

'Can we go to yours? I think we need to sit down with a drink.' He thought it best for Jasmine to be in her own familiar surroundings, not stood there in his newly refurbished kitchen.

'OK.' She frowned, wondering what on earth Robin was about to tell her.

An hour later Robin was holding a shaken, crying Jasmine. He wrapped her tightly in his arms as she juddered in shock and distress.

'Do you think… he–he definitely k–killed Tom?' she stuttered.

'Time will tell, but the police certainly took what I reported very seriously. They have your details too, so could be in touch imminently.'

More sobs followed, making Robin wince. He held her firmly, in some vain hope that he could absorb some of the emotional pain currently wracking her body. He'd do anything to mend her, *anything*. He looked down towards her blonde head resting on his shoulder and instinctively his mouth dipped down to kiss it. Then realising what he'd just done, froze. She hadn't even noticed, and he breathed out in relief.

'Robin?' she croaked.

'Yes?' he replied huskily, fighting his own emotions.

'Will you stay, here, tonight? I don't want to be alone, especially if the police come.'

'Of course I will,' he immediately answered. Then thought about the logistics, where would he sleep?

'I've a camp bed in the spare room,' Jasmine told him, answering his question.

'No problem, I'll be here for you,' he told her, his voice slightly catching.

As he settled down, Robin stared up into the darkness and took stock of the day. It had certainly been an emotional one. Then again, on reflection, the last few days had been rather taxing for him. He pictured himself on Adrian Hall's premises, climbing the roof of his building, opening up his garage doors, then scampering off through the yard. What if someone had seen him, or even worse, told Adrian? Would there be repercussions? He remembered Adrian having a bit of a rough reputation. Was he in for a bruising? But reason kicked in – what option had he but to involve the police? He'd face ten Adrian Halls if it meant doing the right thing by Jasmine. His eyes filled at how she had reacted. Poor Jasmine, he so wanted to care and shield her.

His thoughts took a darker turn. If Adrian was charged, it would be all over the press and get intense media coverage. Road deaths and hit-and-runs happened all the time, sure, and didn't get much coverage, but in their surrounding communities, this had been a huge regional shock at the time – no doubt reporters would want to wrap up the story now it had an ending. Reporters were bound to turn up at the cottages, wanting to snap pictures of Jasmine, even attempt to interview or get a response from her. It was going to be a nightmare. Perhaps he ought to suggest she go back to her parents' house until it all settled? But then, he suspected, the press would already know their address from when the accident happened. A plan was starting to form in his head, which seemed ideal the more he considered it.

Chapter 18

It hadn't taken long for him to crack. Once under the spotlight, Adrian had sung like a canary and wept like a baby. The police had only needed to scratch the surface. When they'd presented the photographs of his damaged white van, he'd crumbled. Yes, it was his van. Yes, it had killed Tom Boyd. No, he hadn't been driving it. That had been a man who had previously worked for him, but after the accident had disappeared.

'Who is he? Where's he gone?' demanded one of the police officers interviewing him.

'His name is Ian Dixon,' cried Adrian. 'I don't know where he is now, honestly.'

'Tell us exactly what happened that night,' barked the other officer.

Adrian looked nervously towards the tape machine and swallowed.

'It was a Friday night. Me and Ian had just finished a big job near Carston.'

'What job?' interrupted one of the officers.

'Digging out a double driveway,' Adrian replied, then continued. 'I suggested we go for a pint, local like, so we ended up at The Mariners on the high street. Only, one pint led to another, and before we knew it, we… were over the limit.'

'How much had you both drunk?'

'Well… I'd say about six or seven pints,' Adrian answered lamely.

'Go on.'

'So I says we'd better get a taxi like, then come back for the van the next day, but Ian said no, he would drive us home, that he'd be fine.'

'What, after *seven* pints?' asked the other officer incredulously.

'Yes.' Adrian looked down in shame.

'Then what happened?'

'I says are you sure, and Ian says yes, he'd be OK to drive, so… I handed him over the van keys.'

'And are you quite sure this happened? That *you* didn't get behind the wheel?' the sceptical tone in the policeman's voice was evident.

'Yes! Definitely!' Adrian shot back in alarm. 'I swear, I gave him the keys, Ian drove.'

'Then what?'

'Well, we gets in the van, start it up and hadn't got too far before this figure comes out of nowhere and the next thing, *thud*, it's on the bloody bonnet of the van! Ian didn't stop in time and the body's then flung into the middle of the road. We panicked, we—'

'Drove off and left a man for dead,' cut in an officer with venom.

There was a charged silence. Adrian broke down in tears again.

'Yes,' he sobbed, 'we left that poor bloke dead in the road… His poor wife…' More crying followed.

'Interview over.' The police officer pressed a button on the tape machine.

Ian Dixon was easily located by the police. As his employer, Adrian was able to give plenty of information regarding bank account details, national insurance number and previous address, even his car registration number.

The hardest job for them would be speaking to Tom Boyd's widow. With a heavy heart the officer in charge cancelled his next morning's commitments. He wanted the full morning free to visit Jasmine Boyd in Samphire Bay.

Chapter 19

Jasmine woke early in the morning. Truth be told, she hadn't slept well at all. The nightmare of Tom's accident dominated her mind. Horrific images of him being ploughed into, his lifeless body cruelly abandoned in the road, tormented her over and over. She had wondered in the very beginning, when it had all happened, how she'd feel if she ever learned who her husband's killer was. Now it looked like she was about to find out.

In a way, she was dreading the police visit, the long-awaited knock on the door, but Jasmine was also experiencing a release, a kind of liberation. If the police had the driver who had ended Tom's life, then it would bring her some small measure of closure to the whole horrendous business. Yet, Jasmine knew she would never seek true closure on the loss of her husband. She would eternally miss him; every birthday, Christmas, anniversary, plus all the other milestones they'd been robbed of. At times, she'd taken to picturing what their children would have looked like. Would they have had his auburn hair, his boyish freckles? Would they have inherited his practical skills, his hands-on approach, his steady direction?

Jasmine smiled to herself at how impetuous she'd been when buying *Moonshine*. In typical fashion she was all in, guns blazing, whereas Tom had counselled patience initially, before being persuaded by her. They'd been opposites in many ways, but that had made them a good team.

Jasmine wiped her eyes and went downstairs to put the kettle on. Tea, that's what people did, wasn't it, in times of crisis, drink tea? She remembered her mum doing just that, pouring countless cups of tea in the aftermath of the tragedy. At the time it infuriated her, now she was doing the same.

On entering the kitchen, she was surprised to see Robin already there. He'd clearly had similar thoughts and was stood with his back to her, waiting for the kettle to boil. She noticed he had put two cups out and was touched by his thoughtfulness. Jasmine stopped moment-arily. He was gazing out of the window, watching how the morning was lighting up into life. His dark curls were ruffled from the night's sleep and he yawned. Then he turned and saw her at the doorway.

'Hey you,' he smiled. 'Fancy a cuppa?'

'I was just about to make one.' She walked over to join him by the window.

They stared, side by side, at the glorious view before them. The sun was up, wide awake and shining brightly on a gentle, blue sea. All was calm. Except it wasn't. Robin braced himself, then spoke.

'Jasmine, I've been thinking.'

She looked up at him. 'So have I,' she said in a deflated tone.

'Of course you have,' Robin said compassionately, then continued. 'Jasmine, if the police make an arrest, the press will soon get wind of it.'

'I know,' she dully agreed, well aware of how they had operated in the past. The nightmare was about to continue.

'Do you think it would be a good idea to get away from here for a few days? Until the news settles down?'

Jasmine considered the question, knowing full well how she and her family had previously been hounded relentlessly.

'Where? Not to my parents', they'd soon find me there,' said Jasmine.

'Yes, they would. I was—' He stopped. There was a hard knock on the front door. Robin looked at the clock. It was just eight a.m. It could only be the police so early. His heart thumped; they must have made an arrest. Jasmine stared at him, wide-eyed in horror. This was it. 'I'll get it,' said Robin.

Sure enough, two police officers stood solemnly on the doorstep.

'Morning, sir. I'm Chief Inspector George Bond and this is Sergeant Lucy Burrows.' They each showed their ID badges. 'May we speak to Jasmine Boyd?'

'Yes, of course,' Robin said. 'This way.' He showed them into the kitchen. 'My name is Robin Spencer, I'm renovating the cottage next door.' he explained.

'Ah yes, the man who reported Adrian Hall,' said the Chief Inspector. 'You did a good job there, son.' This cemented Robin's suspicions. They must have detained him.

Once the officers had introduced themselves to Jasmine and they had all taken a seat round the kitchen table, the Chief Inspector told them the dreaded news. They had arrested two men in connection to the killing of Jasmine's late husband. The two men arrested were named as Adrian Hall and Ian Dixon. Both men had admitted to being in the vehicle at the time of the collision, but each were denying driving the van.

'Does it matter who was behind the wheel?' rasped Jasmine, shock steadily being replaced by anger now. 'They are both to blame! Neither of them bloody stopped, they just drove off and left him!' Tears collected on her lower lids.

'Both men have been detained,' Sergeant Burrows said in a calming tone.

'Absolutely, Adrian Hall and Ian Dixon are each culpable,' stated the Chief Inspector.

Robin coughed before speaking.

'How long will it be before this all gets out? Becomes public knowledge?' he asked anxiously, looking from one officer to the other.

'Imminently, that's why we're here first thing to prepare you for the inevitable,' the Chief Inspector replied soberly.

'Right.' Robin nodded decisively then turned to Jasmine. 'You need to pack a bag, Jasmine. I've a call to make.'

The police got up to leave.

'Mrs Boyd, we'll keep you informed of all proceedings,' said Sergeant Burrows and handed Jasmine a contact card.

'Th–thank you.' Her voice quivered. She chewed her bottom lip.

Robin saw them out, his mind racing. They had to get away from here, pronto. It wouldn't take long for the news reporters and journalists to come sniffing around. He had to act swiftly.

–

Robin drove at speed along the coastal path, enroute to the tidal road, his face set in determination. Jasmine had packed a small suitcase and was sat next to him, staring out of the Range Rover's windows, keeping watch for any sign of unwanted visitors to Samphire Bay.

Once they reached the tidal road, they both sighed with relief. They were safe, driving towards the peninsula. Before long, the tide would come in and reach its peak, totally covering any access to where they were heading, Bunty's house.

Robin had deduced this would be the best place to hide out. The isolated location was ideal, making it practically impossible for any of the prying press to get to at certain times of the day. And, towering high on a piece of land which gave three hundred and sixty degree views of the landscape, any intruders could easily be spotted. For Robin it had been a no-brainer and once he'd outlined the benefits of Bunty's house, Jasmine had fully agreed.

After a phone call to Bunty, arrangements had been hastily put into place.

'Darling, *of course* Jasmine must stay here!' Bunty had exclaimed incredulously. She had been appalled at hearing Robin's revelation and her heart went out to Jasmine. She was more than happy to help in any way possible and, secretly, she was pleased that Robin had had the good sense to involve her, glad that her home could be of good use.

Bunty had immediately started to prepare for her unexpected guest. She pondered over which bedroom to put Jasmine in; there were quite a few to choose from. She settled on the Rose Room, with its pink geometric patterned walls, double bed with oversized plush velvet headboard, matching pink velvet scalloped shell chair, mirrored dressing table and rose-pink cut-glass chandelier. The Burr walnut wardrobe would give Jasmine plenty of storage space; which then prompted Bunty to question how long would her guest be staying? As long as needed, Bunty concluded. The poor girl wanted anonymity – and she'd make damn sure she got it.

It warmed her that she wasn't the only one desperate to help Jasmine. Robin, bless him, was certainly playing his part too. How right she was about those two. They were clearly made for each other; there was no denying how Robin had taken it upon himself to be so caring and protective towards Jasmine. It cheered her soul that there were still chivalrous young men about like Robin.

Bunty had just finished putting fresh sheets on the bed when the doorbell chimed. They were here already. Good timing, she thought, noticing the sea starting to gradually flow forward. Robin wouldn't be going anywhere just yet either. A surreptitious smile spread across Bunty's face. The more the merrier.

She suddenly realised with a poignant pang how lonely she had increasingly become. Living in such a grand house, away from it all, had its drawbacks. Her home may be splendid, with masses of character in a dramatic setting, but rattling around inside alone was proving isolating now for Bunty. She'd never wanted to admit it, to herself as much as anyone else, but as the years tumbled on and she grew older, the impracticalities of coping by herself in such a big, empty place had become… daunting. There, she'd finally acknowledged it. Now came the question, what was she to do about it? Mentally shaking herself, she set off down the sweeping staircase to answer the door to her most welcome visitors.

Opening the door, Bunty was met with two pale faces. Jasmine's eyes were like saucers.

'Thank you so much, Bunty,' she gushed, eager to get in and out of sight.

'Not at all, darling, come in, come in,' Bunty quickly ushered the pair inside.

'There you go.' Robin put Jasmine's suitcase down on the marbled tiled floor. 'I better race back.' He looked over his shoulder to the tide outside.

'Certainly not!' retorted Bunty with force. 'You more than anyone ought to know how dangerous racing the tide is, Robin Spencer. Now go and put Jasmine's case in the Rose Room. I'll fix us all a drink, you look like you could both do with one.'

Robin dutifully did as he was told and set off up the staircase. Jasmine followed Bunty into the drawing room. A part of her was glad Robin wasn't dashing off. She was comforted by his steady calming presence.

'Now, darling, stiff gin and tonics all around I'd say,' said Bunty as she stood by the glass cocktail cabinet preparing the drinks. Jasmine hid a grin; even in such stressful times, Bunty didn't fail to make her smirk. Bunty's joie de vivre and strength of character were attributes that Jasmine was starting to admire in the woman. It made such a stark contrast to her mum, who tended to fuss and faff ineffectually, compared to Bunty's forthrightness. Bunty Deville was a formidable force and one to be reckoned with. She suddenly felt safe here with her, in this fortress about to be cut off from the outside world.

Robin entered the room and rubbed his hands together.

'I could do with one of your G&T's,' he chuckled, knowing how generous Bunty was when pouring out the gin. Not having to drive off too soon meant he could relax and enjoy it. Tension had started to mount up inside him and was building momentum. He badly needed to unwind. Glancing at Jasmine, he noticed she looked more relaxed than she had on the drive over and was knocking back her drink with gusto. Good, coming here had definitely been the right move.

'Come, sit down you two.' Bunty signalled towards the sofa and sat in the opposite chair. 'Now listen, whilst you are here, Jasmine, nobody will come anywhere near you, be assured of that,' she said firmly.

'Thank you again, Bunty, I—' began Jasmine.

'Not at all,' cut in Bunty with a wave of her hand.

Robin looked from one to the other. These two are going to get along just fine, he thought to himself.

'But somebody did promise me a dinner party on Saturday night,' Bunty continued with a wink.

'Oh sorry, I—'

'Not to worry, where better to do it?' interrupted Bunty again with a big beam.

There was a slight pause.

'You mean… me cook here?' Jasmine asked.

'Yes, darling, why not?' replied Bunty, hands spread out. Then, turning to Robin, added, 'And Robin, you must stay overnight. No good throwing a dinner party if you can't relax with a good glass of champagne,' she said sweetly with an innocent smile.

Robin coughed into his drink. He wasn't taken in for one moment with Bunty's butter-wouldn't-melt manner. The old bird was up to her tricks and playing cupid again. But, to his surprise, Jasmine intervened before he had a chance to reply.

'Bunty's right. You can't drink and drive, Robin,' she whispered.

A deadly silence followed. The enormity of the words left a chill in the air. Robin and Bunty exchanged a pained look.

'Of course Bunty's right. I'll stop over,' he agreed.

Chapter 20

Trish gasped as she saw the stack of newspapers delivered that morning. There, waiting to be displayed on the shelves, spread the shocking front-page news of the *Lancashire Evening Standard*: *Killers Caught!* She hastily pulled the top copy out from the pile to read.

> Two men have been arrested and charged with the death of Thomas Boyd, who was killed instantly in a hit-and-run accident in Carston last October. Ian Dixon and Adrian Hall admitted colliding into Mr Boyd whilst being under the influence of alcohol. It has yet to be established who was driving the vehicle. Adrian Hall, from Samphire Bay, employed Ian Dixon, a manual worker, during the time the accident took place. Both men remain in custody, whilst further investigations are made.

Two profile pictures of each man appeared beneath the article.

'Oh my God!' wheezed Trish, hand over her mouth in astonishment. All this time, the killers of poor Jasmine Boyd's husband had been right here, in Samphire Bay. Or at least one of them had, she thought, knowing who Adrian Hall was. He had come into her shop many a time. Trish held the newspaper right up to her eyes to examine the photograph of Ian Dixon. She couldn't in all honesty recall ever seeing his face – and it was one she'd certainly remember; a cruel, gruff-looking man he looked, too. The shot didn't do him any favours with his unshaven face, steely hard glare and thin straight mouth. As for Adrian, well he was looking pretty shifty too, but more in a pathetic, weak way. His eyes seemed to hold an element of sorrow, or shame, in Trish's opinion.

Her first instincts were to ring Bunty. This was hot news, absolute premier gossip! Trish scurried into the back and grabbed the phone. Shaking with anticipation, she punched out Bunty's telephone number. She could hardly contain herself, wait till she told Bunty all the scandal!

–

In the meantime, Bunty was putting the finishing touches on Jasmine's breakfast tray. Deciding she would treat the girl to breakfast in bed, it being her first morning there, she had prepared her speciality, eggs Benedict. A fresh pot of tea had been made and Bunty was just slicing the toast to put in the rack before adding it to the tray. She was so absorbed in the kitchen that she hadn't heard the phone ringing out in the hall, nor the upstairs phone reverberating noisily round the landing.

Jasmine woke to hear the loud, insistent trill. Whoever it was ringing, they weren't giving up, she thought, rolling her eyes. Was it not *obvious* that Bunty wasn't available? After a few more relentless rings, Jasmine got up and stomped out onto the landing, where the phone was loudly buzzing on a console table by a chaise lounge. She picked it up with purpose and was just about to speak when a high-pitched woman's voice blasted down the receiver.

'Oh Bunty, you'll never guess, it's in the papers this morning, that two men have been charged with the killing of that poor Jasmine's husband, you know, Thomas Boyd, and you'll never guess, but one of them was from Samphire Bay. Samphire Bay! I can't believe it, Adrian Hall, he's come into my shop many a time and to think!'

Jasmine froze, unable to move or speak as Trish's tone of excited scandal filled her ears.

'Bunty, Bunty are you there dear? What a do, I couldn't believe the papers this morning when they were delivered, I—'

Jasmine slammed the phone down. Her chest started to tighten and she forced herself to take steady, deep breaths. She heard Bunty call from the bottom of the stairs.

'Oh, you're up, darling! I was just about to bring you breakfast in bed.'

Jasmine turned around ashen faced.

'I just answered the phone, Bunty,' she croaked in a hoarse voice. 'It was some woman, talking non-stop, I couldn't get a word in edgeways.'

'Oh that'll be Trish,' said Bunty dismissively.

'She was going on about the newspapers, how it's all over the news they've caught Tom's killers...' Jasmine's chin wobbled and tears threatened to fall.

'Now just you get back into bed and eat this breakfast,' Bunty gently cajoled. Typical Trish, she thought, blabbering away like that. 'Come on, never mind her, she's just a tittle-tattle. Not worth worrying about.'

Jasmine inhaled deeply again and allowed herself to be herded back into bed. Once nicely tucked in, with the tray on her lap, she delved into the eggs Benedict, while Bunty sat beside her in the velvet shell chair, sipping tea.

'We can't stop what the newspapers print, darling, but we can make sure you're left in peace. Whilst you are here, nobody can get anywhere near you, remember that, Jasmine.' Bunty was looking steadfast, determined to reassure her.

Jasmine carried on munching on her breakfast and bobbed her head in acknowledgment. Now that the initial shock had worn off, she did concede it was fully predictable the story would be covered, after all, that's why she was here. And, like it had last October, would soon be yesterday's news. At least this time there was no room for speculation so the whole episode wouldn't be dragged through the media again. Give it a few days and it would finally be over, she told herself, as her dad had done last night when she'd rung her parents to tell them the news.

They too were thankful the killer of their son-in-law had finally been caught and detained. Her dad had also called Tom's parents, even though he knew Jasmine would be speaking to them at some point, he wanted to share her burden. More than anything they prayed it would aid Jasmine to heal and move forward with her life. They were liking the sound of this next-door neighbour of hers, who, by all accounts, couldn't do enough to help Jasmine. Now it seemed Robin had whisked their daughter away from the dreaded limelight of the media to a safe haven.

Jasmine soon finished her breakfast and felt better already with a full stomach.

'That was delicious, Bunty, thanks again.' She smiled, ever mindful of the old lady's kindness. Then, like it had with Robin, Jasmine began to question *why* Bunty was showing so much compassion… and always had to a virtual stranger. 'Bunty, why did you sell your cottage to me at such a knock-down price?'

'Because I wanted to, darling,' Bunty answered simply. 'Both cottages needed love and attention, bringing back to life, and I knew you were the person to do it.'

'Me and Robin?'

Bunty smiled wryly. 'Robin wanted both cottages.'

Jasmine was shocked by the news. 'Did he?' He'd never once indicated this to her – had she missed something in their interactions? Did he still feel that way?

'Oh yes, he and Jack saw them as a real business venture. Given their way I suspect they'd have created one large country house, the full works.'

Jasmine frowned. 'Then why didn't you sell them both to Robin and Jack?'

'It just didn't feel right. I wanted the cottages to remain as they were, two separate homes.' Bunty gazed wistfully into the distance.

'Who lived in the cottages, Bunty?' Jasmine asked, half knowing there must be an emotional tie.

'Local fishermen,' she replied.

'Perry, the man in the photographs, lived in Robin's cottage, didn't he?'

Bunty's eyes came back to rest on Jasmine's face.

'Yes, he did.'

Jasmine decided to venture further, but tread with care. 'What happened to Perry?' she enquired gently.

Bunty inhaled deeply, then exhaled on a loud sigh, bracing herself for the memories that were, once again, being brought to the surface.

'He sailed away, darling, out of my life.'

'Do you know where to?'

'Sorry?' Bunty's forehead puckered.

'I mean, do you know where he is now?' Jasmine searched her face.

'No, how would I know?' replied Bunty, genuinely puzzled by Jasmine's question.

'There's ways and means, Bunty. The world's a smaller place nowadays with the internet.'

At this Bunty burst into laughter. 'What, you mean track him down, darling?'

There was a pregnant silence.

Bunty looked sceptically at Jasmine. 'Are you serious?'

'Just a thought, Bunty. Supposing he's not that far away?'

'Hmm and married with children and umpteen grand-children?' she said dryly. 'Do you really think he'll remember me?'

'But what if he isn't and he *did* remember you, Bunty?' Jasmine asked in a small but insistent voice.

Bunty didn't have an answer.

–

Robin opened his wardrobe whilst laughing softly to himself. It was Saturday, the evening of the dinner party at Bunty's. Originally, he was sure, Jasmine's offer had been intended to be a simple kitchen supper, but now it had escalated to some kind of formal, elaborate affair. Bunty had even given him strict instructions on what to wear when she'd announced it was a black tie event.

'*Really?*' he'd asked, convinced the old bird was pulling his leg.

Apparently not, if her pursed lips and frosty glare were anything to go by.

So, dinner suit and black tie it was, and he reached into the far corner of his wardrobe to pull out the one and only suit he owned. Good job it was black.

However, once dressed and assessing his appearance in the full-length mirror, he was rather pleased with the finished article. He took in the smooth, fitted contours of his strong physique. The trousers hugged his muscular thighs and the jacket his wide shoulders. The crisp, white shirt complimented his tanned skin and dark hair.

'Not too shabby, Spencer,' he said out loud to his reflection. Then he wondered if Jasmine would be impressed with his look. Would she appreciate him as an attractive, hot-blooded male, or a smartly dressed friend simply making an effort? And, depending which category he fell into, would she let him know? Would he get any inclination as to how she felt about him? Once or twice he had suspected there could be something, some tiny spark in the way she'd looked at him. His mind flashed back to the morning they'd swum in the bay, her eyes had definitely clocked what good shape he was in, and he'd been pleased when her gaze had rested on his bare chest a touch too long. Then, the other day he'd sensed she had been staring at him from the kitchen doorway.

Even if this was so, was Jasmine in the right frame of mind? Robin sighed. He'd actually been looking forward to this evening, but now on reflection he wasn't so sure it was a good idea. Yes, it had been Jasmine's idea to cook for Bunty, but would she have suggested it had she known about Bunty's intent? What would Jasmine really think if she was fully aware of Bunty's agenda? Laugh at an old lady playing cupid, or be mortally offended by her meddling? To make matters worse – or better, again depending on which category he fell into – Robin had fallen into Bunty's trap. He was playing the exact role Bunty had cast him in. He'd fallen for Jasmine. The question was, which role was Jasmine going to take? And more significantly, was she ready to play at all?

—

'Now, darling, I think the gold, strappy number, or... maybe this?' Bunty held out an elegant indigo blue silk gown.

'Oh Bunty, I couldn't possibly wear that!' exclaimed Jasmine in awe. It was one of the most stylish dresses she'd ever seen.

'Of course you can,' replied Bunty waving her refusal away. 'It certainly won't fit me anymore,' she chuckled.

Jasmine imagined a much younger Bunty, just like in those photographs, wearing this exquisite gown. What a beauty she must have looked. Had the elusive Perry seen her in it? Most probably. She faced Bunty who was looking affectionately at her. The old dear was enjoying this, like a child playing at dressing up, she thought endearingly. Then another thought struck her. What company did Bunty have? She was almost stranded out here, in this grand house, living alone, in a pretty secluded spot. God forbid, but what if she had an accident, came unstuck in some way, who'd be here to help?

'What are you thinking?' Bunty's eyes narrowed.

Not wanting to put a dampener on the evening, Jasmine shrugged then smiled. 'What will you wear?'

'Ah, now my outfit is shrouded in mystery,' she said, eyes twinkling.

Jasmine giggled with anticipation, realising how much she enjoyed this lady's company. Bunty was a real mixture. She was strong, forthright, compassionate and most of all *fun*.

Robin was prompt, not daring to be late. As Bunty welcomed him into the hall, he was greeted with 1930s dance band music. It really set the tone.

'We thought of playing daddy's old records on the gramophone,' explained Bunty as she led him through the hall.

We? thought Robin. It seemed Bunty and Jasmine had been hitting it off well.

'I must say, Robin, you cut quite a dashing figure in that dinner suit,' Bunty called over her shoulder as she entered the dining room.

'Why thank you, Bunty. And might I say how spectacular you look too?' He raised a playful eyebrow.

'You may.' She grinned. 'This was my mother's dress, made for her thirtieth birthday party. The house was alive with music, dance and high spirits. She had a passion for the art deco era, as did my grandmother, hence her love of this place.'

Bunty did indeed look spectacular in the cocktail dress with glittering gold beading and swinging black fringe. She wore a silver headpiece with a draped crystal head chain.

Robin pictured the scene of the birthday party like something from an Agatha Christie drama, with chic clad ladies puffing smoke into the air from long cigarette holders, gentlemen in smart tuxedo formal wear, hair slicked back and flamboyant moustaches, band music gently playing from the gramophone, just like tonight.

Then, in came Jasmine, and Robin's jaw literally dropped, bringing a smirk to Bunty's face. The long, blue gown had a cowl neckline, spaghetti straps and an alluring side leg split, revealing a smooth, tanned thigh. Robin's pulse started to race.

'So, let's eat, darlings!' trilled Bunty, pleased with Robin's reaction.

Together Jasmine and Bunty had prepared the starter course of garlic mushrooms. They were ready and waiting on the hostess trolley which Bunty wheeled in. As they sat down, Robin dutifully filled their champagne flutes, whilst struggling to keep a straight face. It really was like a scene from a whodunnit. Would the murderer be Bunty, with the candlestick, in the library? He tittered inwardly.

'Everything all right, Robin?' enquired Bunty with a slight edge to her voice. She'd noticed his lips twitching. Was the boy humouring her?

'Of course, Bunty, and thanks, really, for going to so much trouble.' He gave her a winning smile. That seemed to appease her.

'No trouble, Robin, thank Jasmine, she's the one who cooked the meal.'

Robin turned to Jasmine and they exchanged a knowing smile. He could tell this charade of a dinner party wasn't lost on her either.

'Thanks, Jasmine,' he said, holding her gaze.

'My pleasure,' she said with a smile. 'I propose a toast, to—'

'Happy ever afters,' butted in Bunty, raising her glass.

Jasmine and Robin swapped another look before raising their glasses too.

'Happy ever afters!' they all chorused.

After a splendid meal of beef wellington, followed by cheesecake, they sat drinking Irish coffees, feeling suitably stuffed, if not a little tipsy from all the champagne. Bunty's tongue began to loosen, which didn't take much considering she was already a straight talker. As drink often did with her, it brought to the surface emotions she'd otherwise managed to keep under wraps when stone-cold sober.

'I love this house, as you know,' she started, then hiccupped.

'We know you do,' said Jasmine comfortingly.

'But it cost me to stay here, with daddy,' Bunty continued sadly.

Robin frowned, not knowing where this was heading, and flicked a concerned glance at Jasmine.

'He hated Perry, you see, wouldn't let him near the place,' Bunty carried on in a melancholy undertone. She hiccupped again. 'He didn't want him near me either, but I defied him you know.'

There was a stilted silence before Jasmine spoke.

'Bunty, I think I know where Perry is.'

It took a few moments for Jasmine's statement to sink in.

'Pardon?' Bunty blinked.

'Just a minute,' said Jasmine and got up from the table. Within minutes she'd returned with her laptop. Quickly she found the Facebook page where Perry appeared with three other men. She enlarged it and went to show it Bunty. 'Is this Perry?'

Bunty swallowed. She'd know that face anywhere. Slowly her eyes swept from the screen to rest on Jasmine.

'Yes,' she replied and gulped again. 'I don't understand…'

'He owns a narrowboat. We bought a water pump off him a few years ago and I managed to find him on this group page, then traced his boat and personal details.'

Bunty visibly paled.

'Perry Scholar lives in Lancaster,' said Jasmine in a soft voice.

After a few moments of silence, Robin gently suggested they all turn in.

'It's been quite a night, ladies, I think we should all get some sleep.'

Chapter 21

It was a very subdued Bunty who climbed wearily up the stairs, followed by Jasmine and Robin. The dinner party had ended on a bit of a cliff hanger moment. It had well and truly given Bunty food for thought. Gone was her usual candid bonhomie, to be replaced with a still, reflective mood. She turned to them when reaching the landing.

'Good night, darlings. Robin, you're in the Blue Room.' Then, without another word she disappeared into her own bedroom, leaving Jasmine and Robin staring after her. After hearing the door slam shut, Jasmine looked sheepishly at Robin.

'Do you think I should have told her about Perry?' she asked, eyes searching his face.

'Yes, why not tell her?' replied Robin.

'It's made an impact on her though, hasn't it?'

Jasmine heaved a sigh and sank onto the chaise lounge in the landing corridor. She leant forward and put her head in her hands, feeling fuzzy and confused.

'Oh Robin, what have I done? I shouldn't have interfered with things that don't concern me,' she whined.

Robin almost laughed out loud with the irony of it all. Sitting down, he gently consoled her.

'Listen, Jasmine, you acted with the best of intentions and meant well.' He paused, but deciding to continue,

added in a hushed voice, 'I wouldn't feel guilty anyway…
because…'

Jasmine's head shot up.

'Because what?' she said.

'Because Bunty's done exactly the same with you – us
– actually.'

'What do you mean?' Jasmine blinked, trying to clear
her blurry mind.

'Bunty set us up. She deliberately sold one cottage to
each of us, with the plan of us getting together.' There,
he'd said it. It was finally out in the open. He looked
straight at Jasmine to study her response.

'You mean… romantically?' she asked incredulously. A
bit too incredulously for Robin's liking. Was it so unbelievable they should be linked romantically?

'Yes,' he answered flatly, looking down towards his
black polished shoes.

There was an awkward pause, before he felt Jasmine's
shoulders shaking and heard her restrained laughter.
'What's so funny?' he asked, rather offended. Not only
was it unbelievable, but hilarious too? Charming.

'Oh Robin, she knocked quite a lot off the asking
price, and all because she was playing cupid,' she chortled,
doubled over in laughter.

'I know, ten thousand,' he said with a derisive smile.

'You mean…?'

'Yeah, she did the same for me, reduced by ten grand,'
he answered dryly. He waited for her to stop giggling
and calm down, assuming – hoping – it was more to do
with the champagne than anything else. Once she had,
he dared to ask, 'Aren't you offended? That she's tried to
manipulate us?'

'Not really.' She shrugged. 'It's a bit odd that she felt the need to matchmake, but I suppose it's kind of endearing in a way.'

He stared into those brown eyes and was mesmerised. What a complex creature she was. Jasmine had reacted so differently to how he'd expected. Perhaps because she had recently seen another side to Bunty, and having sought refuge in her home had clearly made her feel safe. She obviously now viewed Bunty as a friend and trusted her. All the same, he was still a little put out that Jasmine found the thought of them being a couple so hilarious. As though reading his mind, Jasmine lent forward to kiss his cheek.

'Good night, Robin,' she whispered.

He stilled. Her lips felt soft and warm.

'Night, Jasmine,' he replied in a hoarse voice, then watched her get up and sashay down the landing in that damned sexy dress. She'd kissed him. Albeit on the cheek, but even so, she'd kissed him.

–

Bunty was unable to sleep. After all this time, Perry had been close by. She'd always assumed he had cast his net far and wide, to some distant place. Now it transpired he had a narrowboat and was living in Lancaster. Still, she told herself, just knowing his location didn't really alter things. He could be happily married, surrounded by numerous children and grandchildren. She pictured them all aboard his boat, rosy cheeked cherubs smiling up at him, steering the wheel, as they chugged merrily up the canal.

A shard of jealousy stabbed her. Oh, to be surrounded by such love, and here she was, all alone. A tear trickled down her face. If only she could turn back time. Another vision of Perry drifted into her mind, on his red sailing boat, presenting her with that sparkling aquamarine ring. If only…

–

The next morning, all three of them sat around the breakfast table in a comfortable silence, while nursing their hangovers. They each had much to contemplate. Robin still hadn't got over that kiss; however innocent it appeared to be given, he couldn't help but hope it was a sign. Might Jasmine possibly see him as more than just a good friend? Could this be the beginning of something? He discreetly stole a side glance at her. She seemed natural and normal as ever, then on catching his eye she smiled.

'Do you want some, Robin?' she asked him.

Did he ever. 'Hmm, sorry?' He blinked.

'Tea?' She grinned, holding up the teapot.

'Oh… yes, thanks.'

Bunty seemed in a world of her own, slowly munching on toast, gazing into space. Jasmine put the teapot down and coughed.

'Bunty, about last night…' she started.

Bunty snapped out of her reverie.

'Yes, darling, what about last night?'

'I'm sorry for mentioning Perry. I should have kept my mouth shut.'

'No, you shouldn't have,' retorted Bunty. 'You followed your gut instinct and I'd have done the same.'

Robin slid Bunty a sly look, which wasn't lost on her. She knew exactly what he was thinking and he was right. She herself had done the very same. Nothing wrong with giving fate a helping hand. And now, she was about to do it once more. She inhaled deeply.

'And I'm about to follow my gut instinct again,' she announced causing Robin and Jasmine to look up sharply.

'What are you about to do precisely?' asked Robin with caution.

'I'm going to contact Perry,' Bunty said with conviction.

–

Bunty sat poised, pen and paper at the ready. She needed time and space to think, so had barricaded herself in Daddy's old study. It was situated right at the top of the house, with a huge picture window overlooking the bay. The surrounding walls contained bookcase cabinets with an upper railing, where a wooden ladder ran along.

As a child, Bunty had had lots of fun, climbing and pushing herself along the track, picking out all manner of books. The Deville family held an eclectic taste in reading. From her father's art books ranging from the Renaissance period to the Arts and Crafts movement, her mother's biographies of the rich and famous and of course, all things art deco whether it be architecture or fashion, to Bunty's childhood reads including *Charlotte's Web, Tom's Midnight Garden* and the full Enid Blyton *The Secret Seven* series.

She'd whiled away many a rainy day here, absorbed in the pages of books, providing escapism and adventure to a child's imagination.

Now though, she was applying her mind as an adult, on a sincere mission. Bunty was at pains to pitch the letter just right. She didn't know what she was dealing with, after all. Not knowing what position Perry was in, meant she had to tread very carefully. Bunty decided to keep it affable and platonic, a case of old friends getting in touch. In many ways, that's what she was – just an old friend reaching out. What could go wrong? *A lot*, she glumly told herself. Supposing he didn't even remember her? *Unlikely!* her instincts snapped back, and, as if in support, a flash of inspiration struck her. She'd enclose a photograph of them, surely that would strike a nerve? Yes, now which one to choose... Once again Bunty had the pictures spread out on the desk in front of her. After glancing over them, she selected the one at the beach, where they were paddling in the sea. What a magical day that had been. Then, with a steely nerve she began writing.

> *Dear Perry,*
>
> *This may come as a surprise to you, but better late than never!*
>
> *I've enclosed a photograph which recently came into my possession. I remember that day at the beach so well; such happy memories created.*
>
> *I often think about you, Perry, and the times we shared. For me, I've never had such like with anyone else. I expect you're happily married with a large family by now and wish you well.*
>
> *If, however, you are in a position where you would like to reacquaint, it would be nice to meet up once again.*
>
> *As you probably guessed, I'm still here in Samphire Bay, living in the 'big house' as you called it, on the peninsula.*
>
> *With very best wishes,*
> *Bunty*

There. Short, sweet and succinct. Not too gushy or pushy. If Perry wanted to respond, he knew her address and could write a letter back. She refrained from giving her mobile or landline number, not wanting to be caught off guard by an unexpected call. No, she had to be prepared, not put on the spot. Perry could read her letter and have time to decide his actions, if any. It would come as a complete shock hearing from an old love after all this time and he would need breathing space to reflect and contemplate. If he was happily married, he could write a jolly letter back, thanking her for getting in touch and explain his circumstances, no harm done. If he was single, living alone, then he might well be glad of her company and be pleased Bunty had contacted him.

Bunty folded the letter and slipped it inside an envelope along with the photograph. Jasmine had supplied his address:

> *Fisher's Cottage*
> *Spinney Lane*
> *Galgate*
> *Lancaster*

Jasmine had also typed in Perry's address into her laptop and got his cottage up on a street view map. There he was, Bunty thought, tucked away in a pretty, little cottage on the edge of a leafy lane. She took in the ivy climbing up the grey stone, its white studded door and its house sign, Fisher's Cottage, carved into a piece of driftwood. All so tasteful. The question was, who else, if anyone, lived there?

Jasmine was also sat taking stock downstairs in the kitchen. Having created graphics to accompany written text for an event brochure, she was in need of a break. Instead of doing the sensible thing and making a well-earned cup of coffee, she had kept her laptop open and searched for news of Tom's killers. There was plenty. Those daunting faces of Adrian Hall and Ian Dixon stared up at her. Bile seeped up her throat, threatening to spew out. She got up, shaking, and quickly switched on the tap. Cupping her hands underneath the cold water, she splashed her face, then ducked down under the stream to gulp a few mouthfuls. That was better. Feeling slightly refreshed, she pushed the laptop cover shut. Enough.

How long would she have to hide out here? Jasmine missed her own home. It was now day three in Bunty's house, undercover on the peninsula. Surely she should be yesterday's news by now? Judging by what she'd just read, Ian Dixon had been charged with manslaughter and Adrian Hall in perverting the course of justice. They had both pleaded guilty and were awaiting sentencing. Jasmine had been contacted by the police so was aware of this development, but seeing it sprawled before her on the screen was too much to absorb.

Her parents had offered to visit, as well as her brother, but Jasmine had put them off, assuring them all she was fine. Which she was. Most of the time. Apart from the occasional wobble like earlier. All she had to do was sit it out, she kept telling herself. Her thoughts were inter-rupted by Bunty entering the kitchen.

'I'm going to the post office,' she told her, waving the letter in the air.

'Good luck, Bunty.' Jasmine smiled, proud of the old lady she was growing rather accustomed to. She had half anticipated being shown the letter and was secretly relieved. It was personal and she hadn't wanted to be privy to its contents. She *was* curious, on the other hand, to its repercussions. Jasmine couldn't help but feel responsible. She hoped and prayed it would all end well for Bunty and Perry. It seemed such a waste to think of two people, who clearly loved each other once, being apart. Of course, this was assuming Perry was available. Even so, Jasmine conceded, there was nothing wrong in just being friends, if Perry did have a partner. It could open up a whole new world for each of them she concluded.

Chapter 22

'She kissed you?' Jack's eyebrows wriggled mischievously.

'Yeah, she kissed me,' replied Robin.

'Where?' He winked.

'On the cheek,' Robin answered flatly.

'Oh.' Jack visibly deflated.

'She was pissed,' Robin continued, making his friend burst into laughter. Jack soon stopped at seeing Robin so pensive.

'Come on then, Rob, tell me all about this bizarre dinner party.'

He put his rubber mallet down. The two were in the new kitchen diner. Having installed the wood burner and the new kitchen units, they were now busy laying quarry tiles on the floor. Robin got up, reached for his flask and poured them each a coffee.

'Bizarre's the word, Jack, you should have seen what Bunty was wearing, she looked like some kind of flapper girl.'

Jack spluttered into his drink.

'But bloody hell, the dress Jasmine had on…'

'Sexy?'

'Was it ever,' Robin stared lustfully into space. 'Anyway, after lots of champagne we all go upstairs to bed…'

'Interesting, go on,' urged Jack.

'Bunty waltzes off and leaves me and Jasmine on the landing. She thinks she's upset Bunty over this Perry business—'

'The guy in the photographs?'

'Yeah, Bunty's old flame. So I sat down on the chaise lounge next to Jasmine to console her.'

'And?'

'Well, I assured her that she'd only acted with the best of intentions and that Bunty wasn't averse to playing cupid either. I told her everything.'

Jack had long since heard from Robin about Bunty's plan to matchmake him with Jasmine. He'd not only found it amusing, but was delighted it had resulted in them paying ten grand less for the cottage.

'And?'

Robin took a sip of coffee, then looked dejectedly at Jack.

'She found the whole thing ridiculous,' he dully answered.

'Why?' he asked, genuinely puzzled.

Robin shrugged.

'She just laughed.'

'But what did she say?' Jack was beginning to feel a little offended on behalf of his mate.

'That it was kind of endearing on Bunty's behalf, but more than anything she found it funny that she'd reduced the asking price of both cottages to carry out her ploy.'

'Hmm, maybe that's what she was laughing at, not the thought of being in a relationship with you?' comforted Jack.

'You think so?' asked Robin, wanting to believe him.

'Yes, especially if she'd had a lot to drink, she was probably just giddy.' There was a moment's reflection before Jack added, 'So how did the kiss come about?'

'She just leant forward and kissed me on the cheek and said good night.'

'You could just tell her how you feel? Put your cards on the table?' suggested Jack.

'Not now, Jasmine's under too much pressure at the moment and…'

'What?'

'I don't want to ruin our friendship.'

Jack nodded, understanding his mate's predicament. He was at least glad that Robin had finally been open and honest about his feelings for Jasmine. Hopefully this could be the beginning of something good for him.

'Give it time, Rob, you'll know when to make a move.' He elbowed him with affection. Then, changing the subject completely, asked, 'Anyway, what are we doing for your birthday?'

'Probably the usual,' replied Robin, then tipped his head back to finish his drink.

'Piss up at The Smugglers?'

'Yeah, why not?'

–

Jasmine had made a decision. As welcoming and lovely as Bunty was, it was time to go home. A few more days had passed. Feeling confident that the press must by now have moved on to fresher news, she thought it safe to get back to her cottage. When voicing this to her host, Bunty had nodded in agreement.

'I think we're over the worst now, darling,' she remarked.

Jasmine thought it sweet she'd used the term 'we' as opposed to 'you', giving the impression she wasn't alone in this.

'I'll get Robin to come and fetch you.'

'No, I'll walk,' replied Jasmine, wanting to stretch her legs and get some fresh sea air.

'You sure?'

'Yes, really.'

'In that case, you'd better wait till after high tide,' warned Bunty.

'I know. I'll get packed and ready,' Jasmine said, then looked Bunty in the eye. 'Bunty, thanks so much for having me. I really appreciate it.'

'Not at all, darling, it's been a pleasure having you.'

Jasmine was once again reminded how much time Bunty spent alone. She only wished this Perry was going to come up trumps.

Wheeling her suitcase down the tidal road, Jasmine breathed in the balmy atmosphere. Samphire Bay was still basking in the summer sunshine. It was now edging towards the end of August and wouldn't be long before autumn put in an appearance, but for now the swaying beach grasses, yellow gorse and plentiful white flowering samphire flourished. Seagulls squawked over the vastness of the sea and a salt-laden breeze filled the air.

Jasmine was looking forward to getting back to her cottage, as well as her new garden studio. She was also excited about seeing Robin again. If being truthful to herself, she'd missed his company. It was odd not having him only next door.

After a good hour's power walking, Jasmine had crossed the tidal road and was making her way down the coastal path. She could see the cottages in the distance and wondered what Robin and Jack were doing. She marvelled at the speed they worked at, and once again thought how fortunate she'd been to have them as neighbours.

A figure came into view, appearing to be looking down the cottage gardens. Jasmine squinted to get a better look. It was a woman with long, dark hair, wearing a white linen jumpsuit. Hardly beach wear, thought Jasmine suspiciously. What was she staring at? A sharp gasp escaped her. What if she was a reporter? No, Jasmine reasoned, this woman was empty-handed, no camera, notebook or pen. She was just staring at the cottages. How strange.

To Jasmine's horror, the woman opened her garden gate and began walking down the path. Deciding to confront her, Jasmine sped up into an awkward jog, dragging her case along the stony path. Getting closer, she saw the intruder come back out of the garden gate.

'Can I help you?' Jasmine called.

The woman turned, saw Jasmine coming towards her and shot off. Jasmine ran faster to try and catch up, lugging her case behind, but wasn't fast enough. The woman was now out of sight as Jasmine bent over and panted to get her breath back. *Who the hell was that?*

—

'Are you all right, Dad?'

'Yes, Emma, just received this letter.' He pointed to the piece of paper on the kitchen table.

'Is it from the hospital?' she asked urgently, sensing something had clearly upset him.

He shook his head. 'No, no.'

'Then what?'

'Perhaps it's better if you read it, love.' He pulled out the chair beside him and pushed the letter across the table.

Emma sat down and tucked her chestnut fringe behind her ears to get a clear view of the letter. Her eyes quickly darted over the bold strokes of writing and the photograph enclosed. Once finished reading, she gave him a surreptitious grin.

'Well, well, who's Bunty, Dad?'

Perry gave his daughter a warm smile.

'Somebody I knew long before I met your mum.'

'An old girlfriend?' Emma was more than interested now, sitting forward to hear all about her dad's past. The picture of him in his younger days intrigued her.

'Yes, love, she was.' He nodded, his eyes holding a sadness that touched her.

'Are you going to reply?' she tentatively asked.

He gave a half laugh. 'Oh, I don't know about that, Emma.'

'Go on, Dad!' she encouraged. 'It'd do you good to get some company.'

He pretended to take offence.

'I *do* have company,' he said indignantly. 'I've plenty of friends down the marina.'

'Yeah, old sailors,' she joked, then added in a serious tone. 'Not female company, not since Mum died.'

Emma eyed her father carefully, knowing she was treading on sensitive ground, but it needed addressing.

Twelve years ago they had lost the most precious person in their lives. Valerie Scholar had been a real trooper till the bitter end, but inevitably breast cancer had claimed her life, leaving Perry a widower and stepfather to Emma, her only child. Although Perry had come into their lives

187

when Emma was just eight years old, he had been so much more than any parent could be.

Valerie was a widow when Perry had boldly introduced himself in the museum. She'd taken Emma out on a visit to the Lancaster Maritime Museum, where Perry volunteered, and they'd clicked immediately with little Emma taking to him like a duck to water. He'd thoroughly amused Valerie and Emma with his animated tales about the history of the port of Lancaster. He persuaded them to step aboard a full-sized Lancaster Packet Boat, transporting them back to the bustle of the Lancaster canal during its glory days with a short film.

It was in the Quayside Tea Room, the museum cafe where Perry was taking his break, that Emma ran up to sit opposite him, followed by a hesitant mother.

'Sit down, please,' Perry had invited. After chatting pleasantly to them and learning there wasn't a husband or father on the scene, he further invited them for a trip down the canal on his narrowboat.

From the moment Valerie and Emma had stepped aboard Perry's boat, they had been enchanted. Emma was fascinated by the fact that he actually lived on such a thing! It wasn't long before they were all setting sail together on weekends away. Valerie had never known such tranquillity, listening to the gentle chug of the narrowboat engine as it drifted down the still waters, dappled sunlight flickering through the trees, the whiff of smoke from the wood burner and, most of all, the cheering smile from The Captain (as they'd nicknamed Perry) safely navigating them all. Such happy, happy days.

They soon married and Perry moved into Valerie's little cottage, aptly named Fisher's Cottage. It was fate, they all agreed, a tight-knit little family living under the same roof.

Then five years later, when Emma was just thirteen years old, Valerie was diagnosed with late-stage breast cancer. Emma had been at such an impressionable age. To be without a mother as a young teenager broke Perry's heart and had unsurprisingly made him very protective of his stepdaughter, who he treated and loved as his own. Emma had only ever really known Perry as a father figure and in turn saw him as her one and only dad.

As the years ploughed on and Emma grew into a young woman, Perry's protection had only increased, vetting all boyfriends she brought back with a watchful eye. He respected her space though, ever mindful of controlling parents, his past having never quite left him…

At times, in his quieter moments, he did think of Bunty, but the memories always turned sour when remembering how vindictive and domineering her father was. Hamish Deville was a selfish old man in his eyes. He'd deprived him and his daughter of any future happiness. Now, reading this letter, it looked like he'd robbed Bunty of any happiness at all in her life, the narcissistic bastard.

Emma watched Perry and the various expressions crossing his face. She sat back and scrutinised her dad. He wasn't bad looking at all for his age, she thought, head cocked to one side. He had style, she had to admit, with his long layered grey hair and colourful shirts. The neckerchiefs he sometimes wore gave him an aged David Essex look which had him chuckling when she'd told him. No, not bad at all, Emma concluded. This Bunty would be impressed with his appearance, she was sure of it. Perry had aged well; the years had been kind. And he deserved a companion. When she wasn't working at the bank, she was performing gigs with her band. Plus, she wouldn't be living here in Fisher's Cottage forever.

'So, what about it, Dad?'

'I'll think about it,' he appeased, knowing his daughter would pester him relentlessly until he gave in.

'Samphire Bay,' said Emma contemplatively. 'I love it there, very atmospheric. But what's this "big house" on the peninsula?' she asked, quoting Bunty's letter.

'Where she lives. It's an impressive place,' Perry said, memories of the imposing home flooding his mind.

Emma took out her mobile and searched Samphire Bay. Colourful, stunning scenery flashed up before her. The huge, white art deco house soon appeared.

'Wow! This is where Bunty lives,' she murmured, still swiping through the images. Then, photographs of the Tea by the Sea event came on-screen. Emma clicked on the parish website they were sourced from. This time, the photographs had captions underneath, with the names of those depicted in the images. It wasn't long before Bunty Deville's name came up, dressed as a fortune teller. 'Dad, look!' Emma couldn't help laughing at Bunty's colourful get-up. She handed him her mobile.

'My God,' Perry stared at Bunty in her costume. It was her all right, he'd recognise that face anywhere, despite all the make-up. She still held an air of mischief about her with those twinkling eyes of hers. Bunty Deville, a real blast from the past.

–

Later that evening, when Emma had gone out with friends, Perry reached for the letter and read it again. Why had she decided to get in touch now, after all this time? And how had she known his address? It perplexed him more than worried him. She didn't know about Val, that was clear, from the sentence, 'I expect you're happily married with a large family by now' and asking if he was 'in a position where you would like to reacquaint'. So she only had limited information about him. The whole thing had him thinking and reminiscing. He looked at the photograph of them laughing together on the beach, not a care in the world. Then, after pouring a large whiskey and downing it, picked up his pen and began to write.

Chapter 23

The pub was heaving. In typical Jack fashion, he had rounded up all their mates and Robin's family for a big birthday bash at The Smugglers. Bunty was sat with Robin's parents, looking in great form. The gin and tonics were going down great guns, being replenished by all and sundry.

Jasmine was due to arrive but had spent a couple of days at her mum and dad's and would be a little late. She'd found it cathartic to meet up with them and Sam; they'd all shown anguish over the arrest of Tom's killer and a heavy burden hung on all the family as they awaited the sentencing of Adrian Hall and Ian Dixon. Once that was over with, they would try to draw a line under the whole shocking nightmare, but they knew they would likely never fully heal from the deep wound of having a precious member of the family taken from them. What they could do was help Jasmine to move forward and by all accounts, that's exactly what she appeared to be doing. Her parents were delighted by the progress she'd made on her cottage and Sam was most impressed to hear the garden studio was fully installed and in use.

'You've certainly been very busy, love,' remarked Jasmine's mum. Then, couldn't resist asking, 'Have you had any more help from the next-door neighbour?'

Despite her mum's casual tone, Jasmine could see straight through her. 'Yes, actually I have,' she replied with a wry smile at seeing her mum's face light up.

'Oh lovely! He sounds such a nice chap—'

'Right, let's put the kettle on,' cut in Jasmine's dad, preventing his wife from asking any further questions. He suspected his daughter could do without the third degree. Surprisingly though, Jasmine continued the conversation.

'It's Robin's birthday today. We're all meeting up in the pub tonight,' she announced.

'Who's "we"?' said Sam, just before her dad was about to ask the same question.

'Me, Bunty, Jack, all their mates and family,' Jasmine replied, happy to be growing her social circle and looking forward to the evening.

They exchanged glances. It sounded like Jasmine was really settling into Samphire Bay.

'Good,' her dad said with a nod.

Later in the afternoon, Jasmine set off home. Her parents and brother stood at the bottom of the drive to wave goodbye in high spirits.

'I think the move to Samphire Bay is doing her good,' Sam stated, watching his sister's Mini drive off down the road.

'So do I,' replied both parents in unison.

–

As Robin downed another pint, he glanced round the crowded pub. Still no Jasmine yet, he noticed. He was expecting her to come later but remained eager to see her walk through the door. Since the dinner party at Bunty's, they hadn't really had a chance to speak. He and Jack had worked flat-out, finishing off the downstairs of their cottage and, now that they had installed a fireplace in the living room and the kitchen diner was complete, it was just a case of sanding down and varnishing the floorboards before decorating the upstairs. Then the cottage would be ready to put on the market. A sadness crept into Robin when considering it. Soon he would no longer have a reason to be next door to Jasmine. Jack's suggestion of him 'putting his cards on the table' and revealing his feelings sprung to mind, but not tonight. His head was already starting to spin a little from all the beer constantly being supplied.

'Come on, Rob, sup up!' chorused Jack and a few others, as they put yet another pint in front of him. Robin's eyes glazed over as he tried to focus, then a voice that was all too familiar to him came from behind, stopping him in his tracks.

'Happy birthday, Robin.'

As he turned, a pair of red lips met his mouth. His eyes widened, but the lips pressed harder, forcing Robin back towards the bar. He stumbled and managed to pull away. Wiping his mouth with the back of his hand he stared into the face of the woman.

'Ellie, what the hell are you doing here?'

–

Jasmine had seen it all. At the precise moment she had pushed the pub door open, she'd witnessed Robin and a dark-haired woman kissing. A jolt struck and her gut reaction was to walk straight out of the place. Nobody had even noticed her, so she left quietly without fuss. Trembling slightly, she sat on a bench outside and tried to steady herself. The last thing she'd expected to see was Robin kissing someone. Stupidly, she'd assumed he'd be glad to see her.

The woman with long, dark hair she recognised. It was the same person who had been spying on the cottages. Who was it? Then, she jumped at the rising voices from the side of the pub.

'Get the hell out of here, Ellie!'

Jasmine quietly moved to the edge of the building and discreetly peeped her head round the corner. Jack had his hands on his hips, staring the woman down.

'You can't stop me being here,' she said, her tone laced heavily with scorn. 'Still looking out for Robin? He's a big boy, Jack, and can look after himself.'

'Robin can't stand the sight of you,' he replied with venom.

'Really?' came the sarcastic reply.

'And there's no way he wants you back,' Jack rasped.

At this the woman gave a harsh laugh.

'Well, we'll see about that,' she taunted, then turned her back and walked away.

Jasmine quickly returned to the bench and pulled out her phone, head bent down so as not to be noticed. She inconspicuously watched the woman strut past. She had an air of conviction about her; shoulders back, long legs in a short, red dress taking confident strides. So, this was the woman who had broken Robin's heart. Judging from the sound of her, she hadn't finished yet either.

Feeling a jumble of emotions she didn't understand, Jasmine decided to go home. A strange anxiety had seeped into her, leaving her numb inside. Jasmine craved solace, yet also felt the need to be alone. So many questions whizzed round her head. Despite Jack telling Ellie Robin didn't want her back, they *had* been kissing. She'd seen it with her own eyes. Did they still have unfinished business?

Walking back along the coastal path, for once the spectacular views didn't lift her mood. All manner of thoughts and sensations passed through her as she plodded on, taking one step after the other until at last she reached her cottage, her haven. Once inside, she slammed the door shut on the whole evening.

–

Dear Bunty,

Where do I start? Firstly, by thanking you for contacting me. Not sure how you managed it, but I'm so pleased you did.

Life without you was tough, I'll not lie, but I did manage to find happiness eventually. I met and married Valerie, but sadly lost her to breast cancer twelve years ago. Thankfully she left me a stepdaughter, Emma, my pride and joy. It's Emma who's always telling me to get out more. Easier said than done for an old sailor boy like me, but now, thanks to you, I find myself in a fortunate position. I'd love to meet up. The photograph you sent kick-started many fond memories we shared and it would be great to catch up and reminisce.

So, where and when Bunty? As ever, I'll be guided by you.

Very best,

Perry

PS You made an excellent fortune teller BTW.

Bunty sat down with a huge beam on her face. Perry had replied! And, more importantly, he wanted to see her. The postscript at the bottom of the letter had made her giggle. He must have had access to the parish website and seen the snaps taken from the Tea by the Sea event. He was evidently 'with it' using the internet, and what did the abbreviation BTW mean? She'd have to ask Robin, or Jasmine. Since her stay, she and Jasmine had exchanged numbers and had often chatted on the phone. The two women were forming quite a bond. In fact, thought Bunty, she'd ring Jasmine now and let her know about Perry's letter. Before doing so, she poured herself a generous gin and tonic, as a celebratory drink. It wasn't every day you reconnected with a long-lost love.

Taking a pleasurable sip, Bunty closed her eyes in appreciation of the zesty fizz, then punched in Jasmine's mobile number.

Jasmine was in her studio working when her phone bleeped into life. Quickly seeing who the caller was, she smiled at it being Bunty, despite wishing it had been someone else – Robin, mainly.

'Darling, I have news!' exclaimed Bunty.

'Oh yes?' Jasmine said with eagerness, hoping it was news on the Perry front.

'He's replied,' she proclaimed with glee.

'Bunty!' gasped Jasmine in delight. 'What did he write?'

'That he wants us to meet.'

'That's fabulous!' Jasmine gushed, truly happy for her. 'When are you going to meet?'

'He's left it up to me,' Bunty said, before adding, 'he's seen the photographs of me dressed up as gypsy Rosy-Lee.'

Jasmine laughed, finding it funny he'd looked her up before replying.

'Hmm, what does "BTW" mean?' asked Bunty.

'Sorry?'

'His letter says... hang on,' she grabbed the letter. '"PS you made an excellent fortune teller BTW."'

'By the way,' replied Jasmine with a grin, liking the sound of the man. He clearly wasn't an old fuddy-duddy, using terminology like that and surfing the net. When she'd said as much to Bunty, she'd gone on to tell her about Perry's stepdaughter, Emma.

'She obviously keeps him young,' Jasmine commented.

Bunty also went on to explain about Perry's late wife.

'Oh, that's sad,' said Jasmine, 'but at least he's had Emma in his life.'

More than I've had, thought Bunty with regret. Then, she forced herself to remain positive. She had to think about future arrangements with Perry, which prompted her to ask for advice.

'Where do you think we should meet?'

'Maybe somewhere neutral?' suggested Jasmine.

'Hmm...' Bunty was racking her brains, after all she very rarely left Samphire Bay.

'What about a tea shop in Lancaster? I could take you.'

'Would you, darling? As moral support?'

'Of course! After all you've done for me,' replied Jasmine with gusto. 'I don't mind spending the day in Lancaster. I'll drop you off, then make myself scarce until it's time to come home.'

'You're sure?'

'Yes, absolutely,' Jasmine said firmly.

'Oh thank you, darling. I'll write back and tell him.'

Jasmine frowned. 'You haven't his number then?'

'No, but then he hasn't mine either,' replied Bunty matter of factly.

'Don't you think you should exchange numbers? It'd be easier when meeting up.'

'Sorry?' said Bunty, a touch confused. My goodness, how would the youth of today cope without their mobile phones? It was as though they couldn't exist without them. How did they think the likes of she and Perry managed all those years ago without one? Set the date, time and place and stick to it. Simple, to her mind.

'Well, supposing something happens and one of you can't make it?' said Jasmine, equally bemused by Bunty's apparent inability to grasp the obvious.

'Like what?'

'I don't know!' she laughed, finding Bunty's obtuseness exasperating, then added for devilment, 'FFS.'

There was a moment's pause. Jasmine could almost hear the clogs ticking in Bunty's head.

'Sorry? FFS?'

Jasmine bent double, trying to keep the laughter in.

'It's another abbreviation,' she replied, but couldn't keep the humour out of her voice.

'Oh I see,' said Bunty suspecting she was the subject to ridicule. 'I'll look it up,' she told her flatly.

'You do that, and in the meantime, I'll find a nice, cosy tea shop in Lancaster for you and Perry.'

'Good. Thank you.'

'BFN,' replied Jasmine, unable to resist throwing out another acronym.

'Oh stop!' thundered Bunty before hanging up.

Jasmine burst into more giggles. But she stopped immediately upon seeing a certain woman with long dark hair walk past on the coastal road through her window. She got up from her desk and went into the garden. Scurrying to the hedge, she ducked down and watched

Ellie brazenly stroll up next door's path and knock on the back door. Jasmine's eyes narrowed as she saw Robin answer. Then, with a heavy heart, she saw Ellie enter and the door close.

Chapter 24

Robin banged the door shut, then turned to face Ellie.

'What exactly are you playing at?' he asked wearily. He really didn't have the time, energy or inclination to bother with her. His head was pounding after last night's birthday bash and the last thing Robin needed right now was Ellie.

She looked at him coquettishly.

'I just want to talk Robin, that's all.'

'About what?' he demanded.

She fluttered her eyelashes. 'Us.'

'Us? There is no *us*,' rasped Robin.

'But there could be.'

'Are you for real?' he replied incredulously.

'Things didn't work out for me with—'

'Yeah, I gathered that,' Robin cut in harshly. 'And I'm guessing you thought, I know,' he put his finger on his chin in mock contemplation, 'I'll go back to Robin after all this time and rip him off again!'

Ellie winced slightly, not quite expecting this reaction from Robin. Yes, granted he might be surprised to see her, a little bruised perhaps, but not this outrage and disdain he was showing her. Anger blazed from his eyes. She quickly changed tack – Robin was her last chance. She was homeless and skint; poetic justice really, that her solicitor boyfriend had proved to be even more mercenary than her. After being booted out of his house, he'd cleared their joint account and took everything he'd ever given her, even the jewellery, back.

'I wanted to talk properly, to apologise, when I first saw you last night,' she began.

'You mean when you forced yourself upon me?' he asked sardonically.

She pouted. 'I mean before Jack frogmarched me out of the pub.'

'Well good for him. If I hadn't been so pissed I'd have done the same.'

Ellie faked hurt, but Robin had seen it all before and was wise to her tactics.

'And it's a bit late in the day for apologies, not that I need to hear any. I'm so over you.' He stared her out.

A flicker of bitterness cast over her face. Evidently, he had moved on from her, she no longer had any pull on him like the old days. This wasn't going according to plan. Not at all.

'I suppose this is to do with her next door?' She tipped her head in the direction of Jasmine's cottage.

Robin frowned. What did she know about Jasmine? He folded his arms and remained silent.

'I've read all about her in the paper. A real damsel in distress, you might say.'

Robin's jaw tightened, but she carried on regardless.

'And who better to be her knight in shining armour?' she taunted sweetly.

'Keep Jasmine out of this,' Robin warned in a low voice.

'I've heard about you skivvying for her, obviously playing the sympathy card, was she?' Ellie asked with spite.

'Right, that's enough, get out.' Robin opened the door for her to leave.

'Oh, and by the way, I don't think she appreciates me being on the scene, not with the way she was skulking outside the pub last night,' she threw over her shoulder whilst leaving, 'or the way she's spying over the hedge right now.' She gave a nasty laugh and marched off.

Robin watched his ex-girlfriend walk away, bold as brass, not a care in the world, and wondered how on earth he had ever loved her. Her words however did affect him. Ellie mentioning Jasmine being outside The Smugglers last night for one. Why hadn't she come in and joined them all? And what was that about Jasmine spying over the hedge? Would Ellie's presence cause that much interest? The sound of the front door opening interrupted his thoughts. Jack had arrived and wandered into the kitchen. They were due to start sanding down the floorboards, but Robin couldn't summon up any enthusiasm at all.

'Hi Rob, how's your head this morning?' Jack grinned.

'Bad, and it's got worse. Ellie's just called round,' replied Robin in a dull tone.

Jack performed a double take, which Rob would have found funny in any other circumstance. 'You what? I don't believe that woman,' he snapped.

'It's OK, she's finally got the message.'

'Good. With a bit of luck, she'll clear off Samphire Bay and never come back again.'

'Hmm.'

Jack eyed Robin, who was looking anything but relieved.

'You all right, mate?' Surely he wasn't about to rekindle any feelings for his poisonous ex?

'It's what she said.'

203

'What?' Jack brusquely asked, not liking the sound of where this was heading.

'She said Jasmine was outside the pub last night, skulking.' Robin turned to Jack. 'Did you see her?'

'No.' He shook his head, then asked, 'But why stay outside and not come in?' They exchanged a puzzled look. 'Unless, she *had* and saw you and Ellie kissing…'

'I wasn't kissing Ellie, *she* was kissing *me*!' yelped Robin.

'Yes, I know, but from Jasmine's view at the door, it wouldn't have looked like that, would it?' reasoned Jack.

There was a short silence.

'Of course, this does beg another question,' continued Jack philosophically.

Robin's head shot up.

Jack's eyebrow rose. 'Was Jasmine jealous?'

–

Meanwhile Jasmine was back in her studio trying to concentrate. She was at least comforted on seeing Ellie soon pass by the window again. The girl even had the cheek to give her a cheery wave! She'd plainly been aware of her all along and Jasmine assumed she'd probably sussed her out last night too, however engrossed in her phone she had pretended to be. Mindful of the way Samphire Bay operated, Jasmine knew full well how tongues wagged, particularly in the grocery shop with a very nosey shop-keeper. Jasmine pictured Trish telling all to Ellie with relish.

Giving up on work, she decided to seek out that tea shop for Bunty. Quite a few came up on the search, but one stood out from the rest. Of course, The Castle Café.

Why hadn't she thought of that? It was ideal, having lots of space inside and a pleasant courtyard in the Lancaster Castle grounds. There'd be lots going on around them, as there were craft shops in the grounds too, so no awkward silences. Not that she envisaged Bunty and Perry being at a loss for conversation, after all they had a lot to catch up on. She reached for her mobile and rang Bunty.

'Bunty, it's me. I've got the perfect venue. The Castle Café,' Jasmine told her.

'Oh yes, that sounds delightful. I'm sure Perry will know it.'

'Even if he doesn't, it'll be easy to find,' replied Jasmine.

'Yes. Oh, I forgot to ask earlier, where were you last night BTW?'

Jasmine smiled at her use of abbreviation and paused before answering.

'I… didn't feel too well,' she lied. It was a visceral reaction she instantly regretted, hating being dishonest with her friend.

'Oh, darling, why didn't you say?'

'I'm fine now, just tired I think,' she tried to ease Bunty's concern, feeling guilty for not being honest and causing the woman undue upset.

'I see,' replied Bunty in a knowing voice.

'Did you all have a good time?' Jasmine tentatively asked.

'Until an unwelcome visitor showed up.' Bunty's tone still held a touch of perceptiveness. Had the wise old dear seen through her?

Jasmine decided to wrap up the conversation. 'Right… well, better get on.'

'Bye, Jasmine, and thanks for suggesting a place to meet Perry. I'll let him know.'

'Bye, Bunty.'

Jasmine gave a heavy sigh, not entirely certain as to why she felt so wound up.

Chapter 25

Perry grinned to himself. So, the date was on, all set and raring to go. He folded the letter and put it in the back pocket of his jeans, not wanting Emma to see it just yet. He preferred to tell her in his own time and had a few days to get his head round the fact he was reuniting with Bunty. As always, when needing space to clear his mind and ponder, Perry decided to retreat to his narrowboat.

The Merry Perry was a real sanctuary for him, a place where time and rhythm calmly slowed down to a restful pace. Somewhere he could just *be*. He looked at his pocket watch and placed it back inside his waistcoat. It was only one o'clock, plenty of time to get there and back and make dinner for him and Emma.

He set off to the marina which conveniently wasn't too far away. Perry walked with a spring in his step. Physically, he was in good shape. Having lived for years on a narrowboat meant he had to be fit and flexible as living afloat required hard physical work. When he moved into Fisher's Cottage, Perry had still maintained a fit and healthy lifestyle. His regular sailing trips kept him agile and he was hardy to the elements. The nomadic existence wasn't for the faint-hearted and Perry didn't mind the cold, wind and rain. He wasn't particularly materialistic either. Storage space was limited on a narrowboat, with room for only the essentials. On the whole, a cruising life had suited Perry, apart from one thing: it was easy to feel lonely on the waterways. Although he did have fellow sailor friends, forming a special, intimate relationship had been difficult for Perry, until, that is, Valerie had come along.

He soon reached the marina and enjoyed the stroll along the canal path. It was pleasant and soothing seeing all the colourful boats lined up. Every now and then someone would call out and wave up at him. Perry loved the connection he felt with other boaters.

Arriving at *The Merry Perry*, he opened her up and stepped into the saloon at the front of the boat, the bedroom being at the rear. A small galley kitchenette separated the two, where Perry filled the kettle with water and lit the tiny gas hob. Whilst waiting for it to boil, he also got the wood burner going and it wasn't long before the boat was snug and warm. Sitting down with his hot chocolate, he took out Bunty's letter again.

> *Dear Perry,*
>   *Thanks for the lovely reply!*
>   *I'm told The Castle Café in Lancaster is a great place to meet up. How about next Saturday at two p.m.?*
>   *I'm also told, by a young friend of mine, that we ought to exchange mobile numbers. So I've written mine at the bottom. Just text me if you need to rearrange.*
>   *See you soon,*
>   *Bunty*

She had included her mobile number which Perry added to his contact list on his phone. It was odd, seeing the name Bunty on his screen. Holding his phone to text and confirm Saturday was good for him too, he agonised over what to type before sighing aloud. This was when he needed Emma's input. He decided to wait until that evening before replying, when he could be guided by his stepdaughter, chuckling at what he imagined her reaction would be, knowing she'd be chuffed for him. This led to him wondering how Emma and Bunty would rub along, assuming they'd meet at some point. They were both lively characters, very alike in many ways. That is, if Bunty hadn't changed. He noted she had mentioned 'a young friend', perhaps she too was being guided by the younger generation.

He stared out of the window, watching the wildlife around him. Dragonflies hovered, elegant blue kingfishers hunted for fish, butterflies flapped prettily on the canal surface whilst bright, multicoloured boats trundled past. An idyllic setting. What would Bunty make of it? Could she fit into his lifestyle? Or did she belong to his past? Would she find him and his life a little too basic? She did still live in that bloody big house with all its extravagant trappings. Perry had grown to resent what the spectacular art deco building represented – a symbol of his inadequacy. He pictured Hamish Deville towering above him on the sweeping stairs, that arrogant sneer on his face. How he hated that man. Even when Hamish had got his own way and he'd disappeared from Samphire Bay, he'd learnt the old bastard had bought the fishermen's cottages, ensuring he wouldn't be able to return and rent his old house. Hamish had had it all covered. There was no easy way Perry was ever going to be his son-in-law. And what of poor Bunty? It seemed nobody had been good enough for her, or, as Perry deduced, it was more pure selfishness on Hamish's behalf. Since becoming a widower, the egotistic old man just wanted Bunty at his own beck and call, regardless of her happiness.

–

Later in the evening, after Emma had heartily eaten Perry's signature dish, Lancashire hotpot, she sat back in contentment.

'Thanks, Dad, that was delicious as usual.'

Perry seized his moment.

'Emma, I've had another letter from Bunty,' he began.

Emma quickly looked up at him with a smile. 'And?'

'We're meeting next Saturday,' he stated.

'Yes!' She punched the air, before going to give him a hug. 'I'm so pleased, Dad. This is just what you need.'

'I hope so…' Perry said cautiously.

'What could go wrong?' asked Emma.

'We might not, well… get on,' he shrugged. 'It's been a long, long time since we've seen each other. What if we've both changed?'

'What if you haven't?' replied Emma, tilting her head to one side. 'Just wait and see. You've nothing to lose, have you?'

'No,' said Perry, seeing the logic in Emma's words. He then showed her Bunty's letter.

Emma quickly read it.

'Oh, you've got her number then?'

'Yep.' Perry winked, making them both giggle. He pulled out his mobile. 'So, what should I text her then?'

'Right, let's keep it simple, how about, "next Saturday at The Castle Café is good for me. Looking forward to it"? Oh, and finish with a kiss.'

'Really?' Perry furrowed his brow.

'Yes! In fact, give her two, go on, xx,' Emma said with conviction.

Perry dutifully did as he was told and pressed Send. There, he'd done it. The die was cast.

Chapter 26

Robin surveyed the work he'd done on the floorboards. Not bad, he thought, rubbing his hand along the smooth sanded wood. Now all he had to do was stain and varnish them and the bedroom floors would look newly polished. Then that was it. Job done. The cottage would be fully renovated and ready to go on the market. It wouldn't take long to sell, he knew that for a fact. Not only was property on Samphire Bay popular and in demand, this particular location on the coastal path was an absolute dream, plus the house had been restored to a very high spec.

When taking all these factors into consideration, Robin couldn't help but consider buying the property himself. He had already decided long since that Samphire Bay was where he wanted to stay. But was he being practical? It was a three-bedroom property with a large renovated loft space, a huge kitchen diner and reception room. Could he really justify living in such a spacious house? Especially when his flat was more than adequate. Then again, an opportunity to buy a cottage like this, in such a good spot, may never present itself again.

He smirked to himself knowing what Jack would say. He'd accuse him of letting his heart rule his head, again. Jack would remind him of what he'd lost in the past after buying the barn they'd worked on. And, Robin conceded, he would have a point. Was the real reason he considered purchasing the cottage because of the next-door neighbour? Deep down, was it more about living close to Jasmine?

Robin kept replaying Ellie's scornful words about Jasmine. Had she really been outside The Smugglers? He hated to think of her alone and not joining them.

Not wanting to put it off any longer, he made the decision to go next door and see her.

As he walked down his garden path, he looked over the hedge and saw she was working in the studio. He made his way through her gate and knocked gently on the window. She looked up startled, obviously deep in concentration.

'Come in!' she called.

Robin entered with a smile.

'Am I disturbing you?' He tipped his head towards her desk which was covered in sketches.

'Not really. I was due a break,' she replied, stretching out her arms.

He admired the toned contour of them. Her morning swims clearly kept her in shape.

'I saw your visitor the other day.' Jasmine looked directly at Robin, taking him slightly by surprise.

'Yes, Ellie.' He sighed. 'She turned up unexpectedly at The Smugglers, then again-'

'She was here, snooping about when I returned from Bunty's,' cut in Jasmine.

'What?' Robin's eyes widened in surprise.

'I saw her outside on the path, staring into your cottage, then she actually went into my garden to get a better view,' she said, still staring at him.

Robin's mouth opened, then shut in amazement. He couldn't believe the cheek of Ellie, to have openly trespassed on Jasmine's property.

'She flew off when I challenged her,' she continued.

'Jasmine, I'm sorry.' Robin felt he owed her an apology, feeling responsible in some way.

'It's not your fault.' She shrugged, not quite comprehending why she was annoyed with Robin. Then to her astonishment, heard herself say, 'But I think you've got lousy taste in women.' Had she really just said that? She blinked.

Robin just stared at her, bewildered.

'P–pardon?'

Oh my God, Jasmine cursed herself, she'd just blown her cover. Now she would have to admit to seeing him kiss Ellie.

She cleared her throat. 'I saw you kissing her…'

'You didn't,' he quickly replied.

'Yes, Robin, I did.' Jasmine moved to sit on the edge of the desk and folded her arms defiantly.

Robin stalled, still a touch perplexed. Was she accusing him? Did she expect an explanation? He exhaled.

'No, what you saw was my devious ex-girlfriend force herself upon me, when I was totally inebriated,' he replied matter of factly, suddenly feeling like a schoolboy in front of the headmistress. Then he frowned. 'You must have been in the pub then?'

Now it was Jasmine's turn to feel uncomfortable. She looked away, refusing him eye contact.

'Jasmine?' he gently probed.

'Yes, I was. Then when I saw how… busy you were, I left.'

Silence fell as each absorbed the information.

'You shouldn't have left,' Robin spoke first. 'Believe me, I would much rather have seen you there than Ellie,' he added, hoping she would at least look at him.

Jasmine's mind was in a whirl, trying hard to digest Robin's account, as well as process her own emotions. Her heart was thumping and instinctively she reached for the heart pendant round her neck, which then triggered even more commotion within. Her eyes began to fill.

'Sorry, Robin… I… You don't have to justify yourself to me,' she choked.

'Hey, listen, I don't want *anyone* to think I still have feelings for Ellie,' he half laughed, trying to diffuse the tension. 'Just putting it out there, she's history.'

Jasmine gave a shaky smile, not trusting herself to speak and feeling a tad foolish now.

'And for your information,' Robin continued in the most jovial tone he could muster, 'my taste in women has somewhat improved.' With that, he looked intensely into those beautiful brown eyes of hers. She gazed back. The charge between them was palpable.

'Jasmine…' he croaked.

The sound of his mobile's ringtone ruined the moment. She wished it would stop, but the ringing persisted.

'You better answer that,' Jasmine said with a grin.

Reluctantly Robin grabbed his phone. Whoever it was, this had better be good.

'Darling, I'm in a bit of a pickle!' exclaimed an alarmed Bunty.

'Why, what's the matter?' asked Robin, then mouthed who it was to Jasmine.

'It's the boiler. It's rattled and creaked for years, now it looks like it's finally given up the ghost.'

Robin wasn't surprised. He and Jack had looked at it in the past and managed to patch it up but, being so old, it wasn't going to last forever. He winced at what a new boiler would cost her for a place that size.

'OK, Bunty, I'm on my way.'

'Oh thank you, Robin!' she gushed.

Jasmine had overheard the conversation on the phone.

'Off to the rescue?' she asked.

'Yep,' he replied, rolling his eyes in good humour. Of all the times for Bunty to call, just when he'd been about to spill all to Jasmine.

'A real knight in shining armour, aren't you?' she teased, then frowned at seeing Robin's face fall.

Those were the very words Ellie had uttered, and some part of him worried that perhaps there was some truth in her snide comments – did Jasmine only care for him as a 'knight in shining armour'?

'Robin?'

He shook his head.

'Sorry, I'd better go.' He paused. There was so much he wanted – needed – to say, but now was not the time. 'Jasmine, can we talk? I mean *really* talk?'

She nodded. 'Yes, definitely.'

'Good. How about dinner tomorrow?'

'Yes,' she repeated, then gulped. They both knew what was going on. They had reached an impasse, and it was time to address how they really felt about each other. 'It's my turn to cook,' said Jasmine.

'No, I've an idea,' Robin replied, suddenly feeling inspired. 'Leave everything to me. I'll be here about six.'

'OK...'

'And don't dress up, keep it casual,' he smiled.

'Why? What have you got planned?' she asked.

'You'll see. Bye!' he called over his shoulder.

Jasmine watched Robin go. Rushing off to the rescue again, she thought. What a truly wonderful man he was. It reminded her of how fortunate she'd been in having such a next-door neighbour. How much easier Robin had made the whole renovating process for her. Yes, she had indeed been lucky.

She looked out of the studio window onto the bay and longed to go for a swim, to help ease the tension that had steadily built momentum since… well, since seeing Robin and Ellie kiss, or, according to him, Ellie forcing herself upon him. Did she believe him?

Yes, Jasmine conceded, she did. Why would he lie? Robin had made it pretty clear he no longer felt anything towards his ex-girlfriend apart from resentment, as Jack's comments had verified. But where did all this leave her?

Jasmine sighed and looked out to sea, as if the clear blue water held all the answers. It did help alleviate some of the troubles on her mind and had a calming effect on her. So much so, she eventually managed to untangle all the mixed-up emotions bubbling up inside her. Like it or not, she was attracted to Robin. And all this pent up stirring inside was in fact jealousy. She had to be honest with herself and accept that she'd developed real feelings for him. She hadn't moved to Samphire Bay intending to meet someone, but she had – the boy next door. She shook her head and laughed, of all the cliches!

A trace of guilt edged across her conscience. Jasmine honestly believed she would never find anyone, ever, to match Tom. And, in a way, that was still true. Robin didn't *match* Tom; he was an individual in his own right. He was *Robin*, every bit as decent a man. Paradoxically she knew Tom and Robin would have been mates had they met.

Jasmine looked down towards her hand, conscious of holding the charm around her neck. She slowly unclasped her fingers from the gold heart. It was time to let go and follow her gut instincts again.

–

Robin heard the old boiler rumble and sing like a kettle and immediately presumed it was to do with the heat exchange. He had been proved right when examining the deposit build up, clogging the flow of water. He'd cleared the pipes and bled the system to get the radiators working at full capacity again, but he didn't hold out much hope for it long term. When saying as much to Bunty, she groaned.

'I thought so. It's as old as the hills,' she said.

'I think it may even be the original. To be honest, it's done well to last as long as it has,' Robin told her.

'Yes I know, but all good things come to an end, eh Robin?' Bunty sounded rather melancholy.

Robin, misunderstanding her, replied, 'Don't worry about the cost Bunty, me and Jack will fit it for free.'

This earnt him a harsh look.

'Indeed you will not, Robin Spencer. You'll get paid just like any other job.'

'Oh, I thought you were concerned about the expense—'

'No, no.' She waved her hand dismissing his remark. 'It's just… another thing that's made my mind up, the maintenance of this place.'

'What do you mean?'

'I'm selling up,' she stated with conviction.

'What, this place?' asked Robin, stunned.

'Yes. I'm going to put it on the market,' she replied with a decisive nod.

'Are you sure?' Robin still couldn't quite believe it. He pictured Bunty staying in this house until her very last day on earth.

'Yes. It's huge, costly and secluded. And I'm not getting any younger, Robin.' She gave him a wary look. 'One day I'll conk out, just like that old boiler.'

'But… where will you live?'

'In Samphire Bay of course.'

Robin frowned. 'But where?'

At this Bunty threw her head back and chuckled.

'Why, in your cottage of course,' she answered with a wry grin.

It took a moment for her words to sink in. So, Bunty wanted to buy back her renovated cottage. Oh, the irony thought Robin. Folding his arms, his mouth twitched.

'And what if I don't want to sell it to you, Bunty?' It amused him to see her reaction; finally Bunty was the one on the back foot for a change.

'Don't play silly buggers with me, Robin,' her voice was playful but tinged with a slight edge.

'I'm not,' he said innocently.

'Yes you are, darling,' said Bunty. He was enjoying this, the swine. 'I'll pay the asking price,' she continued.

Robin forced a laugh. Now where had he heard that before? Not that it had done him any good. He raised an eyebrow.

'Oh stop,' scolded Bunty. 'Who else would you sell it to anyway? Why not me?'

'I was thinking of living there myself actually,' Robin replied. Then couldn't resist adding, 'That was your intention, wasn't it, Bunty? To get me and Jasmine next to each other?'

'To meet yes, but now you're...' She looked at him quizzically. 'What are you exactly, still just good friends, or have things moved on yet?' She remembered the telephone call between her and Jasmine and suspected there was a shifting in the sand, judging by what she'd said. Something told Bunty that Jasmine wasn't her usual self and had wondered if that trollop Ellie had anything to do with it.

At this, all humour had evaporated for Robin, his face suddenly turning serious.

'Let's just say I'm on the case.'

'Meaning?' Bunty obviously required him to elaborate.

'We're going to talk tomorrow.'

'What, have a heart-to-heart you mean?' Bunty's face lit up with eagerness at this.

'Yes,' Robin said quietly. Wanting to distract her, he quickly changed the subject. 'So, are you serious about putting this place on the market?'

The diversion worked.

'The time has come, Robin,' came the sad reply. It touched Robin. 'It could take a while to sell though, darling, houses like this will only attract a certain amount of people, especially it being on a peninsula.'

'Well, they'll need deep pockets,' said Robin, knowing how much the huge house needed spending on it. 'It would make a fantastic hotel. Its location could prove to be a real selling point, a place to get away from it all.'

Bunty's head turned sharply.

'Yes, of course. What a brilliant idea.' She stared into the distance, considering his idea. 'That's certainly something for the estate agents to bear in mind when advertising it.'

It was odd to think of a Deville no longer living in the big white house, standing proudly on the peninsula. This place had been her home since childhood and in the family for generations. A place which held many memories, some good, some bad. Flashes of her mother's notorious parties came into focus, Bunty watching the glamorous guests through the spindles of the banister as she sat on the stairs. Seeing their chic clothes, how they air kissed and sipped from cocktail glasses, dancing so joyfully, it was all magical to a child. She pictured her father, busy painting in the studio, shafts of sunlight illuminating the room; the library full of countless books to escape into; she recalled helping out in the kitchen, standing on a small stool and washing the copper pans in a butler sink. Then she remembered Perry and how small and insignificant he was made to feel, stood at the bottom of the sweeping stairs, while Daddy looked down on him. She remembered crying in anguish, face buried in a pillow at the loss of her one true love. The four walls of her bedroom had certainly witnessed some tears. Yes, it was indeed the end of an era. But, as she had told Robin earlier, all things, good or bad, come to an end.

Chapter 27

Robin was packing his rucksack with sausages, burgers, bread buns and a ready-made salad, plus a few cans of lager that had been chilled. He picked up his trusty portable folding grill and set off for Jasmine's.

His plan was to have a romantic barbeque on the beach. He'd timed it just right for six p.m., as the sun would be setting about two hours later, which by then he hoped, they'd be suitably relaxed to enjoy a magnificent sky.

As Robin drove to Jasmine's, his thoughts turned to the barbeques he'd had as a teenager on Samphire Bay. They'd been riotous at times. He laughed to himself at some of the antics he and his mates had got up to, usually ending in them stripping off their clothes to skinny dip. A far cry from his intentions tonight. His mood went from jaunty recollection to serious deliberation. There was a lot hinging on this evening. Jasmine had come to mean so much to him.

Robin wanted clarity; he felt he'd made his position clear, saying his taste in women had improved when staring straight into her eyes. Did he need to be any more obvious? He had to know exactly where he stood. It was cards on the table time. His expectations were high, why else would Jasmine appear unsettled over Ellie? He dearly hoped Jack was right about Jasmine being jealous, that was some form of indication, surely? He remembered Jack's words, 'Give it time Rob, you'll know when to make a move.' Well, the time had come, decided Robin with determination, gripping the steering wheel.

–

Jasmine was in a quandary over what to wear. Casual had been what Robin told her. Hmm, where were they going? she pondered. At least she'd been occupied with her attire, which kept her mind off The Talk. Not that Jasmine didn't want to talk, but she was, if being truthful, a little daunted by the future. She'd had her life previously mapped out – a lifetime with Tom – but that had changed.

Now, her life was all about learning to readjust, to—

Go with the flow, Jas! There it was again! Tom's voice. She stopped, startled.

'Tom?' she said out loud. But there was no answer, just an empty silence. How she had wanted, been desperate, to hear his voice again, ever since the first time when viewing the cottage. Maybe she'd only hear it at pivotal moments? Was her life going to take another turn after tonight? Funnily enough the daunting sensation slowly eased away, letting her breath come more easily. Jasmine reached for the white cheesecloth blouse hanging in her wardrobe and denim cut offs. She tousled her hair so it hung carefree on her shoulders. There was no need for make-up, just a touch of rose-pink lipstick did the trick. There, couldn't get more casual than that.

There was a knock at the back door, which had Jasmine scarpering down the stairs. Opening it and seeing Robin holding a rucksack and folding barbeque told her everything about what to expect that evening.

She beamed. 'Hello, you.'

'Hi, thought we'd have a barbeque on the beach,' said Robin.

'Great!' she exclaimed, loving the idea. 'Should I bring anything?'

'Nope, got it all sorted,' he replied with a proud grin.

'What about a bottle of wine?'

'Even got the booze, come on, let's go.' He tipped his head towards the bay.

They chatted, walking along the coastal path, enjoying the gentle breeze in the air. The temperature had dropped slightly and the evening light was gradually fading as autumn loomed, but the sunsets were still amazing.

They reached the dunes and Robin unpacked his rucksack, firstly laying out a large picnic rug. He then unfolded the barbeque and set it up with the charcoal. Jasmine was impressed.

'You look like you've done this before,' she smiled, observing his speed and efficiency.

'Many times,' he laughed, digging in his bag for the cans of lager and passing one to her. They both opened them and clinked the tins together.

'Cheers, and thanks for doing all this, Robin.' She threw her head back and took a gulp of lager. It tasted cool and refreshing.

All the time Robin stared, unable to take his eyes off her. She looked beautiful and in such a natural way. He loved her effortless style, so carefree, and once again, he compared her to the stark contrast of Ellie, who had hated the sand messing up her clothes and hair. More and more he was perplexed at how he had ever come to be in a relationship with the likes of her. Jack had been right about his ex all along. He only hoped Jack was also right about Jasmine. He took a long drink and savoured the refreshing taste.

'I really appreciate all the help you've given me over the past few months,' said Jasmine, leaning back on her arm.

'Renovating's what I do,' he replied. 'It's no big deal.'

'But it was a huge deal to me,' Jasmine insisted as he came to sit down next to her. 'You dropped everything to work on my house.'

Robin looked out to sea.

'And all your support when Tom's killers were caught, you've been a rock,' she went on.

He paused before replying. 'You must know why.' His voice was husky. He turned facing her, and their eyes locked. 'I've fallen for you, Jasmine. Hook, line and sinker.' He'd said it. He'd finally come out and declared his feelings. Jasmine's eyes filled and, drawing nearer to him, her lips softly touched his. His heart almost burst. Instinctively his hands went to reach the sides of her face, pulling her closer. The kiss became more urgent, seeking and exploring each other. Robin wrapped his arms round Jasmine, wanting to feel her warm body. Jasmine entwined herself into him, loving the strength and comfort it gave her. She relished the power and safety of being held by Robin. An immense wave of assurance swept over her. They were interrupted by piercing squawks from nearby seagulls.

Slowly pulling apart, Robin grinned.

'They can smell the food,' he laughed, moving to the barbeque to add the meat, now the coals had heated up.

'It is making me hungry,' replied Jasmine as she watched him place the sausages and burgers on the grill.

She helped by getting the plastic plates and putting out the salad and bread buns.

Once the cooking had finished, they sat eating contentedly.

'This is fantastic,' gushed Jasmine, tucking into her burger.

'Food always tastes better when it's cooked outside.'

After thoroughly enjoying their meal, it was followed with a few more cans of lager. They talked about their families. Robin was keen to introduce Jasmine to his parents, which to his relief didn't faze her.

'You're already a hit with my mum,' she remarked dryly.

'Really?' He chuckled but was pleased to hear it.

'Oh yes, she fairly sings your praises, and Sam too for that matter.'

'Well, that's good to know.' He bent down and kissed her cheek.

As if on cue, when they lay huddled together on the blanket in peaceful bliss, the radiant burnt-orange sun gradually started to dip beneath the shoreline, casting amber, pink and red flares across the cloudless sky. All was still and quiet, apart from the sound of the sea lapping against the sand. Robin leant over Jasmine, the last of the sun's rays reflected in those gorgeous brown eyes of hers. She smiled up at him and brushed his cheek with the side of her hand. They would remember this moment forever.

Chapter 28

'Well, how do I look?' asked Perry, standing in front of his daughter, arms outstretched for inspection. Emma examined the figure in front of her.

'Not bad, Dad. Not bad at all,' was the verdict. He really did cut quite an attractive chap, with his dark jeans, brown corduroy jacket, white shirt and red neckerchief. He also had a matching red pocket square. Very stylish, thought Emma. 'I'm sure Bunty will be impressed,' she assured him with a thumbs up.

'She better,' he snorted, 'I've used my best aftershave.' He winked making her laugh.

'Don't worry, Dad, Bunty will be delighted with your efforts.' Then she tilted her head to one side. 'Do you think she'll recognise you?'

'Will *I* recognise her?' came Perry's reply.

'Surely there won't be any other lovesick oldies ready to reunite?' teased Emma, which earned her a threatening look.

'Hey, less of the "oldies" thank you,' warned Perry playfully. Despite his joviality, he was just a touch nervous. He wondered how Bunty was feeling. 'Right, I'm off.' He'd spruced himself up as much as he could, now it was time to go.

'Do you want a lift?' asked Emma.

'No, it won't take me too long to walk there and I'll enjoy the exercise,' Perry said. Besides, he didn't want Emma hanging around, trying to catch a peek of Bunty.

'OK, good luck!' she called as he set off.

He gave her a salute and grinned.

–

Bunty was at fever-pitch. It was times like this that she wished she had someone nearby to confide in. Hoping she'd chosen the right outfit, she quickly downed a stiff gin and tonic to calm her nerves. Then she saw Jasmine's Mini pull up outside on the gravel driveway through the bow window. Opening the front door and seeing Jasmine's face light up, told her she did indeed look the part.

'Bunty, you look marvellous!' cheered Jasmine.

'Are you sure, darling?' asked Bunty, tugging nervously at her amethyst stone necklace.

It was strange to see her acting so self-consciously, not at all like the usual, confident woman she undoubtedly was, thought Jasmine.

'Of course, come here, give me a hug.' Jasmine grabbed hold of Bunty and held her tightly. She found it rather endearing that, despite her age, Bunty was still on edge. She pulled back and appraised her once more. The navy trouser suit hit just the right note, smart yet casual, with a lilac short sleeved top underneath. The amethyst necklace finished the outfit off perfectly. And her hair! Jasmine had never seen Bunty's hair so tamed and glossy, freshly blow dried straight and smooth.

Bunty was pleased with the reaction she'd got, knowing it was genuine and well meant. It gave her that extra boost she'd so needed, along with Jasmine's hug.

'Right, ready to knock him dead then?' said Jasmine with a glint in her eye.

Bunty observed Jasmine's appearance too. Was she mistaken, or did she appear to be especially cheery and upbeat today? Not at all like the subdued girl on the phone from the other day. Perhaps the talk Robin had spoken about had done them both the world of good. She hoped so. It was about time her plan unfolded.

'Yes,' Bunty said. 'As ready as I'll ever be.'

Jasmine started up the car and together they set off for Lancaster.

–

Perry knew The Castle Café, having already been there several times. He opted for a table in the courtyard outside. Not only was it pleasant to be sat in the fresh air, but he had a good view of all the visitors coming into the cafe from where he was sat.

And there she was. He'd recognise her anywhere, the poised walk, the smart suit, her hair looked different though, expecting to see her wild curls. He waited for her to enter the cafe and then kept his eye on the bi-folding doors which led onto the courtyard.

Bunty soon appeared and after a quick scan of the tables saw him wave. She broke into a huge smile. He was here! Perry was right there, waving up at her. She made her way over, all the nerves replaced with excitement. Close up, she could see how the years had been kind to him. What a handsome brute he was.

'Bunty.' He rose up. 'How lovely to see you,' he said, kissing both her cheeks.

He smelt of sandalwood and his skin was smooth and fresh.

'Perry.' She was speechless, unable to say anything else.

'Here, sit down, what shall I get you?' he asked, suspecting she was a little overwhelmed.

'Oh, a cappuccino, thanks.'

She watched the back of him as he went to get the drinks. It was as if he'd never left… Her heart fluttered in delight. Feeling somewhat dazed, she told herself to get a grip. *Pull yourself together, Deville, for goodness' sake!* she scolded.

Perry stood in the queue shaking slightly. My God, she was as striking now as she'd ever been. It was extraordinary how the years had so easily rolled back. He ordered two coffees, when what he really wanted was a double brandy. Thank goodness he'd splashed on his new aftershave, he chuckled to himself.

Once back at the table and seated opposite Bunty, he couldn't resist asking a question which had puzzled him.

'I'm curious as to how you found me, Bunty?' His voice was more good-natured than accusing.

'A remarkable coincidence.' Bunty gave an ironic smile, then proceeded to tell him all about Jasmine and how she had lived on a narrowboat and bought a water pump from him.

'So, after a little research she managed to track you down. It was the name of your boat that gave you away,' she laughed.

'Ah yes, *The Merry Perry.*' He grinned. 'This Jasmine sounds quite a girl,' he added. 'Just like my Emma.' He went on to tell Bunty all about his late wife, Valerie, and how they'd met. His eyes clouded over when explaining how she had died of breast cancer, leaving him a single stepdad. 'I treat Emma as my own. I couldn't love a daughter more,' he finished gruffly.

'Oh Perry, I'm so sorry to hear of Valerie's passing.' Bunty was truly touched. She clearly hadn't been alone in her suffering.

'Right,' said Perry assertively, in an attempt to change the mood, 'so tell me what you've been up to all these years.'

'Well…' It was at this point that Bunty felt her most uncomfortable. Having to admit that nothing had changed much for her; she was still living in Samphire Bay, in the same house, but now alone. On saying as much to Perry, he suddenly looked sad, making her cringe even more.

'Oh Bunty, you were never meant to be alone.' He reached out and covered her hand with his. She looked up and met his gaze. Time stood still. 'I should have stood up to Daddy. I know that now.' She gulped.

'Yes, sweetheart, you should have.' He gently squeezed her hand. 'But we're here now, and you won't get rid of me that easily.' He shot her a wink and Bunty threw her head back and laughed.

'Perry Scholar, you old charmer,' she said, her eyes twinkling.

'You ain't seen nothing yet, doll,' he replied with a wide smile.

–

'So, how did it go?' asked an over-excited Emma later that evening.

'Fan-bloody-tastic,' said Perry, grinning from ear to ear.

'Will you be seeing her again?' she chirped.

'Oh yes,' he nodded.

'And when do *I* get to see her?' Emma persisted.

Perry laughed. 'Give us a chance! We've only just met up again.'

'Oh I'd *love* to visit her house in Samphire Bay!' Emma clapped her hands together in glee.

Perry smiled and ruffled her hair.

'All in good time Emma, all in good time.'

–

Bunty sat calmly in the drawing room sipping a gin and tonic. She placed the glass tumbler on the table and picked up the pack of tarot cards. It was only a distraction, a diversion, she told herself. They would not predict the future or tell her anything she didn't already know on a subconscious level. They were merely helping her to focus on a situation. After shuffling the cards, she pulled one out. The Lovers. A male and female stood in front of the Tree of Knowledge, the archangel Raphael behind them. A smile spread across Bunty's face.

Chapter 29

Jack braced himself as he walked into the empty shop, knowing Trish's sole attention would focus on him.

'Hi, Trish,' he called, darting straight down the first aisle, taking his time to select items. He willed the door's bell to ring and give Trish other customers to keep her busy. But alas, there was no footfall coming through and he reluctantly walked to the till.

'Have you heard about Robin?' she asked, not even attempting to check out his shopping.

'What about Robin?' he said resignedly.

'He was seen the other night, on the beach with Jasmine Boyd. All snuggled up on a rug apparently,' she whispered furtively.

A slow smile crept onto Jack's face. Good for him, about time, he thought, pleased for his mate. Then another thought occurred, which niggled at him.

He narrowed his eyes at the shopkeeper. 'How do you know this, Trish?'

'Can't say,' she answered primly.

This annoyed Jack more so. He was tired of Trish's tittle-tattling and supposed she was behind Ellie's knowledge of Jasmine. The woman was a menace. Ellie could really have screwed things up for Robin. He decided to tactfully address her careless talk.

'Did you speak to Ellie, Robin's ex-girlfriend?' Her blush told him she must have. 'Only she's been in Samphire Bay, causing all sorts of trouble. Apparently she knew all about Robin, that he was renovating a cottage and the help he'd given Jasmine.' He looked at her steadily, waiting for a response.

'Well, she might have come into the shop…'

'Asking questions?' Jack stared her in the face. Did the woman know no loyalty? *Everybody* in Samphire Bay knew how badly Robin had been treated by Ellie.

'Well… yes, as a matter of fact she was…'

'And you filled her in? Told her everything she wanted to know?' he asked incredulously.

Trish looked down, shamefaced.

Jack gave a hard sigh.

'Listen, Trish, a word of advice here,' he lowered his voice. 'You have got to learn to keep your—' he stopped and tried again, 'to keep quiet.' He mimed pulling a zip across his mouth.

Trish's eyes bulged. 'Pardon?' she sounded offended and chastised at the same time.

'You can't go blabbing all and sundry about people, Trish, it could have consequences. How would you like it, if everyone knew *your* every move?' Not that there'd be much to say, he thought. Perhaps that's why the woman was so fascinated with other people's lives.

'I… I…' spluttered Trish.

'Remember, keep schtum, OK?' Jack nodded towards his shopping. 'Now can I please pay for that?'

Trish served him with a crimson, tight-lipped face and Jack left with a sense of accomplishment. All the same, he did drive straight to the cottage to see Robin.

Robin was finishing varnishing the floorboards in the last bedroom. Once that was done, it was time to sell. A sadness filled him. Out of all the renovating projects he'd worked on, this cottage had been his favourite. And why was that? he asked himself with only a dash of sarcasm. Having a gorgeous, blonde-haired, brown-eyed beauty next door had most definitely played a part. He hummed cheerfully to the radio as his brush swept across the wood. Ironically, Van Morrison was singing 'Brown Eyed Girl'. He stopped at hearing footsteps on the stairs.

'In here, mate!' Robin called.

Jack appeared at the doorway. 'Hi, looking good,' he pointed to the shiny varnished floor.

'Yep, then that's it, all done,' Robin said, which prompted him to tell Jack about Bunty's offer of buying back the cottage.

'Straight up?' asked Jack in surprise.

'Yeah, she's putting her house on the market,' said Robin.

'Blimey, I never thought she'd leave that place.' Jack was still in shock. 'Not that I blame her, it's vast.'

'And costly. She's going to need a new boiler, plus the amount that needs spending on it.'

Jack narrowed his eyes. Robin knew instantly what he was thinking.

'No, mate, it's too big a project and we'd never raise the capital to buy it,' he counselled.

Jack nodded his head reluctantly, realising he was being far too ambitious.

'Still, it's a great buy for someone,' he conceded. 'Anyway, I believe you and the lovely Jasmine have finally got it together.' He quirked an eyebrow.

Robin laughed. 'We might have.'

'Come on then, spill,' Jack said eagerly.

Robin briefly outlined the barbeque on the beach, editing out the romantic kiss on the rug. The main thing was that the feelings he had were reciprocated by her. His chest filled with utter joy; he'd never know such bliss. It obviously showed on his face, as Jack came over and gave him a hug.

'I'm pleased for you, Rob. It's good to see you so happy.' Jack smiled and decided not to tell him about his conversation with Trish. Any mention of Ellie would only sour the mood.

'So, what do we do about the cottage? Sell it back to Bunty?' asked Robin.

Jack shrugged. 'Why not? Although I'm not sure for how much.'

'Especially after she knocked ten grand off the asking price,' Robin said, having had similar thoughts.

'We'll do the same, just take ten grand off the current value,' reasoned Jack.

There was a pause.

'How did you know?' Robin suddenly asked.

'What?'

'About me and Jasmine, how did you know?'

'Trish, but she wouldn't reveal who told her,' Jack said flatly. 'Apparently you were seen cosying up on a rug.' He shot Robin a sly grin.

Robin chuckled, too happy to care. So what?

-

Jasmine was working on the cover for a sweet romance, the brief asking for a cross between countryside and

236

vintage. She rather liked choosing colourful, floral bunting to swoop over the title and depicting a young couple sitting at a bistro table holding hands. Maybe it was her frame of mind that made her enjoy the project so much today.

She cast her mind back to the barbeque on the beach with Robin and couldn't help but feel warm and tingly inside. It seemed an age since she had felt anything that resembled passion. Yet passion was what she did feel for Robin, there could be no denying how her body had responded to his.

Jasmine had felt a cocktail of emotions these past few days, longer even. From attraction, jealously, confusion, guilt and now... serenity, happy in her own skin. Love must be in the air, she chuckled to herself, remembering the drive home from Lancaster with Bunty.

Jasmine had dropped Bunty off outside the castle and, after being assured that she'd be fine, had parked nearby and wandered round the shops. She'd picked up a brass table lamp from an antique shop and a pair of brass candlestick holders. Her living room still needed finishing and she thought they'd look good in there once it was decorated and ready for the final touches. She'd also bought, to her delight, a framed picture of Samphire Bay. It was a small watercolour print which captured the beauty of the landscape. She had thought of going on a tour of Lancaster Castle but didn't want to run the possibility of Bunty seeing her and think she was spying. Instead, she opted to go for a coffee on the high street and watch the world go by from a table by the window.

Sipping her latte, she took stock of her life and all that it had thrown at her. She'd accepted the tragic turn of events in her life and had come out the other side stronger than she ever could have expected. She'd got through it. She was now in a good place.

Jasmine reflected on the people she'd met. Robin and Bunty, two people she had grown so close to that it was impossible to think she hadn't even known them this time last year. She didn't want to go back to that harrowing, painful time. Her memories of Tom and their life together would always be precious, but it was time to move on and she felt resilient enough to do so now.

After finishing her coffee, she decided upon a touch of retail therapy and bought some new make-up and a silk nightshirt. On impulse, she called into a nail bar for a manicure. Why not? she thought, it had been ages since she'd pampered herself. The assistant behind the counter grimaced at the state of her nails, making Jasmine smirk. What did she expect when she'd subjected them to ripping out kitchen units, a bathroom, wallpaper stripping, painting and tiling?

'Oh dear, never mind, we'll soon have them in tip-top shape,' the technician promised, lining up a row of colourful nail varnish bottles. 'Now, which one should we go for?'

Jasmine wanted to be daring. 'The bright crimson please,' she said almost defiantly, never having had such a vivid shade before.

'Excellent choice!' exclaimed the beautician and set to work.

It was amazing how just a manicure could give you a boost, thought Jasmine as she pushed out of the glass doors with her newly polished nails.

All in all, Jasmine had had a very productive day and when she'd collected Bunty later in the afternoon, she knew her friend had also had a good time.

'How did it go?' Jasmine asked as soon as Bunty had got in the car.

'Splendid, darling, simply splendid,' gushed Bunty, to Jasmine's delight, then proceeded to give her a full lowdown.

After listening to Bunty's account, sparing no detail, Jasmine was full of hope.

'It all sounds so promising,' she remarked excitedly.

'It was like going back in time, Jasmine. Perry was, *is* still—'

'Full of charisma and utterly handsome?' cut in Jasmine with a giggle.

'Yes,' Bunty said, 'yes, he is.' And with that she sat back and sighed like a lovestruck teenager.

Jasmine grinned, finding the whole thing entertaining. It was good to see Bunty like this, upbeat and positive. She thrived in company. Once again, she considered how lonely Bunty must get, living alone in that great house on an isolated peninsula.

When they'd arrived at the house, she had accepted Bunty's invitation to go inside for a drink but, instead of going to the glass drinks cabinet in the drawing room, Bunty headed for the kitchen.

'I'll put the kettle on,' she said over her shoulder, surprising Jasmine as she followed.

For Jasmine, the kitchen was one of her preferred rooms in the house. Having cooked in there for the dinner party, she'd quite liked its quirky free-standing units, ancient Aga, white pot butler sink and stone floor. A sturdy shelf above the stove held pots and pans of all sizes and a glass cabinet displayed fine bone China. All it lacked was a frilly aproned cook, which she assumed it once had. Even the kettle was copper and had a whistle attached to its spout. It was all so quaint and reminiscent of the 1930s. She found it amusing that Perry wouldn't notice any change whatsoever if he were to revisit the place.

'I take it you'll be meeting Perry again soon?' she asked, whilst Bunty made the tea.

'Oh yes, we both want to see each other again,' replied Bunty. Putting the cups of tea on the kitchen table and sitting down next to Jasmine, she added, 'That's the beauty of being old, you're more upfront, say what you really feel.' She faced Jasmine and looked her in the eye. The statement was clearly loaded.

Jasmine couldn't help but believe there was a message intended for her.

'I hear what you say,' Jasmine spoke in a quiet voice, 'and I now know how I feel, about Robin that is,' she admitted, looking into the wise, old face of her friend.

'But does Robin?' Bunty questioned softly.

'Yes.' Jasmine gave a wobbly smile, not trusting herself to start blubbering.

'Come here, my darling.' Bunty's arms enveloped round her in a reassuring way. She smelt of Blue Grass perfume and compact powder.

'It's a weird feeling, you know, after Tom...' Jasmine mumbled into Bunty's shoulder.

'I know, darling, I know,' soothed Bunty, then pulled away to face her at arm's length. 'But would Tom really want you to live the rest of your life alone?'

Jasmine gulped. 'No, no he wouldn't.'

'Well then.' Bunty smiled kindly, making the sides of her eyes crinkle.

'You've been a good friend to me,' said Jasmine, still on the verge of tears.

'And you me,' replied Bunty somewhat teary herself. Then she inwardly pulled herself together. 'Nice nails BTW.' She winked, and Jasmine couldn't stop her laughter.

Chapter 30

Emma had teased Perry non-stop since his first date with Bunty. Refusing to rise to the bait, he had taken it all in good spirit. Unbeknown to his daughter, he had already arranged to see Bunty again, but this time it wasn't on neutral territory, very much the opposite in fact. He'd suggested a sail on his narrowboat, which she had gladly accepted.

'I'd love to see *The Merry Perry*!' Bunty had exclaimed in excitement. Her response had reminded him of Emma and how she was desperate to see inside Bunty's art deco house.

It was because Emma was so keen to meet Bunty that he had kept a low profile. Not that he didn't want to introduce his daughter to Bunty, but thought it better to wait a little longer, to see how things panned out; the last thing Perry wanted was for Emma to get attached to Bunty if it all ended belly up. She spoke with familiarity about her already and this was before even setting eyes on the woman.

As a result, he'd taken to snatched calls and messages on his mobile when the coast was clear. Like a teenager, hiding from parents, he was in the garden sat on a bench, having just texted Bunty.

'Hi, Dad!' Emma called from the back door, back from work.

He quickly got up to join her in the kitchen, slipping his mobile away in his back pocket.

'What's for tea?' she asked.

'I thought we'd go out,' Perry replied.

'Oh, right.' Emma sounded surprised. 'Any particular reason?'

'Just thought I'd treat you.' He smiled.

Truth be told, he felt guilty not updating her about Bunty. In an attempt to ease his conscience, he wanted to spend some quality time with his daughter.

Emma eyed him suspiciously.

'Go on, what's up?' she said.

'Nothing!' he replied, then his mobile rang. He ignored it. Emma folded her arms and lent on the kitchen worktop. She clearly wasn't going anywhere.

'Aren't you going to answer that?' she asked innocently, suspecting who it was.

'Er... Yeah...' Perry took out his phone and cleared his throat. 'Hi, Bunty,' he tried to sound casual, conscious of Emma's beady eyes on him. 'Yes, yes that'd be great, thanks.'

Bunty's voice was fairly loud and could be heard by Emma, who was taking a very keen interest. 'Yes... bye.' He gave his daughter a sheepish look. 'That was Bunty,' he explained unnecessarily.

'So I gathered,' Emma said.

'I'm er... taking her out on the boat,' he went on, feeling like a naughty schoolboy.

Emma burst into laughter.

'Oh, Dad, you look almost guilty.'

'Hey, I'm new to this, cut me some slack,' he reasoned, still feeling like this was role reversal.

'Well, you look like you're doing just fine to me,' she chuckled.

'I do want you to meet her Emma,' said Perry.

'But just not yet. I understand.' Emma held her hands out in surrender.

'I hope so.' Perry was at pains not to cause any offence.

'Stop worrying, Dad, honestly, I just want you to be happy.'

'Which is exactly what I want for you,' replied Perry with a firm nod.

'Good,' said Emma, then couldn't resist singing David Grey's, 'Sail Away'.

–

Bunty was no fool. She knew full well, judging by Perry's demeanour on the phone, that he hadn't been alone. He sounded a tad awkward, which could only mean he was uncomfortable with his daughter listening in. Whilst understanding the situation, she didn't want to cause any embarrassment for Perry. Perhaps it would be better if she met her? Curious to see Emma, having heard so much about her, she wanted to put a face to the name.

Bunty's thoughts turned to a more serious matter, something that had been on the backburner of her mind for some time – selling her house. It was no good procrastinating; she really did have to start the ball rolling.

Initially, Bunty was going to contact the same estate agents that oversaw the sale of the cottages. However, after giving it more consideration, she realised such an impressive property would need more than just a run-of-the mill agent. The marketing for the exclusive art deco house would require specialists. She went online to research estate agents with the calibre for selling premium properties. Eventually she settled for Grand & Country, an agency offering to make a 'valuable partner' whether buying or selling. It promised supreme efficiency in selling exquisite homes, delivering the three guiding principles to maximising a sale – presentation, exposure and service. Reading on, Bunty was assured her property would be 'portrayed in its absolute best light,' making her laugh out loud – good luck with the old boiler then, she thought with mirth. One thing did stand out, though, which offered some reassurance: when it came to buyers, they guaranteed any offers were valid and that 'potential purchasers were fully motivated and qualified'. In other words, they wouldn't entertain any possible cranks who just fancied a nosey round. Bunty knew there would be a lot of interest and didn't want to waste her time on people who had no intention, or the financial means, to buy. On a more sinister note, there were very valuable paintings and antiques in the house and she didn't want to showcase them to any old Tom, Dick or Harry. No, this did indeed require expert handling.

She scrolled through the website, impressed with the properties they had sold in the past, from penthouse flats in Westminster to country homes in Wiltshire. There was even an art deco house in Devon, set in a quiet, elevated position, a few minutes' walk from the sandy beaches and rockpools on the coastline. Good, thought Bunty, at least they had experience of marketing something similar to hers. She clocked the selling price too, which pleased her even more.

She recalled Robin's suggestion and was convinced her home would make a fantastic boutique hotel, especially with its character and unique features. The place was crying out for the love and attention it so deserved. Bunty rather liked the idea of it being a hotel. Was that because she'd be able to stop over if she wanted?

Confident Grand & Country were the right agents for her, Bunty completed the valuation appointment form, giving her details and a preferred date and time for them to visit. She gave herself a week, time to adjust, to get her head round the fact she was actually selling what had forever been her home. Pressing the Send button made it all too real.

–

Jack and Robin were giving the cottage a final inspection. Jack was downstairs, casting an eye over the newly fitted kitchen, the dining area with wood burner, the living room and its feature fireplace, the hallway and stairs. It was all looking good in his opinion, done to a very high spec.

Robin was upstairs, impressed with what he saw too. The bedrooms were all painted in neutral colours, which contrasted nicely with the darker wooden floorboards. He was particularly pleased with the renovated attic and its skylight. Altogether it made for a splendid family home and he couldn't help but think it was too big for Bunty living alone. Then he laughed to himself; compared to where she was now, it would seem like a shoebox. Still, if she was happy to buy back the cottage, so be it. At least it would give them the cash flow to start a new project.

When Robin had told Jasmine of Bunty's intention to buy the cottage, she was thrilled.

'It makes perfect sense to me,' she'd said. 'I've always been a bit concerned about Bunty being by herself, out there cut off by the tide.'

They'd been lunching in her garden studio, both having worked all morning. Jasmine liked knowing Robin was only next door, but knew it was all about to change, now that he and Jack had completed the restoration.

'You've grown rather fond of Bunty, haven't you?' smiled Robin.

'Yes, I have. She's a lovely lady. Despite the age gap between us, I find her full of life and such good company.'

'She's certainly a character,' he chuckled.

'Absolutely and so interesting,' agreed Jasmine. 'I'm so glad she and Perry are reunited.' A thought occurred to her, and she grinned.

'What?' Robin asked, noticing her lips twitch.

'Do you think she'll end up living with Perry?'

'Next door? I dunno.' Robin shrugged with a smirk. 'Who'd have thought, eh, you living next door to Bunty and her fancy fella?'

At this they both burst into giggles. It was a relief to Jasmine that Bunty was buying the cottage next door. She no longer felt unsettled by having a new neighbour. Her mind cast back to the first day she'd arrived at Samphire Bay, when she hadn't wanted anyone living near her, just the glittering sea. How things had since changed.

Robin saw the expression on her face and wondered what she was thinking. Then he decided to ask her something they had touched upon before.

'Jasmine, are you ready to meet my parents?'

They were dying to meet her, that was for sure. Absolutely delighted by the change in their son, they were more than keen to be introduced to the girl responsible for Robin's happiness. Jasmine looked up at him.

'Of course, when?' she replied, well aware of how desperate her parents were to see Robin. Knowing the interrogation he would endure from her mother, she was putting it off though.

'At the weekend?' suggested Robin.

He could see it now, Sunday lunch, the full works, all cooked by an eager mum. Maybe this would be a bit too soon? When saying as much to Jasmine, she surprised him.

'Hell no, I'd love a Sunday dinner!' She'd leapt at the chance. That was one of the things she really missed not being at her parents' house. Her mum's roasts were legendary.

'OK, I'll let them know then.' He paused. 'But be prepared, they'll be more than pleased to meet you,' he'd warned.

That had been two days ago now, and as they got closer to Sunday, he couldn't deny the nervous butterflies fluttering inside his stomach.

Jack came up the stairs to join Robin.

'Everything OK here?' he asked.

'Yeah, it's all good,' replied Robin with a nod.

'Right, let's give the old bird a viewing then,' Jack said with a grin.

Unlike Robin, who had contemplated buying the cottage himself, Jack was more than ready to get the house sold. Time was money, after all, and they were running a business.

'Now's a good time. She's got someone to value her house next week apparently.'

Jack turned, taking in the cottage. 'It'll be interesting to see who's going to end up there.' He still thought Bunty's house would have been an ideal business venture, if, that is, they could have stretched their finances that far. Out of the two, Jack was more ambitious than Robin, always hunting for the next project. As soon as it looked like they'd be in a position to start another renovation, he'd put the feelers out. As for Robin, well, he was far too busy with the girl next door, thought Jack with affection, chuffed for his mate. 'How's things with Jasmine?' he asked.

Robin's face lit up. 'Fine. She's meeting my parents at the weekend.'

Jack whistled. 'Must be love.'

There was a knock at the door, then a voice called, 'It's Jasmine!' from the bottom of the stairs.

'Up here!' Robin shouted back.

Jack watched as she came in the room and smiled at Robin, then him. Only the smile he got was less warm and still a touch uncertain.

'Hi, Jasmine,' he dipped his head.

'Hi, Jack,' she replied, then faced Robin again. 'Lunch later?'

'Lovely, thanks,' answered Robin, then in an effort to encourage conversation with Jack said, 'We were just discussing Bunty viewing the cottage, weren't we, Jack?'

'Yes, that's right.' Jack smiled again at Jasmine, wishing she'd learn to like him. Clearly, he had given her the wrong impression from day one.

'I'm sure she'll love it,' Jasmine said, seeming to ease slightly in his company. Despite what Jack thought, her opinion of him was on the ascent, ever since he'd told Ellie where to go. She knew that Jack had had Robin's best interests at heart. 'Have you agreed on a price?' she enquired, curious to know. Then she felt a little embarrassed. It wasn't really any of her business, was it?

'Not yet, but we'll honour the reduction she gave us,' Jack stated, further attempting to coax himself into her good books. It worked. He was rewarded with a huge beam.

'That's decent of you,' she said.

'I am decent,' he replied, making Robin laugh.

'Right, I'll arrange a viewing with Bunty, get things moving,' said Robin rubbing his hands together in anticipation.

Chapter 31

The moment Bunty hopped onboard *The Merry Perry* she was enthralled. Holding Perry's hand as her feet gently landed on the deck, she was captivated. She loved everything about the narrowboat. It's cute kitchenette, little wood burner, round windows and cosy living space. It was all so quaint, like another world waiting to whisk you away.

Sailing along the canal, Bunty relished the serenity of it all. Sat outside on the decking, she had time to appreciate all the surrounding wonderful nature and wildlife. Bunty gazed in awe at a kingfisher plunging down to catch food, the silver-backed fish, the frogs hopping in the bulrushes and the shadows on the still water. Birdsong could be heard in the nearby trees, as the sun shone through their green lush branches. It was a different way of life, for sure; one which she could easily become accustomed to. She felt good to be in a small space, comfy and secure. A far cry from rattling around in a huge house like a pea in a drum. A lot less hassle to maintain too, thought Bunty wryly.

'There you go.' Perry handed her a tin mug of steaming coffee, freshly brewed from the stove.

'Ah, lovely thanks.'

He sat next to her on the cushioned seating. 'So, you're selling up then?'

Bunty gave a sigh. 'Yes, it's time.'

Perry nodded sagely, knowing how hard it must be for her.

'The estate agent is coming in a few days.' There was a short silence, before Bunty looked sideways at him. 'Will you be there, when they come, as moral support?'

'Of course I will,' Perry replied without hesitation. He wanted to support her in any way possible, even if it meant revisiting the house where he had been made to feel so inferior. But that hadn't been caused as much by the place as its occupant at the time, when all was said and done, he rationalised.

'Thank you, I don't think I could manage it all on my own,' said Bunty in a small voice, which touched his heart.

'Well, you're not on your own,' he said. 'I'm here, at your service.' He winked, pleased to see it draw a smile from her.

'Where are we sailing to?' asked Bunty blowing on her cup.

'I thought we'd go to Carston.'

'Carston?' Immediately Bunty thought of Jasmine's late husband.

'The market town?' Perry frowned.

'It's where Jasmine lived, when she and her husband had a narrowboat.'

'Yes, I remember. Poor bloke. He was killed outside The Mariners, wasn't he?'

'Hmm, a hit-and-run,' Bunty said gravely.

'Terrible business. I believe they've caught his killer though, pretty recently.'

'They have, thank God.'

When they arrived at Carston, Perry slowed the boat and gently steered it to the side bank. The throb of the engine dulled and then stopped completely. Perry helped Bunty to climb up the steps out onto the canal path. There, they walked contentedly along arm in arm and Bunty realised it had literally been years since she'd had a trip out like this. Samphire Bay was an area of outstanding natural beauty, but it was good to have a change of scenery – and company. She stole a glance at Perry. My, he was good-looking. He wore a grey silk waistcoat over a paisley patterned shirt. Bunty looked down over her blue linen trousers and stripey blue and white top, hoping she looked the part. Drawing the line at wearing a sailor's cap, she'd wanted to create a nautical look.

'Shall we call for a drink?' Perry asked, pointing to a building with 'Bridge 64 Cafe Bar' written in the window.

'Sure, let's.'

Entering, Bunty scanned the place, taking in the old, wooden whiskey barrels used as tables and high stools. The cafe was airy, with a glass gable end flooding in the daylight, overlooking the marina. Perry ordered them a bottle of wine, which they shared whilst admiring the view outside.

Bunty relaxed, sipping cool white wine as any remaining tension in her evaporated. The estate agent's appointment was bothering her. Not really looking forward to a stranger intruding in her home, she was apprehensive of any possible criticism. Although it was her pride and joy, she had begun to see the house from a prospective buyer's eye. Fearing she would take any adverse critique personally, Bunty was mentally preparing a 'tough skin' – something Daddy often referred to. It helped knowing Perry would be about, and it also helped that Robin had arranged for her to view the cottage. At least there wouldn't be any issues there, wise to the excellent workmanship of Robin and Jack. She hadn't told Perry yet of her plans. How would he react, when he learned she was about to live in his old house?

'Penny for them?' Perry watched her, sensing there was something afoot.

'I'm buying back the cottage you once rented,' she said. He stopped mid-drink and looked at her. 'It seems the ideal solution. I know its renovation will be first class and it's a fantastic spot. Besides, where else is there? Property doesn't come on the market that often in Samphire Bay.'

'No, it doesn't,' Perry agreed. And her father made damn sure he never returned, buying the cottage he previously lived in. 'I'm sure you'll be very happy there.' He raised his glass.

After finishing the bottle, they made their way into the historic market town. It was charming with its artisan shops and restaurants. They passed The Mariners pub on the high street and Bunty shivered. Quickly moving on, they called at various charity shops and a deli store where Bunty bought two sandwiches for the journey back. That was the beauty of canal boating, you could sit, eat, drink and relax whilst still travelling. She could see the appeal it held for Perry and Jasmine.

Bunty never wanted the day to end, she'd never had so much fun. Perry made a fine companion. Considering they had so much history together, very little was said about the past, though Bunty couldn't help but detect an undercurrent concerning this. She could only assume it was resentment towards her father. As a young adult growing up, she too had seen Daddy in a different light. Perry's absence in her life had triggered that. On the rare occasion she had challenged his attitude towards Perry, he had dismissed her nonchalantly, stating that the likes of

Perry were not for his precious daughter, and did she really think he'd let his only child go to someone less worthy of her? He'd smothered her in superficial compliments in an attempt to distract her, in order to keep her to himself, she knew that now. Anger started to boil inside her. She had sacrificed far, far too much. She had acted as the dutiful daughter till the end, fetching and carrying for him like a lapdog. Today had spelt out, so starkly, just what she had missed out on. All those years she'd never get back. Well, that dominant figure in her life wasn't here now, was he? And she was going to make bloody sure nobody would ruin her second chance with Perry.

–

Despite Robin's prediction, the Sunday lunch with Jasmine and his parents was not what he had envisaged. Instead of a formal, sit-down affair with a full roast, his mum and dad were busy at the outdoor cooking station on the patio. Making the most of the last of summer, they'd decided to eat al fresco. Robin was secretly pleased, as it created a more casual atmosphere.

'Thought we'd eat out here, whilst we still can,' said Robin's mum, as she came to meet them. 'I'm Ann by the way, pleased to meet you.' She smiled warmly and offered her hand to Jasmine.

'Pleased to meet you too,' Jasmine replied, shaking her hand.

'And I'm John!' called Robin's dad, turning around waving a spatula. He was stood over the grill of the oven, wearing an apron with the words 'Head Chef' stitched across the chest.

'Hi,' Jasmine called back. She marvelled at the outside kitchen, all stainless steel and granite, with an oven, grills and barbeque hood. 'I love that,' she said, nodding her head towards the cooking station.

'I know, it's great,' trilled Ann. 'We've really made good use of it this summer, all thanks to our wonderful son.' She put her hands on Robin's shoulders.

'*Mum*,' Robin muttered in embarrassment.

Jasmine grinned. 'Oh, did Robin fit it?'

'He certainly did!' yelled John, patently keen to be included in the conversation despite his task at hand. 'And he made a brilliant job of it too.'

'*Dad*,' cringed Robin, making all three of them laugh.

'He made a brilliant job of my kitchen too!' Jasmine said, enjoying the banter.

All the repartee proved to be a good icebreaker. The afternoon had been pleasant and easy going, with everybody relaxed in the sunshine. It was blatantly obvious that Robin's parents were delighted with Jasmine, especially his mum.

'I can't tell you how relieved we are he's met you,' she whispered discreetly, whilst the men were sorting out the food. She and Jasmine sat relaxing with a glass of prosecco. Ann rolled her eyes. 'After all the trouble we had with Ellie…'

This was music to Jasmine's ears.

'Yes, Jack isn't a fan of hers either,' she said.

'Oh Jack's been an absolute trooper, always can rely on a chap like that. They've been best mates since we moved here,' Ann told her, furthering Jasmine's opinion of him.

Only much later on, after many more proseccos, when Ann threatened to get the baby album out, did Robin insist on leaving. Enough was enough, he thought, even though Jasmine had been clearly up for it.

'It's been lovely, but it's time to go now,' he said firmly, getting up.

His dad gave a low chuckle. 'I think you're right, son.' God knew what his wife might come out with next – baby album for goodness' sake! He looked fondly at her, chatting animatedly to Jasmine. It was a far cry from all the anxiety his son's ex-girlfriend had given them.

On the way back to her cottage, Jasmine turned to Robin.

'Your parents are so lovely,' she said, feeling just a tad tipsy. She sank back into the passenger's seat with a contented sigh.

Robin grinned, pleased with the way the afternoon had gone. Glancing at the sleepy girl beside him, he felt his parents' approval, and a wave of exhilaration swept over him.

–

Bunty was anything but calm. Butterflies were flapping inside her stomach from the moment she woke up. Today was the day the estate agents were calling. Perry, as promised, had arrived early on as moral support and upon seeing how panicky she was, he'd put a reassuring arm round her.

'Now come on, Bunty, it'll be all right,' he'd said in his low smooth voice.

'Oh Perry.' She looked up at him with wide eyes. 'Do you think I'm doing the right thing?'

'You know you are, sweetheart, it's just nerves, that's all.'

He was right, of course. As soon as the agent rang the doorbell, Bunty slipped into her role, playing the eccentric lady who owned the big white house on the peninsula.

'Come in, darling!' she welcomed, throwing the front entrance door open.

'Pleased to meet you, Ms Deville,' said a very smart looking man.

Expecting to see a younger person, like the previous estate agents, Bunty was quite surprised at the middle-aged, pin-striped suited fellow, with a centre parting and moustache. He had a clipboard clung to his chest.

'I'm Anthony Armstrong-James,' he announced in a pompous voice.

Bunty's eyes flicked sideways to Perry, who was pursing his lips.

'Pleased to meet you too and please, call me Bunty,' she gestured to Perry, 'and this is Perry.'

'How do,' nodded Perry and offered his calloused sailor hand.

Anthony looked aghast at it, before gingerly shaking it.

'My, what an impressive hall,' he stated as his head tilted back to assess the high ceiling, detailed cornices and huge chandelier. He also clocked the sweeping staircase and marbled tiled floor.

'I think you'll find it *all* impressive, Anthony,' countered Bunty, confidence fully in bloom now.

That's my girl, thought Perry, cheering inside.

'May I ask, how long have you lived here Ms Deville?'

'All my life. I was born here. My mother's family built it in the Thirties. They had such a passion for the art deco era,' she told him wistfully.

Anthony looked genuinely transfixed. He too, despite his straitlaced exterior, had a real interest in the Arts and Crafts movement, hence his allocation to this property. Although appearing po-faced, his zeal for selling such properties as this was second to none. He was a stickler and his attention to detail was remarkable. This was evident by the many questions he asked Bunty and the notes he made.

After a full tour of the house and grounds, Anthony Armstrong-James was more than satisfied.

'I shall commence with the marketing campaign, arrange a photographer to visit and draft an advertisement for the website tomorrow. Once you have perused and approved it, Grand & Country will press full steam ahead.' He smiled for the first time, with real gusto.

It confirmed Bunty's choice in estate agents. This Anthony seemed to know his stuff, she thought.

'Rest assured, Ms Deville, your home is in safe hands. Grand & Country will manage the sale of your house and ensure you get the best possible price it deserves.'

Good, thought Bunty, feeling thankful.

'When can we arrange an open day?' asked the agent.

Her head shot up sharply.

'A what?'

'An open day,' he replied calmly. 'A property such as this requires full exposure, an opportunity for prospective buyers to wander round and appreciate the grandeur.'

'But they'd get that when viewing it,' said a slightly confused Bunty.

Anthony gave a tinkle of laughter. 'No, no, no, we need to dress the house and *really* showcase it,' he said with fervour, eyes shining with enthusiasm.

'Dress the house?' questioned Perry, who was a little perplexed too.

'Yes, put in extra pieces, plants, accessories, garden furniture, et cetera. I'm thinking copper moulds for the kitchen, a grand piano for the hall, a gramophone for the drawing room—'

'I already *have* a gramophone,' Bunty cut in tersely, now beginning to feel irritated and a touch defensive.

'Excellent!' gushed Anthony and clapped his hands.

He really was on fire for the place, Bunty admitted to herself in defeat. An open day it was then.

Chapter 32

Waiting for Bunty's arrival, Jack and Robin exchanged grins – they were about to show her round the cottage and were keen to see her reaction. Although they knew the renovation was done to a high spec, they hoped the choice of decor met Bunty's high standards. Both Jack and Robin still found it hard to picture her living in the cottage, it being such a contrast to what she'd always been familiar with. This characterful, flintstone cottage was very pretty, but so small and humble compared to the huge art deco house. Not to mention having been born and raised in the home; inevitably she must have a very strong attachment to the place, and those kinds of emotional bonds were hard to break…

'I just hope Bunty knows what she's doing,' said Jack with unease.

'So do I,' replied Robin. 'I doubt her house will sit on the market too long.'

It seemed so strange to see the imposing house up for sale in glossy brochures and on the internet. He'd got to hand it to her estate agents though, they were absolutely pulling out all the stops. The idea of an open day was genius.

'Maybe that's something for us to think about in future,' Jack remarked, reading his mind.

'Why, what are you planning on restoring next?' asked Robin half laughing. He doubted they would ever be working on something of such calibre as Bunty's house.

'You never know Rob, think big,' Jack answered, ever mindful of expanding their business.

–

Jasmine had viewed the finished cottage the day before and was most impressed.

Bunty was going to love it; she knew for a fact. Then she wondered to herself if Perry might come along to the viewing. How would he feel having lived in there previously? He'd certainly see a difference. She remembered when she'd come to view both cottages for the first time, with their rotten window frames, peeling wallpaper, grotty kitchens, mouldy bathrooms and the pervasive smell of damp. The transformation was incredible and the value of the cottages must have soared, even when taking into consideration what had been spent on the renovation work.

This prompted Jasmine to think about the profound turn of events over such a short amount of time. Bunty hadn't known at the time of selling them that she would in fact be buying one back. And Jasmine hadn't known at the time of viewing how she would meet Robin and form such a good friendship with Bunty. It was funny how life had a habit of working out. Such remarks had been bandied about when losing Tom and she had dismissed them with scorn. She only prayed everything would work out for Bunty with Perry. Things were certainly looking promising so far, according to all the feedback she was getting.

Bunty had had her in stitches when impersonating the estate agent.

'I'm Anthony Armstrong-James,' she'd mimicked in a snooty voice, with her nose in the air.

Jasmine too, had thought the open day a fantastic idea.

'Can I come and pretend I'm interested?' she'd asked eagerly, wanting to share the experience and see the house in all its glory.

'Of course, darling, the more the merrier,' Bunty said, keen to get a full house.

–

As Bunty's Morris Minor pulled up outside the cottage, Robin and Jack went out to meet her. They were taken aback when they saw she wasn't alone.

'Hello, boys, this is Perry,' she said. 'Perry, meet Robin and Jack.'

All three shook hands before making their way inside.

Looking round the kitchen, Perry couldn't help but be astonished. He'd hardly recognised the place. The only thing that hadn't changed was the view from the window.

'Well, you've done a fabulous job, lads,' he said as his eyes took it all in.

'You approve then?' smiled Robin.

Perry nodded. 'I do, it looks so much bigger with the adjoining wall knocked through.'

'Doesn't it?' agreed Bunty.

'Wait till you see upstairs,' Jack chipped in, impatient to show it off.

With pride, Robin and Jack opened the bedroom doors to reveal freshly varnished floors and smooth white walls. They each had the original cast iron fireplaces restored.

'Can they be lit?' asked Bunty in delight.

'Yes, they're in working order,' Jack told her. 'And the chimneys have all been swept,' he went on, pleased at seeing her face light up.

'Very romantic,' muttered Robin, who couldn't resist the mischievous remark. This earned him a nudge from Jack, who was at pains to create the best impression. Luckily it had gone unnoticed by Bunty, but was that a sly smirk from Perry? The old fox!

Perry blinked in disbelief at the transformation of the attic.

'This is incredible,' he exclaimed in awe. His eyes scanned the corners, and Robin saw a frown flicker across his face.

'There were two trunks left behind,' he said, turning to Perry. 'I've kept one of them, if you'd like it back.'

'They had the photographs in it,' Bunty supplied.

Perry gave a knowing smile and shook his head.

'You keep the trunk, Robin,' he replied. 'It belongs to the past.' Facing Bunty, he continued, 'It's the future that matters.'

Once the viewing had completed, in true Bunty style she asked outright, 'So, boys, what are we looking at, price wise?' Her eyes swept from one to the other in expectation.

This was where Robin began to feel uncomfortable, but thankfully Jack took the initiative.

'We want you to get it valued Bunty.'

'Why?' she frowned.

'Because we'd feel better if an outsider gave their opinion.'

'Plus, we'd reduce it by the same amount you did for us,' Robin added.

'There's no need to do that, boys,' replied Bunty shaking her head.

'Yes there is,' Robin and Jack replied in unison.

Perry looked on with esteem, pleased that these lads were doing the decent thing by Bunty. Seeing that she was about to argue, he put an arm round her.

'One good turn deserves another, sweetheart,' he appeased in that soothing voice of his. Bunty turned a shade of pink, making Jack and Robin exchange a grin. Something told them they'd be seeing a lot more of Perry.

Chapter 33

The sun very kindly put in the first appearance on the open day, much to Bunty's joy, which was nothing compared to Anthony Armstrong-James'. He arrived in splendour, followed by a convoy of vans transporting all the 'extra pieces'. Bunty was on the balcony, getting a bird's-eye view. Her jaw dropped at seeing the whole entourage park up on the gravel driveway. Her face creased into a smile as Anthony shot out of his Aston Martin to give directions to the team awaiting instruction.

He was looking extremely dapper, wearing a striped boating blazer and cream trousers. The clipboard was out in good use, and his head bobbed up and down as he consulted his notes. He was pointing to the side garden and talking vivaciously to a group of men unloading a vintage rose bistro set. Anthony then scurried to another van where three young girls dressed in black and white maid uniforms carried various boxes. Good grief, thought Bunty, he's actually got staff to act the part! Putting her cup of coffee on the glass table, she rushed down to meet them all. Out of breath, she flung open the doors dramatically.

'Good morning!' she called out.

Anthony turned and practically ran to her. Gone was the pompous, priggish agent from the first visit, this was an invigorated, excited Anthony, totally in his element.

'What a splendid day for it!' he chirped, arms raised to the cloudless sky. Then a gruff voice shouted out.

'Where's this going, Anthony?'

Two men stood at a grand piano, waiting to hoist it on a wheeled platform.

'Careful now, this way.' Anthony's hands waved them forward. 'We need a ramp for these steps.' He pointed to the front entrance.

Bunty's eyes widened at the beautiful French polished piano and stood back to make way. It took time and effort to get it in place, but it looked the part perfectly standing in the hall.

Then in came the maids. Bunty noticed the copper moulds for the kitchen in the boxes and saw a set of antique balance scales. One box remained closed.

'What's in that one?' she asked the girl holding it.

'Old cookery books,' she grinned. 'Mrs Beeton, eat your heart out.'

Bunty laughed.

'My, my, he thinks of everything, doesn't he?' she said, tipping her head towards Anthony, who was by now overseeing a young man wheeling a variety of plants in a trolley. Huge ferns, aspidistras and parlour maples were being transported to the drawing room.

'I'll need the copper planters and the wooden plant stands,' he was telling the rather harassed looking boy.

'What about the stone urn?' he asked, wiping his forehead.

'Outside and I want it *overflowing* with that false ivy,' replied Anthony, his hands in a circling motion, emphasising the 'overflow'.

Bunty was mesmerised. It was like being on set for a period drama. Her eyes darted from one place to the next.

'This lot going in the cellar?' asked a sturdy man holding an enormous hamper of wine.

'I wouldn't advise it,' Bunty said, 'seeing how it's not been in use for years, apart from maybe by the odd mouse.'

On hearing this Anthony shuddered.

'No, don't open the cellar. Display it in the kitchen.' The last thing he needed was any rodent making an entrance and ruining his day.

Bunty read the labels on the bottles and gasped.

'They're empty,' Anthony whispered with a nudge. 'Purely props. I get them out for most of the open days.'

Bunty chuckled and shook her head. Then in came two ladies each carrying a Tiffany lamp.

'Upstairs, in the master bedroom,' ordered Anthony.

Bunty was slightly alarmed at having her bedroom invaded but she forced herself to take a step back from the proceedings.

'Do try to distance yourself, my dear,' Anthony gently told her. 'Think of this as a showcase for the day, not your home.'

He was right, of course. She wanted to sell the house, after all, and that required strangers coming into her space. At that precise moment, Perry appeared and just seeing him put her at ease.

'The place is a circus!' he laughed.

'Tell me about it,' Bunty said dryly.

'Where. Is. The. Pianist?' Anthony demanded gripping his phone to his ear, showing the whites of his knuckles. 'What?' he rasped in outrage. 'This is a *disaster*!' He hung up abruptly.

'Everything all right, Anthony?' Bunty asked as he closed his eyes in frustration.

'No. The pianist has had to cancel,' he replied in despair. 'The stupid oaf has fallen and fractured his wrist. *How* inconsiderate!'

'Oh, I didn't realise the piano was actually going to be used. I thought it was just for decoration,' said Bunty.

'Both,' said Anthony. 'The idea was to set the scene, by hearing the tickle of ivories as the guests entered.'

Perry disguised his bark of laughter with a cough. Where was Emma when he needed her? She could play the keyboard. Thinking it would be a good opportunity for her to meet Bunty and see the house she was so desperate to step inside, he cleared his throat again.

'Er... I might be able to help there,' he spoke up, causing Anthony and Bunty to stare at him. 'My daughter, Emma, can play.'

'Can she really?' smiled Bunty.

'Well, yes, but probably not to the standard of a hired professional,' he warned.

'Hmph, not very *professional* cancelling at the eleventh hour,' said Anthony tartly. 'I suppose she'll do,' he continued rather ungraciously, 'any port in a storm.'

Bunty and Perry exchanged looks.

'Should I ask her?' Perry's eyebrow raised. 'I know she'd love to see the place.'

'Of course, she should have come with you in any event,' insisted Bunty.

'Thank the Lord, crisis over!' Anthony exclaimed, then checked his watch and scampered down to the kitchen to inspect everything there. 'One hour until blast off!' he yelled to everyone as he sped by.

Bunty and Perry exchanged another look and burst into giggles.

Exactly one hour later, peace reigned. It was a miracle how every single item had been strategically put into place. The house looked truly amazing, inside and out. The lawn was decorated with vintage garden furniture and colourful blooms in terracotta pots. The kitchen was cleverly styled to look like a 1930s working kitchen, with its era-appropriate props. The gramophone was quietly playing in the background in the drawing room and the mirrored drinks cabinet was opened to display the elegant cocktail glasses. The bedrooms had been de-cluttered, with silk throws placed neatly on the beds (Anthony had been disappointed not to have got his hands on a four-poster). However, the pièce de résistance, was the hallway. Not only had Emma saved the day, but, at Anthony's request, had dressed the part. She wore Bunty's mother's gold beaded dress, complete with the crystal chain head-piece.

After a hasty but heartfelt introduction to each other, Emma showed Bunty the music sheets she'd brought with her.

'Just something light and tinkly,' Bunty said, smiling. 'And thank you so much for doing this, Emma.' She gave her a quick squeeze.

'My pleasure.' Emma's eyes shone with glee, she was loving being a part of it all.

The vans and all the team fetching and carrying had left. Anthony gathered the girls in the maid uniforms who were at the ready to circulate with champagne glasses on silver trays. They'd been given strict instructions not to let anyone have more than one. They may be visitors, but they were first and foremost potential buyers and needed a clear head, Anthony had advised.

'And remember, pay attention, girls, eyes and ears open. Listen out and direct me to those sounding the most interested.'

As the clock chimed, Anthony gave the signal and the doors opened.

Chapter 34

A small party of people milled outside, raring to get in the house. One or two were stood facing the bay, taking in the panoramic view. A couple had ventured to the side to look at the gardens, while the rest waited with anticipation on the stone steps. As well as assessing the magnificent facade of the property, they were also sizing up each other – the competition.

The advantage of an open day for such a prestigious property meant that the viewers were vetted. They had to produce financial evidence to prove they had the means to buy it. So, with that in mind, *everyone* was a rival to each other.

Anthony had meticulously collected all the necessary information from every single person stepping foot inside the house. It was a job he thoroughly savoured, being the inquisitive kind. He'd overseen enough open days in his time not to be too in awe of the cliental – dealing with multi-millionaires, the rich and famous were old hat to him now, and he always conducted himself in a business-like manner, no matter who the client or buyer was, refusing to be either intimidated or star-struck.

He welcomed the viewers at the front entrance, along with his trusty clipboard containing the registration list. As each person passed through, they were greeted with a glass of champagne after giving their names. Today there were three couples, a father and daughter and one gentleman. Anthony had instantly recognised a few names, having shown them other properties previously. He had a staple group of potential buyers who, if they didn't like one property or were outbid, would request to see another. Anthony knew that one of the couples today particularly sought an art deco house, having been gazumped on the Devon house which Bunty had seen on the Grand & Country website. The father and daughter he had done a little research on, enough to know that Daddy had very deep pockets. He was in the oil business and his daughter was getting married next year. Anthony assumed they were looking for a potential marital home for her. As for the sole gentleman viewer, he was somewhat of a mystery to Anthony. It irked him that all attempts to glean more information on him had met a dead end. Yes, he had answered all the obligatory questions and more than proved his very solvent position, but that's all he had, the basics. Often when prospective buyers completed the forms, or attended the offices, they couldn't resist boasting, proclaiming how rich and successful they were; it more often than not came with the territory. But not in this case. Whoever Mr Adam F Sinclair was, all Anthony knew about him was that he was rich and currently living in Central London. It further annoyed Anthony that he hadn't yet arrived along with all the others.

After giving a short, potted history of the house, Anthony invited all the viewers to 'wander round at leisure and discover the charm and delights of the place.' Bunty stood and watched the proceedings wondering what her parents would have made of it all. She stole a glance at Perry, who was standing by Emma at the piano. Once the group dispersed, she started to play a pleasant sonata which set the tone beautifully. What a lifesaver she was, thought Bunty, feeling an affinity towards her, like she had with Jasmine.

Thinking of Jasmine reminded Bunty to add her name to Anthony's registration list. Beginning to understand just how fastidious he was, she wouldn't put it past him to refuse her entry.

'Is there anyone else I should be expecting?' he asked a tad primly. He clearly didn't approve of her friend coming along for a nosey.

'No just Jasmine Boyd,' replied Bunty firmly.

Refraining from telling him that this was still her house and she'd have who she wanted in it, Bunty made herself scarce. It was all starting to get on top of her. In desperate need of a gin and tonic, but unable to get to the drinks cabinet, she took a glass of champagne off a silver tray and went out onto the lawn. Discretely, she sat down on a bench behind a gigantic stone urn, bursting with mounds of hideous, plastic ivy. Glad to be camouflaged, she took a deep breath and tried to relax. She could do this. *Just focus on that lovely flintstone cottage waiting for you*, she told herself. After a large gulp of champagne, Bunty began to ease up. She overheard voices and deciding it was in her best interest, sat still and listened.

'Daddy, it's perfect! Hugo's going to adore this house.'

'Now, now, let's not be too hasty, Tabitha. Doesn't Hugo need to see it first?'

'No, he doesn't,' came the petulant reply. 'Hugo says it's up to *me*. It's what *I* want.'

Bunty stifled a giggle and took another sip of champagne.

'All right, princess, let's take another look.'

'Yes, let's!' cheered Tabitha, all signs of tantrum gone.

Dear God, please don't let my house go to that spoilt brat, prayed Bunty. She'd almost finished her drink and decided to get another. On her way back into the hall, she saw that Jasmine had just arrived and was giving her name to Anthony.

'Ah, there she is.' Jasmine pointed towards Bunty and went to join her.

'Am I glad to see you,' said Bunty in a weary tone.

Jasmine gave her a hug.

'It'll soon be over,' she soothed.

'They're crawling around the place like ants,' choked Bunty on the verge of tears.

'Oh Bunty, is Perry here?' Jasmine asked, thinking he'd be good support for her friend.

'Yes, so is Emma, come on, I'll introduce you,' she said with a sniff. She mentally shook herself and ushered Jasmine towards the piano.

Emma was just finishing a piece of music when she noticed Bunty approach with Jasmine.

'Hey, loving the outfit,' said Jasmine, recognising Bunty's mother's dress from the dinner party.

Emma laughed.

'Emma, this is Jasmine,' said Bunty, then linked arms with Perry. 'And this is Perry.'

'Hi,' replied Jasmine, smiling at them both.

Perry reached out a hand.

'I believe we have a connection?' he grinned.

'We certainly do. Fellow narrowboaters,' said Jasmine giving a firm handshake. 'It was Tom, my husband, who bought your water pump through the marina website,' she explained.

'Yes, I'm so sorry to hear about poor Tom,' Perry gravely replied.

They were interrupted by an agitated Anthony.

'Play on dear, *play on*,' he hissed at Emma.

Bunty glared at him. She had an overwhelming urge to empty the contents of her glass in his face.

'I think you're wanted, Anthony.' Perry gestured with his chin towards the entrance, where a tall man wearing sunglasses stood waiting.

Turning sharply, Anthony gripped his clipboard and sped off, leaving the others to swap grins.

'What a man,' Jasmine muttered with mirth.

'I know!' giggled Emma, then dutifully did as he'd instructed and chose another sheet of music.

'Ah, my favourite,' remarked Perry at hearing her choice, 'Pink Champagne'.

'Cheers, here's to new beginnings,' toasted Jasmine raising her flute.

'And second chances,' added Bunty gazing warmly at Perry.

After clinking glasses, they separated to mingle. Jasmine particularly wanted to see how the kitchen looked.

Emma's playing was drawing to an end, when the late arrival wearing dark sunglasses sidled over to her.

'You play well,' he drawled in a deep smooth voice, which resonated with Emma immediately. He lent on the side of the piano.

'Thank you,' she replied, then added a little self-consciously, '"Pink Champagne" is my dad's favourite.'

He gave a dazzling smile, showing perfect white teeth. His face was tanned, but hard to see properly hidden behind the black shades. He had short, black hair, which was greying at the temples.

'Do you know "Champagne Problems"?' he asked.

'Taylor Swift's song?'

'Yeah,' he nodded with a slow grin.

'Er… I'll try…' stammered Emma, taken off guard. Fortunately, she had played it several times before when gigging and felt pretty confident remembering it. 'Do you want the lyrics too?' she asked.

'That would be lovely,' he answered looking straight into her eyes.

That voice, where had she heard it before? thought Emma. She was just about to start the song when Anthony interrupted them.

'If you allow me, Mr Sinclair, I'll show you—'

'Just a minute,' the man cut him short, raising his hand. 'This lady is about to sing.'

'Oh… er… right,' spluttered Anthony blinking.

Emma cleared her throat and began to sing.

Everybody in the hall stopped still at hearing her voice, even Anthony. Jasmine, Perry and Bunty re-entered and were mesmerised by her voice. The acoustics in the marbled hall were superb.

As Emma finished the last line, a round of applause erupted, reverberating round the room. Perry's eyes misted over, he gulped with pride. Anthony seized the moment.

'Well, if that can't persuade you to buy the place nothing will!' he trilled to the mystery man. The very *rich* mystery man. The very rich mystery man, who could earn him a whopping, big, fat commission.

He turned, his dark shades fixed on Anthony.

'I'll take it, on one condition,' he stated.

'Name it,' squeaked Anthony, working up a sweat.

'You leave the piano.'

'It's yours,' shot back Anthony. Hell, he'd throw in the pianist too, for what he was about to pocket! Dizzy with excitement, Anthony produced a document for the man's signature at grease lightning. In the background a very angry Tabitha could be heard.

'Daddy!' she wailed, stamping her foot.

–

The 'Mystery Man' buying the Deville's big, white house on the peninsula was the talk of Samphire Bay. All anybody knew about him was his name, Adam Sinclair, and that he currently had a residence in Central London. End of. Zilch.

Bunty had initially thought that the Grand & Country estate agency were being deliberately evasive in not divulging information. However, after talking to Anthony, she was beginning to comprehend just how enigmatic this Adam Sinclair was. There was no mistaking the sheer frustration in his voice.

'I assure you, Ms Deville, I know practically *nothing* about him!' he whined down the phone. 'And believe me, I have tried my best.'

Bunty did believe him, knowing he'd be more curious than her to obtain any morsal of information going. But seemingly all Anthony's attempts to further his knowledge had been in vain and he was as clueless as the rest of them. Anthony had only given Adam Sinclair's address, which Bunty and Jasmine had looked up on google maps street view. They were in Jasmine's studio, waiting with bated breath to get a good look.

'Here we are,' said Jasmine, homing in on the penthouse suite in Knightsbridge. They both leant forward, squinting to focus on the property.

'*Ve-ry* nice,' remarked Bunty.

'I know, a penthouse in Central London must be worth a fortune,' Jasmine said.

A large roof terrace filled with greenery and a swimming pool overlooked Hyde Park and bustling Knightsbridge below.

'Blimey, and to think he wants to give that up to live here in Samphire Bay,' said Bunty in disbelief.

'Who says he's giving it up?' Jasmine asked. 'Maybe he's buying your house as a holiday home.'

They stared at each other, mouths wide open.

'How the other half live,' muttered Bunty, still staring at the screen.

'Did Emma not glean anything? He did seem quite taken with her,' laughed Jasmine, remembering how he had shut Anthony up to listen to her play the piano.

'Hmm, he did rather, didn't he?' Bunty chuckled. 'But no, Emma says he just remarked on how well she played and asked her to sing that song.'

'"Champagne Problems", very intriguing,' said Jasmine.

–

Meanwhile, next door, the very same man was on the lips of Robin and Jack.

'Yeah, some flash guy turns up late and says he'll "take it", according to Jasmine,' Robin told Jack.

They were in the garden, cutting the adjoining hedge after having mowed the lawn. The cottage was all ready for Bunty to move into and they were just tidying up the outside as a final job. Now that her house was sold, they had volunteered to transport the few pieces of furniture she was taking with her.

The vast majority of the furnishings were included in the sale of the house at Adam Sinclair's request, being in keeping with the property. All Bunty was keeping were one or two personal items; her bed, her father's bureau, her mother's dressing table and a full-length mirror which had belonged to her grandmother, plus a couple of her father's paintings. It would be a wrench to leave behind the stunning glass drinks cabinet she was so fond of (and had put to good use) but, as Robin had pointed out, she could always buy another. He and Jack had promised to keep their eyes open for one in the house clearance and reclamation sites they visited.

'So, who is this flash Harry then?' asked Jack.

'Dunno,' shrugged Robin.

'What, nobody knows anything?'

'Only that he's rolling in it. Oh, and he's tall, dark and handsome, apparently,' Robin said dryly, making Jack laugh.

'Is that according to Jasmine too?' he asked with a sly smile.

'Yeah,' came the flat reply, making Jack laugh even harder.

'I'm sure Jasmine only has eyes for you, mate,' he teased, just as she came out of her studio.

'Hi!' she called, as Bunty followed behind.

Both men stopped cutting as the women approached.

'Just telling Jack about the fella who's bought your place,' said Robin to Bunty.

'The tall, dark, handsome fella.' Jack nodded with a smirk. 'Isn't that right, Jasmine?' He cocked a cheeky eyebrow.

Jasmine gave him a withering look. She was finally learning to accept, if not appreciate his humour.

'Not a patch on Robin though,' she replied tartly.

'I agree,' said Bunty in support.

This perked Robin up no end.

'Do you want me to cut your side?' he asked, pointing to the hedge.

'Oh yes, thanks,' smiled Jasmine. 'I'll cook dinner tonight in return.'

'Sounds good,' he replied. Their eyes locked. Bunty and Jack exchanged a knowing look.

'Will you be having a farewell bash at your house?' Jack asked Bunty, changing the subject.

They all faced her.

'I don't think so,' Bunty replied after some consideration. She really didn't think she could handle any more emotional trauma. The open day was bad enough, without having to endure one last final party at the house. It would be too much of a heartbreaking strain and she hated the thought of falling to pieces in front of everyone. No, far better to go quietly. Her eyes filled as she pictured herself saying goodbye to each room for the last time, running her hands over the elegant, polished surfaces, catching a final reflection in the gold edged mirrors, looking out to sea from the balcony…

'Bunty, are you OK?' asked Robin, noticing her face fall.

'Yes… it's all a bit…' Bunty blinked and looked away.

'I know,' Jasmine said, putting a protective arm round her. 'Instead of a farewell bash, let's have a welcome party at your new cottage?' she tentatively suggested.

'Excellent idea, darling.' Bunty gave a wobbly smile. 'Just an intimate gathering though.'

'Absolutely,' nodded Robin.

Chapter 35

Autumn had fully arrived, turning Samphire Bay's trees russet gold and the hedgerows sparce. The sand was cool and damp, while the bay ran icier and wilder. The shift of season acted as a warning, a foreboding to the changes Samphire Bay was to experience.

Bunty, with the help of not only Robin and Jack, but Perry, Jasmine and Emma too, had managed her move as seamlessly as possible. The angst Bunty had expected to be overwhelmed by had been replaced with distraction. It had been such a hectic, but productive day and she couldn't have done it without them. Having her close friends to oversee the move was infinitely better than an impersonal removal firm. Bunty couldn't bear for her precious belongings to be handled by total strangers. Instead, she had a loving team to aid her, which put everything into perspective. Relationships were what mattered. Not bricks and mortar, or possessions, but *real friends* who cared.

This had been Bunty's mantra, as she locked the door for the last time and walked down the stone steps. She turned for one final look at her family home. Her eyes cast up to the balcony, leading from the master bedroom where she'd been born. A whole lifetime spent there – and yet she knew it was time to go. This stunning house was about to be a new home for another person. Its curved rooms, nooks and crannies she wished would hold future fond memories for other families. Whoever the new owner was, Bunty dearly hoped he had a family to fill the house with love.

Her mood remained positive and almost upbeat when reaching the snug cottage awaiting patiently. Her mind was set to rest, knowing it had been totally revamped with care. No botch jobs here, everything had been lovingly restored to the highest standard. Directing where all the boxes being carried in had to go, she already felt at home. Bunty had chosen the attic room for her bedroom. The skylight in the roof would still give her a panoramic view of the bay, which was imperative for her. One of the bedrooms she had decided would act as a mini library-cum-study and was where her father's bureau had been placed. She'd also brought all the family's books, including her cherished childhood editions. Robin had promised to make bookcases to line the walls, complete with a rail track for a little ladder to run across, just like the one they'd had at her old home.

The new kitchen diner was a dream to Bunty. Instead of a large, cold place filled with nostalgic, aged furnishings, she loved the new streamlined appliances. It was all so easy and practical. A part of her wondered why she hadn't made the move earlier.

Seeing Bunty adapt so well to her new surroundings had been a comfort to her merry band of helpers.

'It looks like she feels at home already,' Perry murmured to Jasmine, as they unpacked crockery from the boxes.

'Careful with that!' shouted Bunty, seeing him lift up a fine bone China teapot.

'Well, she's certainly in control,' replied Jasmine. 'I'm just glad she's not in tears,' she whispered.

'She's made of stern stuff is Bunty,' he winked.

All in all, the day had gone well. Bunty had thanked everyone profusely with the promise of a house-warming party. After waving them off, she and Perry had a celebratory drink alone in the back garden. The patio set that had once stood on the balcony, was now by the rockery.

'Here's to your new home.' Perry raised his glass.

Bunty clinked it against hers. Then her eye caught the anchor which Robin had retrieved from the trunk and placed in the rockery as a feature. She got up to inspect it closely.

'Look,' she said, pointing to it.

Perry joined her before crouching down to inspect it more closely.

'It's my anchor, the one you gave me,' he said in awe. He ran his finger over the engraved B and P.

'I know, after all this time,' her chin wobbled and finally the tears came. It had been such an emotional day.

Perry reached out and wrapped her tightly into a warm hug. He stroked her hair, kissing her cheek.

'It's all right, Bunty. I'll never leave you again,' he huskily soothed.

Chapter 36

As expected, Jasmine's mother was absolutely overjoyed to learn that Robin was now in fact Jasmine's boyfriend. Jasmine had told her parents and brother over the phone. Having met Robin's parents, it only seemed right and proper that her family ought to know too. Insisting that Robin be put on the phone, Jasmine's mum was positively gushing.

'Oh Robin, such lovely news! I always liked you, right from the very start,' she shrilled.

'Er... thanks Mrs—'

'Call me Sue,' she cut in. 'Such a weight has been lifted off our shoulders, I can tell you, isn't that right, Mike?' She glanced over to her husband, who was frantically trying to calm her down.

'Shush, steady on, Sue,' he hissed.

'As soon as you offered to help put her kitchen in, I thought, yes, this is a decent chap, a true gent—' then her husband firmly grabbed the phone off her.

'Hello, Robin, Jasmine's dad here. We're very pleased and look forward to meeting you again soon.'

'Thank you,' replied a relieved Robin.

'Goodbye, son.'

'Bye.'

Mike quickly put the phone down before his wife could snatch it back.

Jasmine was in fits of laughter. Seeing Robin blink in bewilderment could only mean he'd experienced the full force of her mum.

'Sorry about that,' she giggled.

Robin puffed his cheeks out.

'Wow,' was all he could say.

It was early evening and they were about to go next door to Bunty's house-warming party. Although dark by now, with a nip in the air, it was at least dry. As they walked down the garden path, a crescent moon shone and the sound of crashing waves could be heard in the distance. Bunty's kitchen was lit up looking cosy and inviting. Perry was there to greet them with a glass of mulled wine when they entered and Emma was playing a keyboard in the far corner of the dining area and belting out 'Our House' by Crosby, Stills, Nash & Young.

Bunty was taking out a huge dish of chicken curry from the oven, while Jack had been collared by Trish, who was gossiping about the newcomer to Samphire Bay.

'Apparently he's installed security cameras,' she was telling a very bored looking Jack. He turned at seeing Robin and Jasmine and quickly sought his chance.

'Rob!' he called and escaped.

Jasmine wandered over to Emma who was just finishing her song.

'You're brilliant, honestly, Emma, you should be on stage.'

'I love doing the pub gigs, but that's all,' replied Emma with a grin.

'More!' shouted Jack.

'Any requests?' laughed Emma.

'"Pink Champagne"!' Perry called, making Emma roll her eyes.

'Not that again, choose another.'

'"We'll Meet Again",' said Bunty, leaning over the kitchen worktop.

'Aw,' cried Jasmine, turning to smile at her, then Perry. The words weren't lost on him.

Emma started, then they all joined in, swaying in tune.

The end of the song was met with a huge round of applause. Amongst the commotion, Robin gently took Jasmine's arm and led her out to the back garden. They stood by the hedge, where he'd first clapped eyes on her, smelling the lavender.

Jasmine looked up to the crescent moon, surrounded by stars in the black sky. She breathed in the salty air and listened to the sound of the sea. Perfect. Everything was perfect. She saw Robin reach for something in his pocket. He looked intensely at her, those hazel eyes focusing directly into hers, holding so much love. She thought her heart would burst.

'Jasmine, I want you to have this.' He took out a small box from his jeans. Jasmine opened it to find a gold anchor pendant.

'It's beautiful,' she gasped. Then subconsciously her hand reached for the heart charm on her necklace.

'It's not to replace the heart you have,' said Robin urgently, 'but put alongside it? I want to be your anchor Jasmine, let me love and look after you.' His voice cracked.

'Oh Robin.' A tear ran down her face. He *was* her anchor, right from the very start, always there, a steady force, keeping her grounded. He was her *everything* and she adored him.

Jasmine unfastened the necklace she wore and Robin carefully added the anchor pendant. Watching it slip down the chain to land next to the heart, they looked up at each other.

'Let's love and look after each other,' she choked, flinging her arms round him.

As they embraced a gentle breeze passed over them and a faint voice whispered in the air, *Well done, Jas.*

Author Note

I'll not lie, a few tears have been shed writing this book. Not just at the beginning, with poor Jasmine spreading her late husband's ashes, or at the end when his spirit wishes her a happy future, but actually writing the second half of the story.

Around that time my mum was dying of lung cancer and I, along with my sister and brother, all looked after her, with the care of the hospice team.

Besides my husband, mum was my number one fan. She got more excited than me when a new book came out! I know how proud she would have been about this one.

Like Jasmine, she too had been a young widow and it seems fitting to dedicate *Second Chances at Samphire Bay* to her and dad, finally reunited.

I hope you're both looking down on us and I'll be raising a glass on publication day whilst thinking of you. ♥

Acknowledgements

First and foremost I'd like to thank my family, friends, colleagues and the wonderful nurses at St Catherine's Hospice, for their support during the time writing *Second Chances at Samphire Bay*. I'd also like to thank my editor, Emily Bedford, and all the team at Canelo for their hard work in producing this book. As always, a big shout out to the brilliant cover designer, Diane Meacham (love this one the best!). Big thanks to all you readers out there, please keep in touch. Last, but by no means least, I'd like to thank my husband, Alex, for his patience, kindness and always being there for me.

Till the next book,

Love Sasha x